BLACK HEAT

http://COOLGROVE.COM

BLACK HEAT

a novel by

NORMAN KELLEY

All rights reserved under the International and Pan-American Copyright
Conventions. Published in the United States by Cool Grove Press, an imprint
of Cool Grove Publishing, Inc., New York.
328 Flatbush Avenue, Suite 302, Brooklyn, NY 11238

Publisher's Cataloging in Publication Data

Kelley, Norman. 1954 –
    Blackheat / by Norman Kelley.
    p. cm.
    Preassigned LCCN: 96-83821
    ISBN: 1-887276-03-3

1. Afro-American detectives—New York Metropolitan
Area— Fiction. 2. Women detectives—New York Metropolitan
Area—Fiction. 3. Private investigators—New York
Metropolitan Area—Fiction
PS3521.E55b43   813'.54
                                           QBI96-40308

Cover and book design: P. T. Hazarika
Back cover painting: LOIS. by Arthur Coppedge. Oil on canvas
All images courtesy of Nik and Funke Douglas family collection

Manufactured in the United States of America
First Edition: August 1997
10 9 8 7 6 5 4 3 2 1

To my mother, Barbara J. Kelley,
and to Susan V. Smith.

In Memoriam
Dr. Betty Shabazz

 I had not seen Veronica Thorn in almost twenty-five years. When I was a young girl she was the most popular Negro actress, the only black actress to become a sex symbol since Dorothy Dandridge. She possessed a certain sleek, ambiguously beige allure with keen features that made blacks—back then called colored people or Negroes—somewhat more palatable to whites. Whenever *Ebony* Magazine featured its annual, habitually insipid article regarding the attractiveness of black women ("Are Black Women Getting Better Looking?" asked one cover), "VT" was touted as the emblem of black feminine beauty.

Now she was sitting before me. Older, her eyes dark from age. She didn't have that faded movie star look, that kind of gloss-over look that women who are judged solely by their beauty resort to when older. Her face was fuller and her lips as sensuous as before. It was her eyes that showed her misfortune. They were sad, yet smiling; she was still our brown-eyed girl.

Veronica Martin, previously Veronica Thorn, sat next to Anna Gong. Anna and I had been Assistant D.A.'s together in Brooklyn. Anna went into private practice after only one tour in the People's Republic of Brooklyn. Mrs. Martin was a client of Pro Bono, a not-for-profit consortium of law firms and private agencies that engaged in free legal assistance. Nationwide, mental institutions were discharging patients to make way for those convicted in drug cases. Veronica Martin was re-discovered after she had been forgotten. After being locked up for over twenty years, she was released to Pro

Bono. Anna was helping the former star in a matter with which she thought I might be of assistance.

Anna was the "marketable ethnic". A Chinese-American, she could run for mayor and not be viewed as a total threat. We were both plotting her future run for a city council seat and then the mayoralty. A handsome woman, Anna wore her hair long, breaking at her shoulder. It framed her high cheek bones; the lines of her jaw sloped down into a slightly pointed chin. The bridge of her nose had a graceful line, as it flared down into two tiny nostrils. My late husband Lee once described her full lips as a small red rose. The folds of her eyes were truly shaped like almonds. Mixed with her lean build and porcelain skin, at five feet ten inches, she was an easy choice as a Miss Chinatown beauty contest winner. She also loved perfecting her Dragon Lady or Madam Nhu personas.

To relieve herself from the stress and strain of dealing with Chinatown politics, the Greater East Asian Co-Prosperity Association, immigration litigation plus volunteer legal work, Anna's retreat was her upper West Side apartment and painting her secret passion. Lately she had become entranced with a collection of Frida Kahlo's paintings. For years she had been trying to get me to sit for her as a model but I kept telling her that I was "paint-shy". Being seated before a former Hollywood race woman only convinced me that I didn't have the *look.*

I remembered VT as a captivating actress who starred in numerous films in the late 1950s and 1960s: *One Thousand Arabian Nights, Miss Buchanan, King of the People* and *Lianna* were my favorites. Her complexion meant she could portray anything: black, mulatto, Mediterranean, Semitic or Native American.

Mindful of what had happened to Dot Dandridge (too many public affairs with white men and the illusion that she had broken the color line), Veronica let it be known that she was a "race woman," proud of her heritage as an American Negro and a daughter of Mother Africa. She dated white men and had the obligatory public affair with Roberto Massini, the Italian director of her hit film *Lianna.* VT let it be known that while she was being escorted to

2

Hollywood premieres and New York galas by white celebrities, she was black—or at least soulful. "My blackness is inner," she once confessed to a Negro reporter.

She was magnificently beautiful, a goddess—something that I, a little girl at the time, felt I could never be. Veronica had a light complexion and tresses of "good hair" from her Native American mixture. Me? I was a dark- brown skinned girl, with the kinky hair of a Negrita. But I pretended that I was her because she was a "fine Negro actress" as one of my teachers exclaimed. Yes, she was my hero. I loved her in *Lianna* where she played an Italian mulatto who arrives from Italy in 1963 and hooks up with her black American half-brother. The two have a rough time learning to love each other as brother and sister, though eventually they become family.

One evening I was riveted to the television set, watching a broadcast of the so-called controversial film, *Miss Buchanan*. "VT on TV," I said to my brother Gary. In that film, made by independent producers, she played a graduate student from New York City who travels to Mississippi during the Great Depression and becomes a teacher in a small Southern town's black quarter.

What made the film controversial was that Miss Buchanan, VT's character, had taken a gun and gone looking for the crackers who had blown up her library that she had established for black children, children like me. Granted, my circumstances were better than the kids' in the film, but I'd heard the fearful story of the Klan bombing a Birmingham church which killed four black girls.

I was young then, a child vaguely beginning to understand the politics of race from that film's confrontation when my father switched off the set. He commandeered the living room of our modest Washington, D.C. home for himself and his AFL-CIO union buddies. They planned to talk about civil rights, union business, and voter registration. Bo-ring, I thought, as I kissed my "union uncles" good-bye, then pouted upstairs to my bedroom. But after not receiving a sympathetic hearing from my mother, a school teacher, who was correcting papers in the kitchen, I closed my door, cuddled up with my Veronica Thorn doll (now a collector's item) and looked at her winning smile in a special edition of *Ebony* magazine.

That was in the late sixties and Veronica's career shifted due to the "controversy" surrounding *Miss Buchanan*. It was cited as an inducement to Negro violence, causing riots in Watts, Detroit, Newark, and other colored havens. Of course, that charge was ridiculous, but Negroes, as we were then called, were termed "an excitable people." Word was that Hollywood got a message from Washington and Veronica's career in Hollywood started to sputter. She only made two more films, *King of the People* and *Blues in the Morning*. Twice she was cited by the critics as "one of the most dynamic actresses of her generation."

In *King of the People,* she portrayed Esperanza, an innkeeper and lover of a black American college professor who inadvertently became involved in an island's fight against despotism. She also reprised her role of Liz Buchanan in *Blues in the Morning,* a series of vignettes about the migration of the blues from the Mississippi Delta to Chicago. Then she also played the role of Delores Jones, a struggling executive of a small blues record label and seducer of Howlin' Wolf in the same film. She lost her middle-class support with that film. But the colored folks loved her to death. She had reaffirmed the blues as a bona fide legacy of African American culture, one of many musical forms that the lower class had created. It was her work in that film which let colored folks see she was making a change and taking a stand about the black revolution as opposed to integration, and linking it to the issue of class in the black community.

Not as accommodating as her friend and fellow screen actor, Hobart Wilson, to whom she presented an Oscar for his 1967 performance as the patient Negro doctor among hostile whites in *Catch Me If You Can,* Veronica was being shut out of Hollywood because she was becoming "political". The godfather of black thespianism, Paul Robeson, had warned younger black actors about the troubles they could expect for being too vocal and prominent. But Veronica spoke out about the bad scripts offered to black women and about the situation of her darker sisters in the acting profession. She held receptions for Malcolm X, African dignitaries, and Adam Clayton

Powell. It was said that VT learned how to be "black" by swiping a page from Adam's playbook. The story goes that he made sure that he was always associated with the darkest of us.

A graduate of Howard University's drama school, she returned to Washington, where she set up the New African Theatre on Fourteenth Street, near the U Street corridor. Somehow, that building was spared the flames of the '68 riots. Her theatre spawned and showcased the talent of new black writers and actors, many of whom went on to work in television, films and plays throughout the 1970s, 1980s, and 1990s. But things really changed for Veronica Thorn when she met her man, the man who she said gave her 'the sparks', Malik Martin.

She later married the Minister-Brother-Doctor Malik Martin and became "Sister Ronnie." Transcending her sex symbol persona, she became the de-sexualized Mother of the Nation. She wrapped herself in bright, vibrant traditional African colors from head to foot, giving support to her man and presenting herself as a model black woman. It was during the nationalist period that Veronica Thorn married the man who carried the weight of Malcolm X and Martin Luther King. But after Malik's death Veronica Thorn Martin shifted in our minds to a new role. No longer the sexy VT or the Mother of the Nation, she became a black Madonna, a woman who epitomized stoicism. She carried her grief silently, as her noble black man was consumed by history and myth.

But being a black Madonna drove her to a mental institution. Actually, it was the post-traumatic stress of witnessing the assassination of her husband that led to her subsequent institutionalization, and the demands of being a symbol for black liberation. Malik's most trusted lieutenants were bickering amongst themselves; they wanted his grieving widow to validate their arguments. Huey P. Newton needed her to help him raise funds for his defense. Stokely Carmichael wanted her to write him letters of introduction to some West African presidents. Black colleges wanted her to speak at their forums. Black student unions at white colleges wanted her to sanction their takeover of administration buildings. Nervous about her evolution as a new black symbol, the FBI, it was later revealed at a Congressional hearing, floated the rumor that she might have had something to do with her husband's assassination, that she was having an affair with someone on his staff. Innuendo destroyed her, crippled whatever fortitude she had left for herself and her young daughter. It was reported in the press that she tried to kill herself repeatedly, distraught over the rumors implicating her in her own husband's murder.

My mind's eye remembers her holding little Malika, both dressed in Christian black, as television cameras showed her listening to a colleague of her late husband's, intoning about Malik as the promise of the race. She held that child and rocked her, smoothing her face, wiping away a tear. I remember seeing her straightening her dress after they stood up from sitting in the pews, leaving the church.

"Is it Miss or Mrs. Halligan?" the former actress asked me. Her eyes shifted quickly, taking in the pastel colors and the black and white photographs decorating our favorite bistro, Pamela's, in the Flatiron district of Manhattan.

"Neither."

"Neither?" She looked at Anna who explained that since the 1970s a number of women use the title "Ms." rather than "Miss" or "Mrs." She smiled slightly at herself for being out of touch. I felt as if I were watching her in one of her films of years ago.

"Why don't you call me Nina?" I said, wanting to reach out and touch her hands which were folded over her black leather clutch bag, but our drinks arrived. We were all served white wine. Anna raised her glass.

"Welcome home," toasted Anna.

Mrs. Martin looked apprehensive. She raised her glass and quickly smiled; the wine passed over her lips and disappeared. Since Anna was acting as Mrs. Martin's counsel, she broached the subject of the meeting.

"Mrs. Martin, as you know, Nina, was released a few months ago; she's trying to pick up the pieces of her life and—"

"My daughter," blurted out Mrs. Martin. Her eyes shifted warily about the restaurant again.

"Ma'am?" I asked. "What about your daughter?"

"I'm trying to locate her, Ms. Halligan. I've lost contact with her."

"Oh?" My attention was slightly distracted by a tune I heard coming over the restaurant's music system, "Children's World" by Maceo Parker, a former sideman of James Brown. The tune is a re-working of Brown's classic "It's A Man's Man's Man's World."

"Malika," interjected Anna, "used to come to visit her, but she stopped a year or so before Mrs. Martin's release...."

"I haven't been able to locate her since then."

I was about to sip my wine but noticed I had rimmed the glass with lipstick. It was then that I realized that I didn't like the recently purchased shade. I also noticed that Anna seemed to think I wasn't as interested in following up on what was being presented to me as she thought I should be. She raised an eyebrow.

"A year ago? Hmmm. Where does she live?" I looked at Mrs. Martin, but Anna answered.

"Here, in New York."

"Did you try her address? Call her on the phone?"

She nodded. "I tried to get in touch with Roy Hakim. He was made her legal guardian when my husband was...." Her voice trailed off into the surrounding din.

"She tried to get in touch with Dr. Hakim, but he has been unresponsive," added Anna.

"Do you think something is wrong?"

"Wrong?" The woman looked surprised at my use of the word.

I looked at Anna, hoping that she had explained to the woman that I was an investigator.

"Have you called the police?"

Mrs. Martin looked at Anna.

"That's why I called you, Nina."

"Oh?" I instinctively arched my eyebrow and began fingering a lock of my braided hair.

Anna placed her forearms on the table and leaned over to me as if we were in a plea bargaining conference.

"Yes. Considering the circumstances of the minister's death...."

With as much bitterness and grief as if her husband's death were only yesterday, Mrs. Martin said, "They killed him!"

Her formerly passive, post-incarcerated demeanor was pushed aside. The rage in her stirred at the memory of her slain husband. I should have been more sensitive and realized that she was dealing with a bout of residual grief, but I went into my interrogation mode and asked: "*Who* are *they*?"

Anna quickly shot me a frown from across the white draped table. She etched a forbidding look with her eyebrows and the turned-down corners of her mouth.

"The police," Veronica Masters Martin hissed—too audibly for her counselor. Anna looked around the room.

A few heads turned looking in our direction; some faces scrutinized the still handsome actress. She was wearing a smart tropical wool blue suit and her hair was shorter than the way she had worn it years ago as an actress. It was salt and peppered and combed back. Back in VT's heyday, an actress had to have had lots of hair—and a colored actress had to have had "good" hair, of which VT had an ample head of gloriously thick black locks.

She became agitated. Her mouth contorted slightly and her eyes stared past me and were fixed, focused, on the past. One of her hands gripped a butter knife before her.

I reached over and placed my hand over her free hand while Anna placed hers over Mrs. Martin's forearm. I gently rubbed her hand and Anna did likewise on the woman's forearm that held the knife.

Anyone who suddenly saw us would have thought they were witnessing two friends comforting each other. Anna slowly worked her hand down to Veronica's and removed the knife. I kept mine over her other hand and looked into the sad eyes of the woman who many years ago represented the new black woman.

CHAPTER 2

Malik Martin was murdered in 1971 minutes before he was to unveil a new program that was to clarify the confusion and mistrust that had grown up between the civil rights moderates and the nationalists. Both Malcolm X and Martin Luther King, Jr. had been assassinated and those who remained, the Black Panthers, Stokely Carmichael, Black Liberation Army and countless others, were talking about what they perceived to be *serious* black power, the gun.

What the brothers hadn't realized was that the police and both state and federal authorities were up to their challenge. Rumors about spies and police provocateurs were rife in both the moderates' and the nationalists' camps. The Panthers were getting busted and were shooting back. At some point almost every ranking Panther member was in jail or was dead. People were getting killed and even those who were not advocating the overthrow of the state, men such as Malik Martin, were viewed as a threat because they were leaders with a pro-black agenda, who could not be bought or sold, men of unquestionable integrity.

Malik Martin was the link between two political trends that perpetually excluded one another: integrationism and nationalism. He was trying to link them with his Nation movement, an amalgamation of black Christian nationalism and Nation of Islam grassroots capitalism. He preferred to call it "social capitalism." He spoke about love and redemption like Brother King, but also preached black self-respect and determination like Brother Malcolm. Malik Martin was the man in the middle. A visionary distrusted by both camps because his philosophy encompassed elements of both schools of thought, Malik sought to develop a spiritual base that spoke of the old and the new, and was in the process of offering an actual economic program to the masses.

The story went that he had gone on a retreat with some of his lieutenants to develop a unifying program which addressed the next phase of the black agenda: economic development. He was killed backstage at Howard University moments before he delivered his speech. It was rumored that he was going to expose treachery within his ranks as well as plots concocted against him by the FBI's Counter Intelligence Program, COINTELPRO.

The assassination, like Lee Harvey Oswald's, was televised. Dressed in his uniform for public appearances, dark suit and black turtleneck with a gold Ankh hanging around his neck, the minister arrived backstage with his wife and daughter Malika. As the gunfire started, he quickly handed the child to his wife and got them out of the line of fire. The killers cried "Die! Nigger die!" as they descended from the ceiling on ropes. It was quite clear to everyone who was there exactly who the target was.

The television news showed the minister's body being riddled with bullets and being thrown several feet due to the force of the assassins' M-16's. Three hooded men were seen committing the murder, but were never caught. Television cameras seemed to capture every moment of the pandemonium: the fear, the blood, people running and screaming, dazed spectators.

In the aftermath, accusations about security or the lack thereof flew. Claims that the police knew of an impending hit but did nothing were bandied about by Martin's security people. There was also widespread speculation that his security forces were goofing off, busily rapping to some "fly sisters with big 'fro's" moments before the hit.

That the killers were never caught added fuel to the charges of a conspiracy. Oddly, since the race of the assassins was never known, no major riots ensued; no black mob seeking retribution against "whitey." Blacks folks were truly shocked that three of their giants had been lost.

The lack of violent reaction was also due to the fact that America had just gone through Watts in 1965, Detroit and New York in 1967, and Washington, D.C. in 1968. There was plenty to burn but the energy was spent. The black nation had lost three of its statesmen. The young warriors, the brothers and sisters who wanted to smash the racist state, were being chewed up by the state and spat out like a nasty black after-taste.

It wasn't long after his death that the Nation, formed by Dr. Martin, split into two diametrically opposing wings. Rev. Paul Tower, the Nation's treasurer, took over the assets of the Nation: their publications, bank accounts, mailing lists, etc. With this firm ground beneath his feet, he created the Black Christian Network, better known as BCN. As owner and chief executive officer of BCN, the righteously Reverend Paul Tower set about the business of reinterpreting Malik Martin's social capitalism. Offering conservative Black gospel preaching 24 hours a day, within a few years the BCN was turning huge profits. Paul Tower became the darling of conservative Republicans across the country.

The other half of Dr. Martin's Nation was led by Dr. Roy Hakim, chief theoretician of black nationalism. Hakim was to have been the heir apparent of the late leader. He tried to keep the Nation going, but he lacked the minister's charisma and eloquence, not to mention his Paul Robeson-esque, West African good looks. Soon, internal squabbling over African socialism versus social capitalism eroded the ranks, with multiple off-shoot parties preaching that they were the true disciples of Minister-Brother-Doctor Malik Martin.

As the years passed the name and legacy of Malik Martin slipped into obscurity. But roughly 15 years later the interlocked MM initials began to appear everywhere in America's urban Bantustans. Young blacks from the middle class who were searching for either meaning or authenticity found the legacy of MM appealing: he was a "real black man" cut down before delivering the word. Many of the survivors of his generation had crossed over and integrated. To the youth they were beginning to look like sell-outs whose greatest accomplishments were their high-paying jobs at white institutions. Something began to smell and the younger generations, both the lower and middle classes, soon began romanticizing the last great black man, Malik Martin.

A veritable cottage industry kicked into production, with books, articles, plays, and television programs. The new jack post-civil right black intellectuals lined up to either denounce Malik Martin for his alleged sexism (the minister sired an illegitimate daughter by a white woman!), or for his naive faith in social capitalism. They claimed he hadn't developed an understanding of the intellectual systems of domination and the theories of power. On the other hand, the cheap intellectuals, those who couldn't develop their own original ideas or theories, picked over Malik Martin like vultures stripping a dead animal's carcass.

One could not walk down the street without seeing MM scrawled on a wall or stitched into some hat, skirt, jacket or whatever. The snakes had even gotten so low as to claim that M & M candies were being dedicated to the man who just happened to share the same initials.

Pushed aside and forgotten was a destroyed family. A father killed, a mother left incapacitated, a child packed off to another household. Veronica Martin suffered a nervous breakdown, a violent mental collapse that left her unfit to be the Mother of the Nation. She was stripped of her kente cloth and easily shoved aside when she could not learn the new role expected of her, the strong black woman. She couldn't hack it in the eyes of the public. Her once adoring black audience deserted her.

The "brown-eyed girl" had lost favor with her white fans when she married Martin. When she exhibited signs of emotional stress due to rumors and innuendoes, especially about her being in on the plot to kill her own husband, news of her nervous breakdown spread throughout the Black community. They claimed she was always a white man's colored girl; she wasn't really black. Did she have black skin and true African features? Who elected her Mother of the Nation, anyway? If she was so sexy, why couldn't she keep the good brother doctor from chasing white thighs? She could satisfy those ofay Hollywood chumps, but couldn't do anything for a real black man.

If nation building came with a high price, showing a lack of strength, in the eyes of the black public, equaled nothing less then failure.

"Do you have children, Nina?"

Veronica Martin had returned from her grief and now she was unwittingly pushing me into mine. I wasn't interested in turning the meeting into a seminar for displaced mothers. She had asked a simple question and I wasn't interested in coughing up the emotion to deal with it. She'd had twenty or so years to deal with her pain; I was just beginning to come to terms with mine.

I sighed, poured each us of some more wine and briefly glanced at Anna. She was as sorry as I was to hear that question.

"I had children, Mrs. Martin." I doused the roof of my mouth with the wine, wanting something stronger. Mrs. Martin was looking at me in an inquisitive way that implied she was expecting further elaboration. I knew that if she had been in circulation she would have understood why that was a sensitive topic. The art of social small talk requires constant practice and she was practicing her strokes with me. I smiled and said, "Let's not talk about me. Let's see what we can do for you. Hmmm?"

She looked at both Anna and me. "You two are very kind. I know I'm really acting like a reject...but...." Tears appeared in her eyes. "But it has been so long...since I've seen my daughter and I'm just trying to...I mean...I didn't handle myself too well...when...."

Anna was very quiet, which is unusual for her. She can be a mouth-o-rama. Her head was slightly bowed, looking down at the table. I wasn't sure if I wanted to deal with this. It seemed like a straight missing person case, but nothing in the world is ever straight, is it?

After we came back to normal, I took down some particulars regarding Malika's last known address, the telephone number and address of Roy Hakim's home and workplace. Mrs. Martin handed me two photographs of Malika, taken within a year.

Outside of the restaurant the sun was moving out from behind a bank of clouds. It was a nice spring afternoon as I said good-bye to Veronica Martin and assured her that one of us, either Anna or myself, would be in touch with her in a couple of days. Anna excused herself from Mrs. Martin and walked a couple of paces with me to my black box, a Dodge four-wheel-drive.

"I'm sorry about that little personal history foray," she said.

I shrugged my shoulders. "I'm a big girl," I lied. "I'll let you know what I find." I looked over Anna's shoulder at Mrs. Martin, who was watching people do their mid-town strolling. "Are you sure she's ready, Anna? I mean being here in New York?"

Anna turned to look at Mrs. Martin. "Yeah. She can deal with it. It's not easy. You know that. She wants to get on with the rest of her life and find her daughter. You can appreciate that."

"Don't rub it in, Anna." I was feeling a wee bit vulnerable.

"I'm sorry," she said.

I patted her face. "Ciao, girl."

"Bye Nina." Anna did an about-face and clicked her heels back to Mrs. Martin.

The two of them caught a taxi and drove into the afternoon sun. I sat at the wheel of my car and held onto it, shaking uncontrollably. My furies raged at the very core of my being, calling, pushing me, badgering me about not getting on with my real work. Beginning to perspire, I opened the collar of my blouse. My forehead was moist and my upper lip was also beaded. The last time I felt this way my assistant found me crumbled up on the floor moaning like a wounded mad woman. A gaping bloody wound...Veronica Martin opened it again for me. It was such an innocent question.... I leaned back into my seat, feeling exhausted. Too tired to drive, I got out of the car and leaned against it. I felt as if I had been in a fight, the same recurring bout since my special day in Brooklyn.

CHAPTER 3

Before returning to my office I stopped at the Manhattan branch of the public library at Fifth Avenue and East 40th Street, returned some books, and then swung around and headed back downtown to my office on West 14th Street. Meeting Veronica Martin was a bit of a jolt. Here was a woman I had worshipped as a little girl, now a woman in her fifties with the best years of her life gone. Freshly booted out of a mental institution, she was a wounded lioness searching for her cub. Her exclamation about "them" killing her husband was still fresh in her mind, and something I could identify with.

Yes, it also happened to me, but I wanted to believe that my childhood idol was immune to such mayhem. Obviously, I knew that the murder of Malik Martin had taken place, but I didn't want to deal with the reality that no one is completely immune to violence, to the havoc it visits upon one's family. The grown woman in me knew that the world wasn't a user-friendly village. As a former prosecutor, I did my part to put some of the badness away, but the little girl who once wore long thick plaits still wished that Veronica Martin could have been as triumphant as the character Miss Buchanan. Then I recalled Liz Buchanan's triumph: the confrontation with the town's rednecks ignited a race riot which caused her best pupil's father to be killed. I parked the car while searching through my memory banks for a better movie ending.

I had to unlock the door which meant Donna, my assistant, wasn't minding the fort. She was probably in the field doing some assignment. I couldn't remember whether or not she was in class, but was glad to be alone. The answering machine in my office was flicking its red message-received light. I had been expecting some return calls regarding assignments but wasn't in the mood to listen. I checked the mail and was glad to receive payments from some clients. I tossed the checks into the desk's top drawer and went out of my private office to an area near Donna's desk where a makeshift kitchenette stood.

The larger room was painted an off-white color. The general tenor of the place was nondescript. Within the last year or so I had lost my enthusiasm for home decorating. Anna would always shake her head whenever she walked into the place. She thought I could do better than merely placing a Persian rug in the middle of the floor. I had some used black leather chairs brought in with a small table between them. The tables were usually stacked with magazines and flowers once a week, but I had lost any feel for the so-called woman's touch. Fuck Martha Stewart. I didn't even have photos or pictures on the walls. A stereo system, a television and VCR unit were in my office. They sat on a black metal shelf with some law books and the New York Criminal Codes.

I went over to the table we had set up with a coffee machine, a small refrigerator, and a microwave. I popped open the jar of coffee and heaped some grinds into a filter while waiting for the water to boil. The afternoon sun was shining through the window. I walked over to the large window and looked down onto the street. The glow of the sun felt good, like a child's warm hand caressing my face. I needed the warmth; I was still shivering from that slight attack I had while sitting in my car. My own unresolved anger troubled me, but it is an emotional scab I enjoy picking at and peeling off.

The kettle whistle blew and I poured the water into a Melitta funnel and then some cream into my cup. I ambled back toward my office but stopped momentarily to gaze at a book that was laying on Donna's desk, *Black Love, Black Trust*. Donna was recovering from her time on the street, I thought. At first I didn't want her hanging around me, but I had interceded and rammed my fist into the pimp who was slapping her a third time for not properly depositing her money into his account.

People were passing by and were not doing anything. The man was so brazen; a police station was only a block or so over. It was a "black thang" and the pimp was stripping the black off Donna's face. He was about to hit her a fourth time when I caught his arm and slammed him against a parked car.

What shocked and caught him off guard was that a woman was bogarting his MP—his male prerogative. He wasn't a big man, average height. He looked like he had been drinking. The pimp was denim down, wearing a hooded sweatshirt underneath a large oversized jacket; a baseball cap covered his head. His jeans were almost drooping down to his behind. But despite the way he dressed, he was no youth.

He called me a bitch and lunged at me. I answered back with my foot in his groin. That caused him to double over and I applied the coup de grace with a downward blow with my bare fist, which hurt me as well as sending him to the pavement. Knocking someone in the skull with an exposed hand can do serious damage.

I collected Donna, who was sobbing, and took her back to my office. She was only eighteen years old, a child on the verge of womanhood, but in some ways already a woman. In a cynical and calculating way, she had marked me as a softie. Not long after this first encounter with her I found some things missing from my office after I took her there. I knew who had cased the joint.

Even when I was a prosecutor I wasn't good at social work and I wasn't going to start with some street punkette. I thought about finding her and kicking her behind, but I figured that she was in her element and I was given a cheap lesson. The things that were taken, an answering machine, a coffee maker, a telephone, could be easily replaced but the lesson was invaluable: I learned to be more selective with whom I gave assistance, and I had to learn how to control my rage. I was still seeking Nate Ford, and that's who I was really slugging when I hit Donna's pimp.

Weeks later while sitting at a window table of an 8th Avenue bar with Anna, I saw the little tramp hanging onto a lamp post. It was raining and the streets were slick. I watched her make her way across, staggering until a car whose brake didn't hold bounced her a few inches, knocking her off her feet. The driver at first was concerned but became less so when he realized that he had only hit a black junkie. He climbed back into his car and veered off, screaming and swearing at her. The girl was having a hard time getting up. I left the bar and went out into the pouring rain and hauled Donna to her feet.

Donna was sick and smelled bad. I could barely keep from retching. I didn't take her inside the bar. Instead we stood in a doorway sheltering ourselves from the rain.

I held her head up in my hands. "Do you know who I am?! Do you remember me?!" Trucks rumbled by so I had to yell to be heard.

She looked at me and mumbled. "Yeah...You the lady who helped me wid Tyrone...Please...I'm sick...I'm so sick...I got some bad shit...I'm sorry 'bout your things, lady...God, I'm really sick...Please help me." She started to convulse and clutched my clothes.

By this time Anna had left the bar and arrived with my raincoat and purse.

She looked at us. "What's the deal? Who's she?"

"This is the little street bitch who I helped and was then ripped off by her. Give me a hand, Anna."

"A glutton for punishment, huh?" winced the former Miss Chinatown.

We threw my coat around her and took her back to my apartment. She was cursing God, her mother and father, the Zulu nation, and anyone who happened to pass us as we got her upstairs to my third-floor apartment.

It was now or never: she was going to kick her habit. We put her in the unfurnished back room that I was going to turn into a study. I uncovered the futon from my bed and dragged it into the room.

Anna became concerned. She thought that this was out of our bailiwick. I was stripping the putrid-smelling clothes off of Donna when she suggested that perhaps a hospital would be better.

"I've dealt with junkies before," I countered. "She'll cold turkey without a substance replacement. She just needs to be fed, watched, and get some rest."

Anna wasn't convinced. "I don't know, Nina." Donna's moaning was unnerving. "As an officer of the court...."

"Go turn the fucking shower on, Anna," I snapped, "or go home!" She hesitated for a moment and went to the bathroom.

We stripped off her dirty gray underwear and I pushed her into the shower and she slid down to the floor, too weak to stand up.

I left the bathroom and quickly put on a sweat suit and went into the shower and scrubbed Donna, trying to make sure she didn't pass out. I sent Anna out for some food.

It was a long weekend. After the shower we got her into warm clothes and placed her in bed. She retched and vomited, kicking up the poison and the bad food she had been eating. By Saturday evening she was able to consume some chicken soup and drink some tea. She still rocked from side to side, holding her stomach, but she was doing it less often as the weekend wore on.

Surprisingly, Anna spent the weekend with me—us. I told her to go home. She has a pretty active social life and I didn't see the point in disrupting it because I decided to play street mama with a vengeance. But she insisted on staying and only went home to get some things for the duration. We took turns feeding Donna, getting her to the bathroom, making sure that she didn't injure herself from her thrashing about.

At one point while she was shivering I wrapped her in more blankets and held her to let her know that she wasn't alone, that someone, even a stranger, cared about her. Suddenly it occurred to me that the reason I may have been asked to take the Martin case was because of the way I had handled Donna. I had become an "expert" in handling damaged and fragile beings. I knew what to say and how far to push...weaving them away from those obstacles that were impenetrable. The question that remained had to do with me being capable of dealing with my own issues, my own damage, my own rages.

CHAPTER 4

Sometimes I think that Anna was really concerned that I have might done something to Donna. She has seen me at my worst: the time that I went over the wall when I suppressed evidence that could have cleared an alleged drug dealer. Anna caught it and confronted me. I had begun to act with prosecutorial zeal, using the system to get back at every cheap punk with a Glock or Mac-10. I had just returned from my two-month sabbatical, enforced by the Brooklyn District Attorney, mind you. Like Donna, I also have my street scars.

The reason for the enforced sabbatical? One evening I rushed home to my Park Slope brownstone after I received a disturbing phone call at work to find my husband, his hands tied behind his back, his face repeatedly punctured by gunfire.

What the killer did to Lee was nothing compared to what he did to my babies, my children, Andy and Ayesha. The word splattered will only give you a vague idea of what was done to their bodies. They were six and seven years old.

Nate Ford, a West Indian posse leader and Brooklyn's big time cocaine dealer, only smiled at me when the jury announced the verdict: guilty of murder and conspiracy to sell and distribute cocaine. Called the Ice Man, always cool and suave, a slick and sick mulatto, he spoke in a polished British clip, never the patois of the island. He had been running a string of small businesses that fronted for money laundering and narcotic distribution in the Crown Heights and Flatbush section of Brooklyn. His major slip-up was not killing Toro De Gama, his main man, a Marelito from Cuba. Toro had been dipping his hand into the Ice Man's wallet pocket and the Ice decided that it was time for De Gama to go. He gave the assignment to a sub-lieutenant, Colgate, and he botched the job, wounding Toro, who decided to turn state's evidence.

At Brooklyn County Court, with Judge Beth Tyndale presiding, Ford's attorney, Bill Sackman, painted Toro not as the consummate narco-trafficker he was, but as a striving member of the emergent Caribbean middle class that was making the American dream come true. It was the American blacks who were the slackers. Under my questioning, Toro started dropping bombs: the amount of drugs that passed through the organization; which places were fronts; how the money was laundered; names of posse members; where the bodies were hidden; who said what and gave what order: Nate, Nate, Nate. We had seized records and other documents, had tapes and videos of Nate and his operation. The jury didn't have to sweat this and engage in jury nullification; their neighborhoods had been tyrannized by knuckleheads who sprayed the streets in Wild East shootouts, killing children and grandparents. Ford was guilty. Case closed.

"I'll be sending you a little something," he directed at me after the sentencing. He would have sauntered off but the court officers cuffed him and sent him upstate.

I'd been threatened before as an Assistant District Attorney and didn't think anything more about it—until my family was murdered.

The whole thing was planned. The killer even called the newspapers which had sent reporters to the scene. They arrived with the police moments before I was also called by the killer. The press got a good shot of me on my knees wailing before the covered bodies of my children, my hands covering my face. *The New York Post. New York Newstime. The Daily News.* All the tabloids ran front-page photos. *The New York Times* was kind: it only printed a photograph on the front page of its Metro section.

I returned after two months. I was back at work but emotionally damaged. How could I not be? I was the plausible black woman who was considering running for Mayor of New York City, an idea I have since bequeathed to my good friend Anna Gong. I wasn't soft on crime. I had good middle class credentials, went to elite undergraduate and law schools. I married another black professional and had two children attending private school, and we resided in fashionable, liberal Park Slope, Brooklyn. I had it made because I worked for it.

I knew it was Nate Ford. It was his signature form of killing: mean and nasty, to attract the attention of others and get their minds right. He had learned a lesson from the Colombians: don't even spare the children.

When I returned I was called the "Mad Woman." I no longer engaged in plea bargains. Even the conservative judges who loved me as the slam-'em-behind-the-bars-Democrat were beginning to find me a nuisance. I was clogging up their calendars with more cases because I didn't want to cop a plea. Every hood, pimp, dealer, cut-throat, punk, whatever, was fair game to the Mad Woman. It had been suspected that I had suppressed evidence before, but I wasn't caught until Anna. She was a friend and my soul during my ordeal. She was caught in a dilemma when she found out that on the Kevin Bundy case I'd stretched the law to get a conviction due to vengeance, not justice. She offered me a choice: resign or she would have to report it. That was her version of tough shove.

And it worked. I left the D.A.'s office and every litigation law firm wanted a piece of my fine legal ass although I wasn't fit for the law. Inside, I was corrupted by vengeance. Unlike my legal colleagues who remained in the secular priesthood for profit and power, I choose not to hide behind the facade of the law. I admit I'm maladjusted.

Months later Detective Frank Johnson called me to let me know that Nate Ford had escaped. The vehicle that was transporting him and others from one upstate prison to another had been purposely sideswiped. Ford had been slipped a gun; he killed the guards and the driver on board, then jumped into a waiting vehicle. That's when I knew what my real work was: finding that son of a bitch. I went back to his old haunts and began accosting his old gang members, staking out ex-girl friends, shadowing known fences and dealers, trying to learn where he was. I often thought I heard him laughing behind my back, snickering over what he believed was my self-induced misfortune: the nerve of a "bitch" taking on a black man—and winning, or so I thought.

Meeting Donna also saved my soul; she has been my good work. Helping her in trying to clean up her life has made me somewhat less vindictive. But I still get those bouts of murderous rage. I still keep my ears attuned to the street for the slightest info on Nate Ford. I want him so bad that I can taste my own death in trying to ensure his....

For a moment I felt one of those monomaniacal rages about to erupt so I switched my thoughts to Veronica Martin. I had to distract myself, get on about someone else's problem. I was about to make a phone call to Roy Hakim's office at City College when I heard the door unlocking and opening.

"Donna?"

She stepped into the office. "Word. What's up?"

Donna was munching on an apple and looking regal with her shaved black head, a hair style she had taken to wearing lately. She also wore a stud in her nose.

I asked her to sit down and she parked herself next to my desk.

"What's up?" she asked, which is her standard way of asking a question.

I told her about Veronica Martin and her daughter, how we have to ask some questions in order to find her. I wanted her to go to a couple of bars where some black bohos hung out and see if she could learn anything about Malika Martin. Her mother said she was known on the black art circuit.

"You mean un'cover work?" She brightened at this prospect.

I shrugged my shoulders. "Well, yes and no. You'll just be going in and seeing if you can make contact with some folks who may know her or where she's at. Be casual. We don't want people to think you're a cop."

"Me, a cop?!" she exclaimed. "Be for real, Nina! Nobody's gonna think that I'm a cop!"

"Okay, maybe not a cop, but people sometime act funny when they are asked questions by someone who they don't know."

"Should I pretend that I'm a cousin or what?" She was eager and wanted to know what type of story we should concoct for her.

The "problem" with Donna was that she was very street, very hard. She wasn't hard or tough looking; actually she was a very nice looking young sister. It was the way she carried herself, sometimes she walked and talked like a man. What little femininity she exhibited was sometimes undercut by her street edge: loudness and lack of manners. She was ghetto. It was a class thing and I didn't know how to deal with it— or even if I should.

"I got it! I got it! I'll say that I got some tapes for her."

"Huh?"

"Yo, Nina, that I'm a rapper. You know, into music and made some funky tracks for her. How's about that?" She was pleased with the idea.

"Okay, go with it." I reached into my purse and pulled out photos of Malika that her mother lent me. I handed one to Donna.

She studied the face. "She looks like she could be in a Spike Lee Joint production."

Malika Martin, age twenty-two, had her mother's features and her father's complexion. He was a brown-skinned black man and his daughter had a delicious appearance.

Donna kept looking at the photo. She placed the photo against her forehead. "What are you doing?"

"Burnin' her into my mind's eye. What time do I do?"

I told her to get there at about nine o'clock and hang out for an hour at each place. One club was called "For Art's Sake," in the East Village, the other was called "Tempus Fugit," located in Soho.

"Huh? What does that mean?"

"Time flies," I answered.

I gave her fifty dollars and told her to eat a full meal at the apartment before she left for the night. I went back to making my phone call to City College, trying to get a lead on Dr. Roy Hakim.

As she headed to her desk to type up reports and invoices, I called out, "Meet me at Byron's, at eleven thirty!" After snooping up at City College and teaching my class, I was going to treat myself to some j-a-z-z at my former brother-in-law's club. The mistress of music was going to be there and I needed her.

CHAPTER

Over the phone I was informed that Dr. Hakim was on sabbatical at an undisclosed retreat. Apparently he'd left no forwarding address or number where he could be reached. I asked if there was a colleague to whom I could speak to about the professor, and was given the policy reply about university personnel not disclosing the whereabouts of unversity employees to unknown persons.

I decided to go uptown and present my body—something they couldn't ignore. I would also present myself as a fellow instructor of the City College community; lowly adjunct that I am.

I arrived at the Gothic-looking campus and walked over to the Black Studies department. Students were passing through the halls; most of them were wearing oversized, baggy clothing, which would have labeled them as "mutts," a term favored by the NYPD. The atmosphere within the department was subdued, no doubt due to the fact that the department was being rolled into another department's program.

I stopped a young Latina, asking her where to find the department office. She pointed up and held up three fingers. Then turned up the volume of her Walkman and kept diddy-bopping down the hall.

Entering the department's office, a medium-sized room with posters of black heroes, clusters and stacks of papers on desks, tables, on the floor and in corners, I presented myself to the first body I saw: a young woman who was turning from a computer terminal and placing down the phone.

We both looked at each other with a hint of recognition.

"Professor Halligan?" She wasn't quite sure it was me or what I was doing there.

I looked at her and snapped my fingers. "Denise Newman," I said. She had been a student of mine two years ago at Borough of Manhattan Community College, in my black history and law courses. Denise was a round-faced, ebony dark woman with bright eyes. She was a so-so student, very quiet but with potential if she applied herself. Unfortunately for her both my courses entailed a great deal of reading and she wasn't into that, as she told me later.

Denise smiled. "What are you doing here? Are you teaching here?"

"No, Denise. I'm trying to find Professor Roy Hakim. I called here a half an hour ago—"

"Was that you on the phone?" She smiled, embarrassed. "I'm sorry, professor. I didn't know it was you. I thought you were the media or something."

"Oh?" I knew my right eyebrow had arched upward. "Why would the media be calling this office?"

"You know, Dr. Ben Mohammed," she said, her voice lowered. There weren't that many people in the office. "The stuff he's been sayin' about white folks."

"Oh, yeah," I intoned. Dr. Ben Mohammed was the controversial head of the Black Studies department. He'd made some impolitic statements regarding other ethnic groups, denigrating them as gangsters and gutter tradesmen who have conspired against the black race. Dividing humans into "ice devils" and "natural people" was his contribution to intellectual thought and discourse. His academic head was called for by both the governor and the junior senator from the state of New York, known in Washington as "Mr. Cash and Carry."

"Does this have anything to do with Dr. Hakim?" I asked, warming to the thrill of new-found scuttlebutt. Denise nodded and her voice became even lower than before.

"Dr. Hakim was leading a faction that was trying to have him removed. He thought that Dr. Mohammed was spending too much time on television arguing with white people and not developing ideas to advance the race."

Advance the race. I thought the phrase had a certain premovement quaintness. Now, it was more a matter of buppies advancing themselves—ourselves—and crying when we realize that they don't want us around.

"I don't suppose he won?" I asked, referring to Hakim's difference with Mohammed.

Denise slowly moved her head back and forth indicating "no." "The rest of the students rallied behind Dr. Mo and some called Dr. Hakim an Uncle Tom."

I stepped in with my $64,000 question. "Is that why he took a sabbatical?"

"Yeah."

"When?"

"Let's see." She picked up a large red appointment/diary book and flipped back and forth through the pages. "It started last September, Professor Halligan."

"Call me Nina." I smiled and asked quickly, "No forwarding address?"

"No, Prof—I mean, Nina." She giggled. "I'm not used to calling you Nina."

"You'll get used to it. Does Hakim have any close colleagues around? You know, drinking buddies?"

"Professor Rudy Downs..."

"Where can he be found?"

"Well, usually he's in his office, Room 312, but he's on a panel at the Postmodernist African-American Intellectual Symposium," she said, letting out a wind of air.

"Good God, sister," I chuckled, "you said a mouthful. Where are these black geniuses convocating?"

"Way downtown at the Rosa Luxemburg Institute," she answered.

"I should have known: the usual suspects." I opened my purse and withdrew a calling card and handed it to her. "If and when Dr. Downs should return, please give him this and have him call me."

She took the card and read it and was about to put it away but then read it again.

Denise looked up at me. "Is this real from the get-go? Are you really a private investigator, Nina?"

"Yes, ma'am."

I was also able to ascertain that Hakim did call in from time to time to get his messages. Denise said that she would tell him that I stopped by. We chatted a few more minutes about her life. Denise was in the first months of her pregnancy, and both she and her husband James worked at City College to defer the cost of their education.

Leaving the campus I wheeled my black box over to Broadway and West 80th Street. I parked in front of the building where Roy Hakim lived and noticed that it was posted by a bored-looking middle-aged doorman.

I got out of the car and walked down a street of scrawny-looking trees. I stopped at the door and announced that I was Linda Wayne and that Dr. Hakim was expecting me.

The doorman wasn't putting out much energy on this fine spring day in April. He was a portly type; as I took in the scenery of the lobby he eyed me suspiciously. He didn't move to announce me over the intercom phone. "Well?" I asked indignantly. "What are you waiting for?"

"The doc ain't in, lady. I don't know whatya tryin' to pull, but he ain't been in for awhile, soz I know he ain't expectin' nobody."

Somewhat satisfied that Hakim was not at his abode, I returned to the car and drove down the West Side Highway, back to my neighborhood.

By five o'clock I was walking down West 22nd Street, heading toward St. Peter's Episcopal Church. Actually, to the rectory where I had a pastoral session, what Catholics called confession, with Father David Margolies. He has been counseling me about my "bad girl" feelings.

Since the murder of my family I've known that I was no longer the same woman I had once been. I had always been called cool and aloof—even cold, although my husband and my children hadn't found me so. What I had become was a wounded animal seeking revenge. I'd taken to liking hunting down Nate Ford, travelling to any city on the slightest pretext of finding him. Once, I went as far as beating a man with a metal trash can in an alley trying to get him to cough up information about Ford. On another occasion, I almost pulled another man's arm out of his shoulder socket when he tried to chump me off for being a woman. He didn't think I would take him on to get what I wanted, information on Ford. Unlike most men, on either side of the law, I don't use guns. I have two; one at the office and one at home, but I don't carry them and haven't had to use one to date. Seeing what they can do to human flesh hasn't made me want to join the N.R.A.

But I have discovered that I do enjoy going up against knuckle-heads who think they can get away with anything. In Chicago I viciously raked a man's face with my nails. His vertical scars now make him look like an African nobleman. My technique is known as "the Halligan touch" in some circles.

I don't think I'm a sick bitch but I know I do have a problem. Once upon a time I used to concern myself with my career moves. Now I have erotically violent dreams about killing the man who sanctioned the death of my husband and children.

I started coming to St. Peter's because I didn't want to do the middle class thing and see a shrink. Sadie, a friend, mentioned the church, and I needed a place to get down on my knees and beg God's forgiveness. I knew when my family died I must have done somebody wrong—and Mr. Ford said amen to that.

St. Peter's is an old church and years ago it was more or less a family church, and more middle class. But that changed over the years; the congregation is now considerably smaller and older with a sprinkling of blacks, but mostly attended by young whites and the gay community.

I began going on Sunday when Donna started living with me. Soon she even started to come, and she practically had no religious instruction, let alone a family life. We would moderately dress up, attend the church's service and tea, and then go to brunch by ourselves.

Father David Margolies, called Father Dave, led me into his office. He's an older man in his sixties with a weathered craggy face and very warm blue eyes. The office is somewhat shopworn but tidy and has comfortable old leather and wooden furniture. The yellow paint has lost it brightness, aging into amber. Since the rectory is on a side street, his office isn't well illuminated by natural light, making the room somber; a place where crying and confessions would seem normal and appropriate.

Father Dave offered me a seat and asked me about myself. I told him I was still having those murderous fits, attacks of wanting to find and kill Ford. I mentioned the attack I had earlier during the day, how I sat in the car and broke out in a cold sweat.

"What about Donna?" Father Dave leaned forward, his elbows on either side of the armchair and his fingers clasped together.

"She's good. Doing very well." I shrugged and smiled. "She's attending an alternative high school and continues to work with me in the office. Sometimes she assists me on cases...."

"You know," he said, pausing thoughtfully, "when you talk about her...your demeanor changes."

"How so, Father?"

"Don't you know?"

I suppose I did but was reluctant to admit it and much preferred to revel in my thoughts of mayhem. They weren't passive like an aching guilt but in a way expiated the guilt I felt regarding my family.

"Well, having her around has been good for me," I confessed. "She's somebody I can do things for. I feel the need to be needed, Father."

"Nina, have you been...uh...dating?"

"Seeing men? No." I shook my head. "I've been too busy beating them up."

Like a sweet old man, a gentleman, he shook his head. "Dear, dear, we're definitely going to have to do something about that."

After class I remained in the Tribeca area of lower Manhattan and ambled over to Lord Byron's, my brother-in-law's club. It's a small, two-storied but well-attended funky place. Its kitchen offers African food from the continent, as well as Caribbean, Southern and Cajun dishes.

I took a seat at my usual table, tucked away in a semi-dark corner. The club is one of those exposed brick joints with a bandstand and permanent baby grand piano near the back; the place is more narrow than wide.

Upstairs there is a lounge decorated like an old-style gentlemen's club: burgundy-colored overstuffed chairs and couches, pseudo-plush carpets, and bank lamps with green glass shades on end tables. The curtains are always drawn. Busts of classical thinkers are placed around the room and William H. Johnson and Romare Bearden paintings adorn the walls. It's known as a cozy place for lovers who want to engage in some serious saliva exchanges.

I was working on my second Jack Daniels and listening to the Cuban emigre pianist firing up the ivories when Byron, the owner and my late husband's brother, sat down at my table. He kissed me on my cheek.

"How you doing, Nina?" Five years younger than Lee, and cuter in his youngishness, Byron had a certain understated matinee idol look that most but not all black women would find droolingly attractive.

"Not bad," I said. It was eleven-fifteen. I was scanning the crowd for Donna.

"What have you been up to?" he asked as he sat down.

"You know. Work, work, and mo' work."

He simply nodded. "You keep busy, Nina—and away from me."

What could I say to that? I knew what he meant. At one time, Byron had tried to entice me into an affair. It was during a period when Lee and I were having problems. I refused to be shocked or scandalized. Since my widowhood he's been trying to fill up the void in my life with his—I presume—six inches or more of manhood.

I felt his hand caressing my thigh. I shot him a nigger-move-it-or-lose-it-look, but he wasn't deterred. I gripped my hand over his and lifted it from my person and placed it on the table. I wanted to pull his thumb off, but he was family.

"Honey, I'm damaged goods. "

He was about to answer but I pressed a whiskey stained finger to his lips.

"Look, By, you're a successful young entrepreneur, featured on the cover of *Black Enterprise,* profiled as an eligible black bachelor. You have lots of good-looking women walking through here, younger and finer-looking than me. What do you want with me?"

"I've always cared for you, Nina."

"Well, that's a good place to start, but your fondness for me exceeded a certain limit. Tu sabe?"

"I know...It was kinda stupid on my part, sibling jealousy," he admitted.

"Yeah," I countered, "and I didn't want to get caught up in your and Lee's shit. I'm not the prize, Byron. Half the problems in the world stem from you guys always trying to trip up one another. Fine. But it's the women and the children who are caught in the middle of your testosterone firefights."

"It wasn't all about that, Nina. I was in love with you...still am," he said.

"You were in love with me at the wrong time then—and now."

He looked away from me and I began concentrating musically on his face.

My eyes began gliding over his eyes, nose, and lips. The

candle's light on the table brought out the redness in his skin. Now that Lee was gone Byron's features were beginning to act as a substitute for my deceased husband's. Byron was clean shaven; Lee had worn a beard. I loved stroking his fur, feeling it against my thighs as he searched for my pearl.

The Cuban was rippling through a piece which reminded me of Ellington's "Single Petal of a Rose." We often made love to that song; Lee planting kisses and needling bites over my breasts, shoulders and abdomen. Like a rose losing its petal, floating downward, captured by a time-elapsed camera, I unraveled and descended, my passion tumbling when I arched my back and he would sear into me.

When the Cuban finished the piece, Byron rose and looked down at me.

"Can we get together and talk? I mean just talk....I need to talk to someone." For a moment his slick man persona was gone.

"Are you in trouble?" I asked, ready to come to my late husband's brother's aid.

"Do I have to be?" There was a tad of pain and innocence in his reply.

"No," I quietly answered. "Sure, Byron, we can talk. Call me. Okay?

I smiled, and it was a sincere one.

He said he'd call and walked into the approving din that was for the pianist and his sidemen.

Pushing her way though the crowd was Donna, looking hot. She wore a natural-colored macrame bodysuit top that had a molded cup bra. Faded jeans with the requisite tears at the knees completed the ensemble. Her lips were embellished with fellatio red lipstick.

"So what's the 411?" I inquired as she sat down.

Always a hustler, she replied: "Buy me a beer."

I had given the girl fifty dollars and she wanted me to buy her a beer. "Okay, but you're paying for the cab ride home."

Luckily, a waitron was near by and I was able to catch her and asked for my night's third and a beer for my gal wonder.

Donna drank and reported:

"So like, at 'For Art's Sake,' she be a regular, you know, or was. She stopped hangin' there sometime ago, 'round October. People said she was political, hanging 'round with some brothers and sisters who were talkin' about a thing called the New Nation."

"What's the New Nation? "

"Dunno, boss. Just some brothers and sisters talkin' 'bout takin' it to the next stage, that's all. They seem to be Brooklyn based."

"Get any names? Any friends?"

"Oh, yeah." She produced a notebook from her kente bag. "Check this out: Mbooma Shaka, the rapper, has some connection with the New Nation. Also, a dude named Roy Hakim is called 'The Elder.'"

That was more than mildly interesting, I thought. "Anything else about Malika?"

"Well," she said as she slurped her beer, "I met a friend of hers, Jackie Shandlin. She's a sister who works at an African art gallery down in Soho."

"Good work, what about Tempus Fugit?" Speaking of flying, my third Jack was beginning to spin my head.

"Check this out, Nina. It's been rumored that Malika Martin was connected to an art theft!"

"Oh?"

"Yeah. She also belongs to another black group that talks about re-painting black art."

"Re-painting black art?" I threw back at her.

"Yeah, taking it back to Africa."

"Oh, repatriate," I corrected. "Repatriation."

"Yeah! Yeah! That's it. Anyway, Malika and another group, called BATA, Black Art to Africa, have staged demos at galleries and museums. They demanded that things taken from Africa be returned. They've been accused by some of stealin' works of art and sendin' 'em back to Africa."

"Get any names?" I was beginning to sound like a stuck record needle.

Donna smiled. "Uh-huh. Only one."

"And the lucky contestant?"

"Rudy Downs."

"Hmmm. He's a colleague of Roy Hakim at City College. How did his name come up?"

"He's an advisor to the group BATA," she said, checking her notes. "An art collector."

I wondered if there was a connection between Hakim, Malika, and Rudy Downs. Presently, I couldn't figure out the art heist angle. I also wanted to check my head. The liquor was smacking around the last surviving neurons of the day.

I offered her my hand and we shook. "You did good work, sister."

My watch read one o'clock. "Let's git, Donna. We have a long day ahead of us later on." I paid the bill and said goodnight to Byron as we squeezed our way out of the club.

We caught a cab home to Chelsea, with me nodding off in the back seat, my head resting on Donna's shoulder.

When we arrived home I crash landed into my bed, barely taking off my clothes. I was right about the day being a long one, but what I did not foresee was that it would begin at three a.m. with a phone call from Anna telling me that Veronica Martin had been arrested as a murder suspect.

CHAPTER 6

Arriving at a midtown police station, I approached the night sergeant's front desk. Sgt. Petroff, a hairline-receding man of about forty years, was wearing his early morning hooded look: eyes at half-mast but nothing escaping his scrutiny as it passed through his front door. When he saw me his eyes went on alert.

"Halligan?" He looked at his watch. "What got you here at this ungodly hour?"

"Anna Gong," I replied sourly, and began signing the registry.

"Oh, yeah." He rubbed his early morning shadow. "She's in with a suspect, right?" Petroff opened a drawer and fished out a blue visitor's badge. He checked the number and wrote it down beside my name. I noticed that Anna had already signed in.

I looked around as he continued signing me in.

A few night denizens were parked on some benches. Most likely they were relatives waiting to hear about loved ones who'd been brought in.

Finally, Petroff handed me the visitor's badge. I clipped it to the collar of my denim jacket. "What did you hear about this, sergeant?"

"Don't know nuttin', counselor—'cept...." Petroff looked around and shrugged his shoulders. "I heard the victim was shot in the chest several times, but no one heard any gunfire." He shrugged his shoulders again, making his information seem potentially worthless.

"That's what I heard," he continued. "The suspect was found

unconscious in the door of the apartment, but no weapon was discovered."

"Hmmm. This sounds interesting. Buzz me, sergeant."

"Sure thing, counselor." Petroff activated the security latch and I entered into the restricted area of the station.

The door closed behind me. I walked down a corridor that had been painted institutional green but was faded with grime and age. Burly men in blue uniforms, their bulletproof vests slightly outlined, were bum rushing handcuffed young brown and black perps, the night shift's catch. My ears picked up heated and muffled voices. Officers, attorneys, and suspects were engaged in animated and subdued conversations. A few people nodded to me. During my D.A. days I often had to come to Manhattan and interview a suspect who had been a bad boy in Brooklyn. Someone was screaming out the latest rap song. A couple of hookers, barely out of their teens, were seated along a wall, dressed in a gaudy version of Victoria's Secret lingerie. Seasoned veterans, these young girls had been through the routine.

"Hey Charlene," said a youngish cop to one of them as he passed her.

The girl looked up. "Yo, Mazurki," she answered back. "Talk to your boy Esposito. He takin' this shit too seriously! I gotta eat, too!"

Charlene and the other looked no older than sixteen but had that street weariness that ages people quickly. She reminded me of Donna a few years ago, not in her looks but in circumstances.

I proceeded to the Homicide Unit and saw Lieutenant Chuck Murchison conversing with some other detectives. He turned as he saw me coming out of the corner of his eye. Murch is a coal-colored man, the kind I have found to be, uh, lip smacking. He was tall and slender and I could have easily imagined him standing watch on an African savanna, his gaze scanning his livestock, wives, children, and yams.

When he saw me he said, "I know you're coming down here for me, Nina. You ain't interested in no stiff this early in the morning."

"Well," I sighed, "I have been known to entertain some stiff elements in the wee hours." I was trying to be funny but it was too, too early for wit.

"Follow me, lady." Murch led me down a row of desks where some cops were typing out reports and talking about the night's war stories and sports. We turned a corner and went into another room.

Peering into the window of the interrogation room, Captain Harold Kirby serenely rocked himself back and forth on the balls and heels of his feet. Kirby was a short man who was tall enough to squeak through NYPD's physical requirements. His large head sat on his shoulders and he wore a gray buzz cut. A former wrestler, he took pride in his bulldozer physique with no neck. Behind his back he was called "five-by-five."

"Captain?" said Murch.

The man turned in our direction. The most prominent thing about the captain was his incredibly bushy eyebrows. They hid the Celtic bulge that was in the center of his forehead. Kirby's countenance was a mixture of stubbornness and serenity. He grunted more than he spoke and when he did speak it was like some deep fog emanating, a rumbling belch pushing up from his abdomen.

"Halligan, your pal Gong is in there with this Martin woman," Kirby said. His words were more an accusation than a statement of fact.

I stepped over to the dark glass and looked in. The light was low but bright enough to make out Sgt. Dan Burchett questioning Veronica Martin. He was seated across from her at a small gray metal table. Anna sat at the end of the table. I couldn't see her eyes.

A squawk box carried the interrogation into the room where Murchison, Kirby, and I stood:

"Okay, from the top. You said you received a phone call from Ralph Conway."

"Yes," answered Veronica Martin, who looked tired and very disconcerted.

"You received this call at the halfway house that you're staying in, correct?"

"Yes, sir."

"And the call was made at about four p.m.?"

Mrs. Martin nodded.

"The man," continued Burchett, "identified himself as Ralph Conway, a former security personnel of your husband's?"

"That's correct."

Burchett shifted in his chair. "He said that he had some information regarding your husband's murder and wanted to speak to you about it?"

"Yes." Her face began streaming with tears.

"He asked you to meet him at his place at one a.m. because he got off work at eleven thirty. Correct?"

"Correct," replied Veronica Martin.

"When you arrived at the appointed time, you found his door open?" asked Burchett.

"That's right," answered the former Mother of the Nation.

"You then entered the apartment and saw Conway dead on the floor?" Burchett continued.

She nodded her head.

"Then you passed out from shock? Is that correct, Mrs. Martin?" the detective pressed.

"It was seeing him on the floor...bleeding...It was Malik all over again, all over again." She kept repeating the words "all over again" and sobbed heavily.

I turned to Mr. Five-by-five. "Are you taking that as an admission of guilt? A confession?"

"Oh, hell, Halligan," he grunted. "That woman's a wreck. She didn't kill Conway. According to our stiff specialist, Conway had been shot an hour or more before she showed up and passed out. Nobody heard any shots or remembers seeing or hearing anything in the apartment. A tenant discovered her passed out in the hallway as he was returning home."

"Robbery?"

Murch pitched in. "Don't think so," he answered. "The man didn't have much in his apartment and nothing was rifled or anything. It looked as if he was popped when he opened the door. Blam!"

"A hit?" I continued.

"Who would put a hit on a seven-dollar-an-hour security guard—and for what?" asked the captain. He continued looking into the room as he spoke.

I didn't know, I thought, but that's what he's paid to find out.

A door opened that led into the room and Burchett's head appeared.

"Let her go or what, captain?" asked Burchett.

"Yeah," said Kirby, disgusted. He quickly turned to me. "I want you and Dong—"

"Gong," I corrected. "Gong."

"Whatever! In my office!" He wheeled around quickly and moved toward his office.

When Anna and I entered his office, Kirby was seated at his desk reading a file. He grunted something about us sitting; we looked at one another and did so. To my left was an old style book cabinet, the kind you find in schools or law offices; they were wooden and had glass-pane covers. Kirby's cabinet had three compartments and on the very top sat trophies, pictures and knickknacks. Above the cabinet itself was a picture of Kirby's police academy graduating class. The rest of Kirby's office was thoroughly nondescript.

"Okay, ladies," he said almost sneeringly, his massive hands moving paper about, "what the hell is going on?" He glared at me.

"I'm just here for moral support," I innocently piped up. I pointed to Anna. "She's the boss."

Kirby's head remained facing me but his eyes slowly shifted to Anna. "Well, madam counselor?" There was an annoying touch of sarcasm in Kirby's voice.

"Mrs. Martin received a phone call at four p.m. yesterday," she started.

Kirby, exasperated, slammed his desk with an open hand. We both jumped.

"Don't recite me the interrogation!" he snapped. "She's Malik Martin's widow! What's she doing up here?!"

Anna was perceptibly shifting into her steely mode. I've seen her do it many times. She becomes slow and methodical, deliberate in her movement, her voice measured, talking through her teeth as if she's hissing.

"Not that it's any of the department's business, but Mrs. Martin is here looking for her daughter. Ms. Halligan has been retained to make some inquiries as to her whereabouts," answered Anna. Her jaw line was becoming prominent. "Satisfied?"

"No, I'm not."

"Then, that's your problem, Captain Kirby. We're finished."

"I'm not, Miss Gong." He pronounced the "G" in her name harshly.

"Well, let's get this over with," I said. "We have a client who's stressed out; we'd like to get her home."

Kirby paused for moment, then went on the attack. "Is she still whacked?" he delicately asked.

"What?" said Anna whose face screwed up in disbelief that the man asked such a question so callously.

"Whacked?" I echoed.

"Yeah. A nut job. She flipped out and went bazooka over Martin and to the funny farm. Is she alright?" he demanded. "I don't want any nut jobs connected with the Martin case."

"The Martin case?" I asked. "The Martin case is closed—isn't it?"

Kirby's Celtic bulge formed into a "V," meaning he was figuring out his next move. The man was subtle. "You ladies care for a little wake-me-up? A shot?"

Anna and I looked at each other. Kirby was becoming cuddly or this was his variation of showing warmth.

Anna shrugged. "Sure," she said. "The morning has already been ruined."

"What about the Martin case?" I asked.

Kirby opened the bottom drawer of his shopworn desk and pulled out his private stock and three glasses. He poured the liquor and assumed the role of a roughneck gentlemen. He handed us glasses. Then he lifted his to his lips and drank. Anna and I shrugged at this inclusion into some sort of male ritual and drained our glasses.

Anna was the first to speak. "The Martin case, captain?"

Kirby became uncharacteristically relaxed. He opened up his collar, revealing a profusion of gray chest hairs. He even smiled—or made some attempt at turning up the corners of his mouth. "Nothin' much...."

I went on the attack. "Do you do this to your wife?" I began to demand. "Get her all hot and bothered and don't deliver?"

He smiled. "Look, we got a communiqué from Plaza One," he said, referring to the NYPD's headquarters downtown near City Hall. "It seems that somebody has been making threats to Paul Tower...."

"And...?" Anna asked. "What does this have to do with Mrs. Martin?"

"Well, Mrs. Martin shows up and Ralph Conway is shot."

"Huh? I'm thick, captain," I said. "What does that have to do with Paul Tower?" I had asked the question, but a more important thought occurred to me and I added: "Wait a minute. Who was Ralph Conway?"

His smile disappeared.

"Ralph Conway was a former police officer who—"

Anna snapped her fingers. "He was the mole!"

"What mole?" I asked.

She turned sideways in the wooden chair and faced me. "Two years ago there was a profile on him in one of the tabloids when the Malik Martin craze was at its height. He was interviewed and talked about being a police agent who had infiltrated the minister's security team," she said. "Martin was killed in Washington, but his headquarters of the Nation movement was in New York, and that made him an object of surveillance. Right, captain?"

Kirby was stone faced. "This department does not comment on former or current police operations. But I will tell you this, Conway was a former member of this department who could not conduct himself as a professional. He was an alkie, a drunk, unreliable in the performance of his duties," replied a man who detested personal weakness.

My mind began to click, whir, and spin. Ah, that's the connection with Tower. Somebody's been making threats to him, then Conway winds up dead—with Veronica Martin at his feet. Now I understood why Kirby wanted to know about Mrs. Martin. He wanted to find out if she was this year's Unabomber.

As I sat spinning my internal wheels, Anna said, "Look, captain, she's just a mother looking for her daughter."

But Kirby wasn't going for the mother and child angle.

"Shee-it," he said. "Excuse my parley-vous, ladies, but is that supposed to assure me that she's as gentle as a lamb? Humph! We all know what a woman is capable of when she sets her mind to it."

His face was turned to Anna, but his eyes slowly shifted to me like ball bearings in mechanical slots. "Isn't that so, Mrs. Halligan?"

His was another throat I wouldn't mind wrapping my black hands around. "If you think she's guilty," I said, referring to Mrs. Martin, "why don't you arrest her?"

"No evidence. No weapon. No motive," countered the policeman. He stood up. "Good night—and good morning, ladies." The session was over.

Within half an hour's time I was back in bed tossing and turning. Questions kept popping up: what kind of threats had been made to Paul Tower? Did Ralph Conway make them? How did he know where to reach Veronica Martin? What did he want to tell her? Who killed him? Did she?

Before Donna rose I had gone out and purchased the morning newspapers. I turned on the jazz station that broadcasts from Newark, New Jersey, WBGO, and plopped down on the couch. Scanning the columns I came up with zero on finding a mention of Conway's death. Too late to have made this morning's papers, I thought.

"You been up all night?"

Donna was standing in her nightshirt, sleepily rubbing her bald head, yawning. She looked like an over-sized but adorable brown baby.

"Naw," I said. My eyes were going over the good, gray *New York Times.* "I caught some Z's, not much but some."

"What happened this morning?" She sat down in the armchair that was draped with an African print.

I told her that Veronica Martin was found unconscious near a dead man in his apartment.

"No shit!" she said loudly. Too loudly. I had about three or four drinks within the last six hours and not enough sleep.

"What happened?! Tell me!!" She perched herself on the seat and drew her nightshirt over her knees. "Is it in the papers?"

"No." I rose and went into the kitchen and started to make breakfast.

I removed from the refrigerator eggs, milk, cheese, bacon, and English muffins, brought down a mixing bowl from the cupboard and cracked in four eggs and began stirring them. While preparing the coffee I started thinking, reminiscing, about how Andy and Ayesha used to hug me in the morning while I cooked, wrapping their young arms around me. Sometimes we all would pile, Lee included, into the bed on Saturday morning and read the newspapers, magazines, the kids would do their homework, and we'd graze the channels.

"Donna," I shouted from the kitchen, "call your auntie!"

She placed down the newspaper and pulled the telephone over and began dialing.

"Morning..." I heard her say. "She told me to wake you up!"

I picked up the phone in the kitchen. "Okay, bitch," I said to Anna, "what's the real story?"

CHAPTER 7

 I arranged to meet with Anna and Veronica Martin at my office at 11 a.m. Donna wanted to be present, but I needed her at the library scouring back issues of newspapers for articles on Ralph Conway. Anna wasn't too keen on the idea of meeting so soon after Veronica Martin's police interrogation but I insisted. I had a couple of concerns: Did the Conway killing have anything to do with my present assignment? Why didn't Mrs. Martin call either Anna or me before she went gallivanting on some nocturnal mission?

Counsel and client arrived at the appointed time. I served them amaretto coffee before starting my inquiries. Mrs. Martin looked better than she had earlier. She was rested, and more composed. I began with what we all knew—or what was told us: Conway had called Mrs. Martin.

"How did he know you were at the halfway house?" I said, making sure to include Anna in the questioning since she had made the arrangements with the committee that sponsored Mrs. Martin's release.

"It was mentioned in some newspaper, in the *Times'* Chronicle section," replied Mrs. Martin.

"That's right," Anna added. "She was in a public institution and her release was made so by Pro Bono. They issued a statement to the press."

"They issued a press release?" I asked.

"Yes," replied Anna.

"Why?"

"I think," she began, "they did so because the organization is primarily staffed by young hotshots who want to make a name for themselves by highlighting Pro Bono's work."

"Okay," I sighed. "We now have an idea of how he possibly got in touch with Sister Ronnie—Mrs. Martin."

"Sister Ronnie?" echoed Anna.

I turned to Mrs. Martin. "I'm sorry, Mrs. Martin." She acted as if she barely heard the old nom d'affection. That was a different world for her back then, as it surely was for us. She had been locked away for over twenty years, and some of us hadn't gotten over the disappointments of the "revolution." It was that aspect that had me concerned. Some people, like Conway, might be inclined to want to get in touch with her.

"Mrs. Martin, why didn't you call Anna or me?"

She stared at me blankly. "I—I...he—Conway—wanted to see me alone." Momentarily she wore that same vacant, hesitant look she had when I first met her. Leaning forward with my hands clasped in my most lawyer-friendly manner, my brow furrowing, I said, "Mrs. Martin, you still should have called us."

"Well, I didn't think he'd be murdered, Ms. Halligan," she replied defensively. "He told me that he wanted to speak to me, that it was about my husband's...." She stopped and the stillness in her eyes revealed that she had traveled back to a moment she presently couldn't mention, the assassination.

"Mrs. Martin," I said, "we know that you didn't expect to find him dead. But the point is he was and *you* were found next to his body. The body of a man you hadn't seen in almost twenty-five years. Are you even sure it was him? That it was Ralph Conway?"

Agitated, she sat the cup of coffee she been holding down on the corner of the desk. "Look, Ms. Halligan," she snapped, "I'm not a retard!"

Anna and I both popped quick glances at her and at each other.

"Mrs. Martin, that's not what Nina was implying. I know she wasn't," countered Anna. "It's just dangerous for a woman such as yourself...."

"And just what kind of woman is that?" A certain stiffness registered in her voice.

Yes, I thought. This is a different Veronica Martin—at least for the time being.

"Well, you've recently been de-institutionalized. Which might encourage people to try to take advantage of your...disorientation. Going up to Hell's Kitchen at one o'clock is not a good idea," replied Anna.

"Look, I didn't hire you two to be my nanny!" VM said. "I'm a grown woman! I've had enough institutionalized care to last me a lifetime. When it comes to looking into the affairs of my late husband, that is of no concern to either of you until I broach the subject. Is that understood?"

Both Anna and I were nonplussed. We looked at each other, trying to figure out who this Veronica Martin was. Of course I could understand her feelings about wanting others to butt out of her business in regard to her husband's death. I was doing the same thing. The only difference being, that my intentions were definitely homicidal.

"Mrs. Martin, do you still wish for me to pursue the matter regarding your daughter?"

"Yes."

I turned to Anna. "Counsel, do you have anything to add to this meeting?"

Anna gave a breezy "no." The tone indicated that this was the last freebie she would ever handle for the Women's Committee on Therapeutic De-institutionalization of Pro Bono. It was also additionally clear that Anna was washing her hands of some aspect of this assignment. This was pro bono work for her, but I was getting paid time and expenses. Our client was left a trust that had appreciated nicely; she could be ripe for the plucking by some enterprising person or persons. But she insisted upon her rights as a free agent and I would not deny her that.

"Well," I said, "this meeting can come to a close. I'm sorry to trouble you, Mrs. Martin, and it won't happen again."

Later Donna arrived with photocopies of news articles and lunch, she plopped down the information on my desk and pronounced judgment on Ralph Conway.

"The motherfucker was a traitor!"

I began sorting through the material. "Who was, homegirl?"

"That Conway dude!" She pulled up a chair and brought out sandwiches, beverages, and afternoon treats. "The nigga deserved to die!" Donna entertained very primitive political ideas.

Munching through the meal I read Conway's mea culpable interview. He had been a member of NYPD's Bureau of Special Services, known as BOSS, an intelligence unit that gathered information on so-called subversive organizations, groups and individuals. As a BOSS operative, Conway infiltrated Malik Martin's inner circle as a member of his security team. In the article, Conway confessed about reporting Martin's liaison with a woman other than his wife; he thought that the information had been used against Martin. It also seems that the NYPD knew of a forthcoming attempt on "the prince of the Black Nation," as Martin Malik was called. Yet no precautions were taken. The minister himself decided against police protection and the hit was made. Conway was transferred to other assignments but lost his bearings after Martin's death. He became an alcoholic and lost his job, his family, and himself. According to newspaper accounts, he worked sporadically as a security guard.

"So now what?" asked Donna. Her legs were stretched out before her and she wiggled her feet, encased in thick-soled urban wear. Her face also had crumbs on it.

"Nothing, gal wonder." I swallowed the last bite of my country paté sandwich on whole wheat with lettuce.

"Ain't we working on the Martin case?"

"Honey, our marching order is to locate her daughter."

Donna pointed to the articles. "What about this stuff, then?"

"File it under Martin, subheading ES."

"ES?"

"Yeah, extraneous shit," I answered. "Case closed." But I wasn't quite sure about that.

At the House of Olodumare, a Soho gallery specializing in African Art, I found Jackie Shandlin minding a combination display case and work counter while her boss explained the difference between "African art" and "art from Africa" to prospective yuppie buyers. I gazed at some interesting gold earrings from Africa that I wouldn't mind getting my hot little hands on.

"Can I help you with something?" asked a petite women with walnut-colored skin and curly black hair.

"Well," I said, hemming and hawing. There was that set of earrings that really would look good on me, I thought. "I would like to speak to Jackie Shandlin," I said, trying to make sure that she was the person. She was the only black person around and Donna reported that she worked at this gallery.

"I'm Jackie Shandlin," answered the woman.

I pulled out my investigator's ID. "My name is Nina Halligan. I'm trying to locate a friend of yours, Malika Martin."

"Oh, God," she let out in an exasperated tone. "What did she do *now*?"

"Nothing that I know of, Ms. Shandlin. I'm working for her mother—"

"Veronica Martin? Is she out?"

"Yes, she is. Did you read about her?"

"No. I'd gone to the hospital with Leeka a few times and met her mother. I knew she would be getting out, being released soon. How is she adjusting?"

"Fine. She has been trying to locate Malika who hasn't been heard from since October. Have you heard from her or know of her whereabouts?"

Jackie bit her lower lip. "I—"

"Jackie!" a sing-song voice called out. The owner, a middle-aged woman with short blonde hair, very chic in her Soho attire, trailed after her voice. She approached the display case where we were standing with a large mask in her hands and the two yups behind her. The way the two of them smiled, apprehensively. I gathered that this was their first time into the deepest, darkest world of African art—or art from Africa.

"Jackie, be a dear and write this up." Madam assured the couple that they would have many years of pleasure and good harvests with the spirit that dwelled in the mask. Then she turned her market-oriented gaze toward me.

"May I help you, miss?"

"Uh, no. I'm just browsing. Do you mind?"

"No, no. House of Olodumare welcomes the curious. I'm in my office if you need any questions answered. Jackie rings up the sales," she informed me.

I nodded my thanks and the madam of Olodumare left. Jackie wrote a bill of sale, wrapped the mask in vibrant kente cloth wrapping paper, and money—plastic—was finally exchanged. The couple left. Jackie nodded her head in the direction of a corner that housed some artwork and I followed her over there.

"When did you last see Malika?"

"God...uh...I don't know...last fall?" she replied, more of a question than an answer. "We had coffee..." Jackie stopped and looked over her shoulder at the niche that madam called her office. She beckoned me to walk with her to a more spacious area that was further away from Madam's earshot. We stood amidst stone sculptures from Zimbabwe.

"My boss hates Malika and her BATA group..."

"I've heard about it."

"Are you really working for Veronica Martin?" she asked tentatively. "It's not that I think that you're lying, but two men came here last week asking about Malika."

"The police?"

She negatively shook her head. "They wouldn't identify themselves; they were really aggressive in their gestures, trying to scare me."

I noted that but pressed on about Malika. "What about Malika? When did you see her? Roughly."

"Haven't seen her since the fall, probably October...since she went underground."

"Underground?"

"Yeah." Jackie looked over her shoulder before she continued. "Miss Halligan, Malika was having, in my opinion, a nervous breakdown."

"Please continue," I said.

"She was becoming increasingly angry and paranoid..."

"About anything in particular?"

"She talked obsessively about getting the men who killed her father."

"Did she mention any names," I asked.

"She would bug out over Paul Tower—the black television preacher."

"What did she say about him?"

"Jackie!"

"Madam Olodumare" had stepped out of her office and into the muted glare of the track lights. Slung over her shoulder was an expensive-looking Coach bag.

"I'm going out to lunch." She looked at her watch. "I'll be back at four p.m., after my massage." She looked at me. "Seen anything you like?"

I pointed to one of the Zimbabwean stone sculptures. "Jackie is filling me in on this. I can see she's learned a lot from you," I lied. "Enjoy your lunch—and the rub." The woman left, and Jackie and I continued.

"What did Malika say about Paul Tower?" I didn't know if that had any relevance in locating her, but it sort of whetted my curiosity.

Jackie mulled over my question as she circled one of the African *objets d'art*. "She basically called him a traitor to the black revolution and to her father."

Traitor was a word that I had heard twice today. "Did she ever mention a Ralph Conway?"

Jackie waved her head again. "No...I don't remember."

I told her that a former bodyguard of Malika's father had been killed. That he'd also been a police agent who spied on Dr. Martin. "You don't think she's...?"

"She talked about killing traitors...."

"What about her guardian, Roy Hakim?"

"Oh, the two of them are on the outs. She was pissed at him for not wanting to help her avenge her father, for talking theory and not organizing."

"Mbooma Shaka?"

Jackie sucked in her breath and rolled her eyes at the mentioning of the name. "Bogus revolutionary. Just a hustler with a bunch of black radical wannabes. It's people like Mbooma who messed up Leeka's mind."

"How so?"

"Telling her that she was the daughter of the revolution! That she had to avenge her father and purify his death by eradicating those who betrayed him! I mean the girl was already scarred by the fact that she actually witnessed him getting killed....She didn't need to hear that!"

"Did she believe it?"

"Miss Halligan, being the daughter of a famous black man is a bitch."

"Meaning what?"

"Meaning that she felt that she had to live up to some ideal. Her mother was hospitalized...her father was murdered...the black

52

movement had frittered away....She wasn't happy with what was going on with black people."

I stood silently. "And you haven't heard from her?"

"Not since she went under....She still keeps her apartment."

"Really?"

"Yeah. She wrote about eight months' worth of checks and I just mail them off to the rental office. I also collect her mail."

This was the time to see whether or not we had bonded. "Can I look at her apartment?"

Jackie bit her lower lip again. "I—I..." She stopped and walked back over to the display counter and unlocked a drawer and pulled out her clear plastic purse. By the time I got over to the counter she was slipping a set of keys over the glass top to me.

"I worry about her, Miss Halligan. If you weren't a sister I wouldn't be doing this." She wrote down Malika's address on Olodumare Art Gallery stationery. Her building was located in a section of the East Side called Alphabet City. I took the keys and placed them in my purse.

"I'll get these back to you either later today or tomorrow. I really appreciate this. Thank you." I was about to start walking, but a sudden thought occurred to me. "Oh, by the way, the men who were here, asking about Malika? What did they look like?"

"Both were black. One had a bald head, completely shaved. One side of his face looked paralyzed. The other guy was kind of ordinary...dark complexioned." She shrugged her shoulders. "I really can't remember anything else. Sorry." I thanked her again and left. I got inside my black box and rolled over to Alphabet City.

CHAPTER 9

Alphabet City roughly encompasses an area that runs from Avenue A to FDR Drive, the neighborhood's western and eastern borders, respectively; East 14th Street is its northern border and East Houston its southern demarcation. Bordering FDR Drive were the projects, predominantly peopled by Nuyoricans: American-born Puerto Ricans. Many of the tenements east of the park had been abandoned and were taken over by squatters during the 70s and 80s. Around the turn of the century, it was home to Italians, Jews and other ethnic immigrants who came to America during the country's expansion after the Civil War. They used it as a launching point to other parts of the city or escaped to the suburbs. Prior to the go-go eighties it had been a very Bohemian place with clubs, restaurants and cafes; Charlie Parker had resided there. But lately it had become a coveted area in the eyes of yuppies and that upgraded the police's attention and increased tension. The center of activity is Tompkins Square Park, a hotly contested space where a riot occurred, pitting the police against street people. The area's claim to fame was a drug film called *Panic in Needle Park,* filmed in the park, and starring a then young Al Pacino. The place had that kind of history, that sort of ambiance. Recently it had become somewhat pacified, the urban funk reduced and contained to make the area hospitable for yuppydom.

I pulled up in my black box and gazed at the neighborhood. It was a rather depressing array of tenement buildings with idle looking men hanging around. They were mainly my brothers and my cousins, Puerto Ricans. I parked at East 5th between Avenues B and C. A mucus-encrusted winehead was propped up against the side of the door as I entered Malika's building. The ground floor landing was dark. I could hear hot salsa music coming from down the hallway. Jackie had mentioned that Malika's apartment was on the second floor, so I ascended the stairs.

Malika's place was a small efficiency that probably had been part of a larger unit years ago. A futon was on the floor in one corner. I was about to go to the desk, which was near the bed, but an arm was suddenly around my neck. I began gagging for air that immediately became a precious commodity. The grip was fierce and I was trying to get my hand in edgewise or reach up behind me and strike my attacker. But every attempt I made was met with an ever tightening grip. I raised my legs and for some inexplicable reason my attacker tried to ram me against a wall. That worked to my advantage. By placing my feet against the wall, I pushed off with all the force I could muster. We both went flying back into the door and I rolled to the floor, gagging and trying to breathe in as much air as possible.

A foot smashed into my head as I was rising to my feet, sending me rolling again. I couldn't afford to black out, so I tried to get up again but his foot hit me again in my face. That blow slammed me into the desk. I grabbed the chair, whipped it around, and threw it at him. He ducked, and the chair crashed into the kitchen space.

The man, hooded, pulled out a huge father-fuckin' knife. He sliced the air, jabbed at me, judging how I moved, and lunged at me. I sidestepped him, grabbed his weapon hand with my left , slammed his face and then his solar plexus with my right hand. The knife dropped as I grabbed his collar and went down on my back, flipping him over. I thought that would stun him but he was quickly on his feet.

He charged at me, using his head as a ram, and I rolled away, cracking the refrigerator door open and slamming it on his head. Quickly I gripped his arm behind his back and yanked him out and pounded him repeatedly, finishing him off with a blow to the base of his skull. That laid him prostrate at my feet. My face was sore and my ribs ached. I was about to stumble to the bathroom when I heard sudden movement behind me. Immediately I went into a crouch, threw up my left arm as guard, and was about to throw a metal Chinese star from my belt only to find that the door was opened and my attacker in flight. I dashed out the apartment. Bounding down the stairs after the man, I saw him shove aside a pregnant Latina. She was about to go over the railing until I grabbed her.

"What da fuck!" she screamed.

I didn't stay to get her settled but continued down the stairs. By the time I reached the street, a dark 1993 green Buick was speeding off. I thought I saw a bald-headed black man behind the steering wheel but wasn't sure.

Inside Malika's apartment I tried to put the small place back into some order. I went into the bathroom and looked at my face. My lips were swollen, and the area around my eyes and my forehead was bruised. I sat down at her desk and looked around. There were scattered papers everywhere, Malika's attempts at stories and poems. I opened drawers and found nothing telling. Then, I looked at the bulletin board. An old newspaper article was tacked to it. The article was about Paul Tower's forthcoming celebration of his stewardship of the Black Christian Network. The celebration was scheduled for May of this year. I stood up and checked her bookcase. Many of the books—and she didn't have that many to begin with—were about the civil rights movement...not an unusual subject for someone like her.

The volume that caught my eye was Elijah Muhammad's *Message to the Black Man.* I picked it up, leafed through the paperback copy and thought of old college debates regarding Muhammad's shopkeeper nationalism versus Malcolm X's pannationalist views. Either a couple of train tickets were being used as bookmarks, or the book was a convenient place to keep old train stubs. One was a stub from Amtrak to a Philadelphia station, the other was for a local train line in Pennsylvania that originated in

New Jersey. As I went through several other books, a pattern was taking form. The ones that had a more nationalistic slant had old train stubs in them. One was dated September of last year, roughly when Jackie said Malika went underground. I took a last look around the flat and locked up.

I left the building looking for a bodega. Finding one, I purchased a Dos Equis. The chilled bottle of beer against my forehead and lips felt like a gift from God as I sat in my black box.

CHAPTER

I returned to my apartment and attended to my temporary defects. It wasn't until I got home and looked at myself in the mirror that I noticed that my white blouse was ripped, stained with blood. This meant I was inadvertently exposing some hefty cleavage. No wonder the brothers and cousins in the bodega were grinning at me when I left. Slowly, Andy and Ayesha came to my mind. Whenever the children came home from a fight or had fallen off their bikes, I was there to bandage them, kiss their pains and scrapes away. Who was here for me? Who was going to kiss my forehead? My bruised lips? Nobody.

The blouse slipped off my shoulders and I examined the area near my left bra strap; it was scratched. Satisfied that I hadn't sustained any serious damage, I walked into my bedroom and tossed the blouse into the hamper. I put on a sweatshirt, closed the door to my room, kicked off my flats, and laid down on the bed.

It was dark when I woke up. A noise I heard outside the bedroom had disturbed my sleep. I guess I was still in a combat mode, still reacting to the afternoon's assault. Reacting to the sounds I heard—voices and movement—as a threat, I slowly reached under the bed and pulled out the 9mm automatic pistol that was attached to the bed frame. I don't like guns and never carry one when on assignment, but since my family was murdered in my last home I've become quite vigilant about protecting my hearth.

I went to the door and slowly opened it, and listened. No one was in the living room. As I stepped out, my ears picked up voice and sounds coming out of Donna's room. Slowly, inching my way, my eyes adjusting to the darkness, I heard a crash or something being knocked over. My foot—my bare foot, mind you—kicked open the door.

"Freeze!" I yelled.

"Nina!" screamed Donna. "Don't shoot!!" She switched on her night lamp.

"Oh God!" cried a pretty-faced, nappy dread boy of nineteen or twenty. "Don't shoot!! We're using protection! We're using it!"

He held up a torn foil wrapper of a condom. At first I couldn't figure out why he was showing me that, but then it dawned on me that my previous lectures to Donna about protection must've been passed on to him during the negotiation for some "skin." He thought he was being inspected by a gun-toting den mother. Donna was hysterical; she assumed I was moments away from firing on them. I was in more command than she realized, but that didn't calm her down.

"What the fuck are you trying to prove?!" she screamed at me.

I mumbled my apologies and left. I went back to my room and holstered the pistol beneath the bed. On the edge of the bed, I wondered about the day, particularly the minutes when I received a fierce head whipping.

What began to annoy me, anger me, was that Donna didn't even notice my lumps. Granted, she was more focused on the pistol. Then I realized that I was becoming upset over the fact that she was getting serviced by some dude (Bokeem, I was to learn later).

Someone was paying attention to her. What about me? Parts of me had been left in a pool of blood in Park Slope....

It was Friday night and I decided that I wasn't interested in listening to their sexy noises. I was going to leave them the apartment. I called Anna and told her that I wanted to crash at her place. "Okey-dokey. You got the key, Nina," she said and we hung up. I left Donna a note, stuffed a few things in a gym bag, headed uptown. I left the car and caught a subway to the Upper West Side.

Anna lived in one of those pre-World War One buildings that was designed for the middle class when they were serious about family life and children. She had rooms. The girl had *serious* rooms. The kitchen was large enough to cook and eat in, with a dining room. These were holdovers from the era of gracious living. She had a spacious living room that could hold a Steinway, plus three bedrooms.

Anna was a painter at heart. Her apartment was decorated in various Asian motifs and classical designs with paintings from Italian masters. Oriental lanterns and bamboo screens decorated the living room. Huge antique Chinese vases were placed strategically throughout the apartment.

When I walked in she was painting in the studio, wearing a paint-splotched, baby blue mandarin-style dress over her even more splotched slacks; her feet were bare. When she dressed like that she looked Chinese *Chinese,* reminding me of Gong Li, the featured actress in Zhang Yimou's films.

"What the fuck happened to you?" she asked when she saw my face. Finally, attention. I felt better already. I told her about my encounter with the hooded hoodlum while searching Malika Martin's flat.

"And Donna didn't do anything after you had arrived from fighting that male dragon?" she asked. She placed down her brush and was examining my face gently with her finger tips.

"Donna was getting her needs met," I reported, not too acidly.

"Ungrateful bitch," sucked in Anna.

"Don't be too hard on her," I said. I told her about how I had burst into her room, brandishing my sidearm. But Anna was not in the mood for granting slack.

"You've been too nice to that girl," she said. "Get her out of your apartment."

I shrugged, ambled into the kitchen and fixed us both a stiff drink. I took Anna's drink back to her and left her painting. I'd brought some of the articles on Ralph Conway with me and was reading them when the telephone rang. Anna picked it up in her studio. I could hear her voice becoming louder and agitated in Chinese. That conversation ended but the phone rang again and she became even more louder—in Chinese, Mandarin dialect, mind you—during the ensuing conversation. She hung up and stormed out of the room, her bare feet slapping the wooden floor, swearing in Chinese.

"What's up?" I asked, setting the Conway articles aside.

"Mama Gong sends her love," she said, ignoring or not hearing my question. Anna walked, then stopped. "You want a refill?" She was holding the glass I'd fixed for her.

I nodded yes and handed her my glass. She padded off, continuing to curse in Chinese.

Anna came back into the room and handed me a newer and more deadlier version of my drink. She sat in a chair, crossed her legs, dangling a bare foot. Silently cursing under her breath...in English.

"Mama Gong?" I inquired.

"With the perennial question!" she spat. The perennial question being when was she going to marry. Like yours truly, Anna was approaching her middle thirties and was unmarried. She was dating Winston Chao, a very handsome and successful investment banker.

I kind of nodded, since I had been privy to this discussion many times before, and went on reading the Conway articles. Anna kept nervously dangling her foot, staring blankly at some object in her living room.

"I'm no longer seeing Winston," she announced out of the blue.

"What happened? Did anything happen ?"

"Yeah, something happened. I've been experimenting," replied Anna. She stood up and sat down on the couch that was holding me.

"Uh-huh," I said. "Who is he?"

"It's not a *he*, Nina."

I had heard what she said and didn't want to hear. The room became very, very, very quiet. My eyes had focused for a very long time on a period at the end of a sentence I'm quite sure I read ten times during the respite.

Anna cleared her throat. "I said...."

"I heard what you said."

"Well?" she demanded. "Are you going to denounce me? Disown me? Report me to the Correct Sex Patrol?"

I decided to be cool. I had been physically slammed around earlier and I had pulled my gun when I thought my household was in danger. "Honey, it's none of my business. The only thing that concerns me is finding our client's—"

"Fuck her—them!" Anna snapped. "This is Friday, the weekend! Workers of the World Night! You're off duty! I'm off duty!" Anna reached over and turned my face toward hers. I winced.

"Sorry," she apologized. "I've got some mainland ointment that stinks, but will make you even prettier than before, Ms. Halligan."

She stood up and went to the bathroom, returning with something that claimed to be mountain ox ointment. She opened the jar, doled out a small pat on her index finger and applied it to the bruised spots.

"Come tomorrow, you be a strong, progressive black woman," she said in a deep, mocking voice.

Okay, I thought, she was mommying me. Should I oblige and ask her about her experiments? I held my breath. "What's with the experiments?"

"I thought you'd never ask," she said gleefully. "I've been seeing women...."

I closed my eyes and shook my head. "Anna...Anna...." I heard myself say.

"I'm a chink dyke," she confessed. "I don't want to have children. My paintings are my children."

"Well, every woman isn't meant for motherhood or the mommy

track," I offered.

"You miss being a mother, don't you?"

"The best years of my life," I smiled slightly. "Brief as they were. It's interesting how God works."

"What do you mean?"

"He took my family away, but still has given me something to live for, namely killing Nathan Ford."

Anna held my hand and kissed it. "Nina, I love you," she said. "I love you so much."

I patted her hand, smiled. "I love you, too."

"No...no...." She shook her head. "I really *love* you."

"Honey, I love you—" I suddenly stopped before I finished. It wasn't until I wiped away a tear from the corner of her eye did I understand what type of love she meant: L-O-V-E like my J-A-Z-Z, a consuming passion, something that you needed, couldn't do without.

Earlier I was feeling sorry for myself because I had no one. It seemed the gods were presenting me with either a gift—or a curse. The room was becoming very warm, even though the windows were open. Somehow, Anna's hands had slid up my face and were fingering my braided strands. This was a little too quick for me.

"Am I the object of your desire?" I asked.

"Yes, dear. Does that sound sick?"

"No, just different. Anna, I don't think I can give you what you want or need...."

"What do you want, Nina?" she asked, ready to accede to my wish or wishes like an enchanting jade princess.

"I just...I just...I don't know...sometimes I don't think I'm capable of real human feelings, one on one. I'm just so angry, suspicious and cynical." I put my hand to my mouth, my eyes were filled with water. I heard my voice cracking. "I just want someone to hold me, Anna. I can't go on like this...I just can't...." I wanted to scream. I was shaking again, those murderous shakes I get from time to time.

Anna pulled me to her and we both reclined against the couch with me on top of her, our legs entwined. She held me as I listened to her heartbeat, her breathing a lullaby.

She was very good to me. I felt her arms around me as I slept. There were times, indistinguishable from dreams, when I felt my breast in her hands, and I returned the caresses. She did things to my body, to my skin, that hadn't been done in two years or more, hands in crevices that I lost count of, external and internal. She was good to me, kissing my wounds and scratches.

CHAPTER 11

Anna was still asleep when I got up and went into the kitchen. She kept her coffee in the freezer. I pulled out a brown bag marked "strong stuff" and heaped it into the coffee machine.

By this time in the morning her Saturday *New York Times* should have arrived. I went to the front door and found it lying in the hallway, ready and waiting. While perusing the "gray lady", gone insipidly "user friendly" of late, I turned on the kitchen radio and got some early morning urban contemporary hip hop blasting my ears. Not in the mood, I quickly found the National Public Radio affiliate, WNYC. It was passing through the continuing sagas of Haiti and Bosnia when I heard that Rev. Paul Tower had been shot at.

The shooting had occurred outside of his townhouse on the upper East Side. From the radio broadcast I learned that he was unharmed. It seems his assailant had fired but missed. The shooting didn't have any bearing on finding Malika until the radio announced that eyewitnesses reported a "black female" fleeing the scene. The assailant wasn't apprehended. Then Paul Tower's voice came on, sonorous, in the cadence of a black preacher. First, he assured his flock that their shepherd was safe and then he went into his standard rant:

"They can't stop my work, my mission—these black fascists!! They tried to stop the ideas of Malik Martin but I built upon them, became his Peter! These black fascists can't stop me or my ministry! I will continue to speak against rap, hip hop and the insane cult of Afrocentrism! I will wage war on the Afrocentric agenda!"

The radio went on with other news. Anna shuffled in wearing a red kimono robe and slippers. This was the morning after, I thought. She looked at me.

"Good morning," she said. I must have been wearing an uneasy look. "What's up, girlfriend?"

That last remark had a new meaning after last night. "Morning, Anna," I finally answered. I was thinking about last night—and this morning, the news about Tower. "Tower was shot at," I told her.

"What?" Anna's face scrunched up, as it usually did when she heard something she thought was wild, incomprehensible or gauche.

"Tower was shot at," I repeated. I began taking cups down from the cupboard but stopped. "This place is yours," I said, referring to the fact that I had taken command of her kitchen as though it were mine. As my last act of commandeering I began pouring coffee for her and myself when I suddenly felt her embracing me from behind and her lips on my neck. I was an odd mix: it felt comforting yet alien.

"Uh-oh," said Anna, noticing my reaction. "The morning after..."

I handed her coffee and a kiss. I nudged her over to the kitchen table and we sat. She was stirring her coffee and making goo-goo eyes. Anna was obviously very happy about last night but I was less than sure. I was also more concerned about the implications of the Tower shooting.

"Anna, we have two things to discuss," I started.

"Two?"

"Us and the Martin case."

"Okay, us first," she smiled, offering me that look of love, the kind only a woman could smile—and only another could read.

I breathed slowly before I spoke. "Last night was very innocent and very tender..." I began, " but we have ten years of friendship as well as a professional relationship--"

Anna abruptly stood up. "May I sit on your lap," she sweetly pouted.

"Huh?"

"I want to sit on your lap. May I?" she asked again. As she stood, her robe had slightly opened and revealed the breasts I had sucked and kissed during the night. I knew this maneuver and I had used it on Lee and former lovers. I was tempted, but as a strong, progressive black woman I had to remain cool.

"No." I pointed to her chair. "Sit down. We gotta get our shit straightened out, Anna," I said firmly. She returned to chair and sipped her coffee.

"Look, I don't deny that I love you as my friend. You're my friend *first*. We have a bond of trust and friendship, girl, that's ten years old. Ten years, Anna."

"I know, Nina," she said solemnly. "I know."

I went on talking about our years together in law school, how we became pals, sisters. Years later she caught me committing professional suicide: suppressing evidence. She knew I was on a vengeance streak, after every drug dealer that came across my path in the wake of my family's execution. She forced me out for my own good. It was the last act she could do as godmother to my son Andy: save his mother from destroying herself.

"We've always been straight with one another, Anna—no pun intended.."

"Then I better tell you this," she interrupted.

"What?"

Anna looked contrite. "I lied about experimenting. You were the first...."

I looked at her. My anger came out slowly.

"You deceitful bi..." I started but didn't finish. "You set me up!" I accused her, feeling like a sucker, a chump for wanting—no, needing—physical and emotional comfort. I got it but at a price I hadn't imagined. "Jesus...."

"If I had said that I wanted to sleep with you—"

"I don't mind cuddling!!" I shouted. "I'm not into cheap sex, but I don't mind cuddling!" I felt used, dirtied. "I bet you're still seeing Winston, huh?!"

She shook her head, acting like a nineteen-year-old ingenue. "No. I wanted to know what it felt like...being with another woman...I—I felt I could be with you—"

"But you lied about it!" I reminded her. "Ten years..."

"Nina, I'm sorry."

Coffee time was over. I got up and went into the bedroom I hadn't slept in to pack my bag. Anna stood in the doorway watching. It was a quick job since I hadn't brought much.

"What about the case?"

"I'm off it!" I snapped. "Excuse me."

She got out of my way, following me at healthy distance down the hallway that had huge prints of Japanese and Chinese erotic art, the kind with folds and folds of clothing and obscenely engorged male organs.

"You mean you're quitting?"

"Uh-huh! I'm not working with you! I can't trust you!" As I walked by the coffee table I scooped up the Conway articles and stuffed them in my bag.

"Don't leave like this, Nina. Let's talk! I'm sorry! I was wrong—selfish," she confessed. I wasn't in the mood to talk. I unlatched the door and left.

Outside the morning was chilly and gray. Winter was still fighting for dominance, throwing a few weak punches. People were bundled up in jackets and sweaters. Some years back it had even snowed in April. I passed a newsstand and saw the tabloids were heavy with the Tower story. I purchased a *Newstime,* hailed a yellow cab and went home.

The apartment was quiet when I arrived. Donna had left me a note apologizing for the night before in her bad scrawl and fractured sentences. I felt better after a shower. I thought about calling Anna, but realized my anger was still too fresh. She used me to figure out her sexuality at my expense. And I was supposed to be her friend. Typical situational ethics of my generation, I thought.

Sifting through the newspapers I remembered that I had Jackie Shandlin's keys to Malika's apartment. I called the gallery to make an arrangement to drop them off.

"Jackie Shandlin," I asked over the phone.

"Speaking."

"Hi, Nina Halligan."

"Miss Halligan, did you hear—" she tried to get out.

"Yeah, I heard, and read." I was out of it, but had to warn her about her friend's apartment. "Jackie, I was attacked when I visited Malika's apartment."

"Oh, God! Are you all right?" she asked.

"I made it through. Seems as if it might have been the same guys who were at your gallery earlier."

"Miss Halligan," she said, her voice lowering probably because of Madam Olodumare's nearness, "I'm really worried about Malika."

"Well," I said, tired of the Martin madness, "I'm probably the wrong person to discuss it with. I'm off the case."

"What happened?"

"The attorney who is handling Mrs. Martin's affairs, who hired me...well...we had personality problems..."

"Oh, I see." Her voice became very small. There was a pause.

"Miss Halligan, I would like to hire you to find Malika."

I almost laughed. "You?"

"I don't have much money, but...I'm really concerned about her."

Thinking about my spat with Anna, I said, "Well, you sound like a true friend."

"It's much more than that," said the woman over the phone.

"You see," she said, her voice became even lower, "Malika and I are half-sisters."

"Come again with that bomb," I requested.

"Malik Martin was my father."

A big boom went off.

Before I left for my meeting with Jackie, Anna called and left a message. It was an agonizing one begging a thousand pardons, and telling me that Mrs. Martin had left the halfway house. I don't like playing the hard bitch, but it was no concern of mine. I had a new client—and a new angle on the Martin mess. Counsel would have to find someone else to assist her.

Jackie worked a half-day at the gallery on Saturdays. We agreed to meet at the Peacock Cafe. I only asked Jackie for two things: One hundred dollars and proof that she was the daughter of the last great black man.

CHAPTER

The Peacock Café is one of my favorite spots in the Village. It's the kind of establishment that is based on Old World principles: you purchase your cappuccino and they leave you alone. It's not unusual to see coffee lovers sitting, reading, or scribbling at the round, rectangular, and hexagonal wooden tables for hours. The tables were placed along the walls beneath large paintings. The ambiance was *sotto voce.* The front was a non-smoking area and the back was the slow death chamber.

Jackie showed me her birth certificate from Philadelphia attesting to her being the daughter of Malik Martin and Eve Shandlin, her white mother. There was another attesting to Dr. Martin's paternity. She showed me photographs of the three of them, *en famille*. She even had photographs of her parents taken during the sixties and earlyseventies. Jackie's mother, a radical history professor, was of old mainline Philadelphian Yankee stock. She had for years advocated the rights of blacks, eventually becoming a part of Malik Martin's informal "think tank," a series of free floating meetings that took place in New York, D.C., and Philadelphia.

"I suspect," offered Jackie, "that's where my mother and father felt an attraction to each other. She told me that he was always reading and trying to absorb information and turn it into real programs. I think my mother gave him some sort of intellectual stimulation that he wasn't getting at home."

"That's quite a statement—and implied accusation."

She shrugged. "Miss—"

"Call me Nina."

"Nina," she said, trying it on her tongue, "let's be for real. My mother was involved with the black struggle, more so than Sister Ronnie, an actress."

"Sister Ronnie paid the ultimate price, though. She watched her husband being gunned down, murdered before her eyes," I added, as the devil's advocate. "Did you tell Malika that?"

"Yeah, and how," she said, raising her eyes to the ceiling. "Malika and I were trying to work out a relationship. You know, we're both seeds of the same man. We're both black women who are the only children in our families. There's a couple of years between us; she's the oldest. I was told that my father wanted to marry my mother but thought—for political reasons—that blacks wouldn't go for a black leader married to a white woman. Of course, I'm considered less *authentic* than Malika." She laughed, but it was without humor. "She was called 'The Princess of the Nation.'"

"By Mbooma Shaka's organization?"

"Yeah. They just kept filling up her head with this crap about her being a warrior princess because she's the slain daughter of the last great black man. They claimed she had a mission to fulfill."

"And what mission was that?" I asked before sipping my last taste of cappuccino.

"To save the black race," she answered in a mocking tone.

"Have you ever met Roy Hakim?"

"Malika's guardian? No."

"So you don't know about her trips to Pennsylvania?" I asked, referring to the train ticket stubs.

"No, I don't." She laughed. "She wasn't going to see my mother, that's for sure."

"Does your mother reside in Pennsylvania?"

"In the funky city of brotherly love."

"Okay, here's the real question: Do you think Malika's capable of killing?"

Jackie's face became a solemn mask. She glanced around the café. "She's angry enough, Nina. She feels as if she has to live up to the dictates of the black revolution."

"And the Tower shooting? You think it might have been her?"

"I don't know..." she said, sounding less sure. "I know she mentioned some people would like to take him out."

I leaned back in my chair, letting that last statement sink in. I would have to find Malika's New Nation playmates or Roy Hakim. My gaze was darting around the room when it landed on two windows of storefront size which flanked the door. The windows formed little niches where two small tables stood. It created a cozy, intimate feeling. Jackie and I were sitting on the right side of the cafe, three tables away from the window. A black man was standing outside looking at the menu. He was dark-skinned, of average height, and dressed in a suit covered by a long, light-colored duster. He also wore sunshades. This was the weekend, I thought. It wouldn't be surprising seeing "suits" during the weekday, for this was a middle-class residential area as well as a Bohemian enclave, but on a Saturday?

My hands went into my denim jacket. I pulled out an aluminum case which held my "special eyes"; they look like a normal pair of sunglasses. I put them on, casually looking out of the window at the man who was supposedly reading the menu. Pressing the right temple, I activated the X-ray mechanism. My special eyes told me the man was packing a Mackie, a Mac-10, in the coat pocket of the duster. I failed to detect any other metal like a police badge or any plastic that might identify him with a legitimate law enforcement agency. I deactivated the X-ray, touched the left temple and the glasses magnified his face. It appeared that the man face's was slightly bruised around the eyes, lips, and cheekbones. I clicked off my shades, and placed them back in their case. I turned to Jackie.

"Be cool. Do you recognize that brother at the window?"

Jackie followed my lead and glanced up at him. "Yeah, it's one of them."

"He's the guy I took boxing lessons from yesterday in Malika's flat. He's packing, too."

"A gun? What about you?"

"No."

Suddenly, the corner of my eye detected a flash of black metal coming out of his natural-colored duster. My arm went into Jackie's chest, knocking her onto the floor. I went down with her, kicking up the table as a weak deflector. Shards of glass and wooden splinters flew as the dude's Mackie kept popping.

People were screaming, and with good reason. Some were burned, others were bruised and wounded with blood spewing forth. Bedlam was everywhere, even though it had been less than a minute of mayhem.

CHAPTER 13

"Mrs. Halligan."

I turned to see a fresh-faced officer who was holding the door open to John Matucci's office, the commander of the 6th Precinct. I walked across the room sluggishly; internally I felt wobbly. That attack unnerved me, the vicious disregard for human life...I stopped in my tracks when I entered Matucci's office. Ordinarily I'd be happy to see him, but he had a visitor, and it didn't take long for me to figure that something was funky. Very funky. There was Kirby, outside his jurisdiction. A moment ago, I was tired, feeling vulnerable, but Five-by-five's mechanical slots snapped me into red alert—or black alert. Kirby's presence was beginning to connect the dots: Malika's disappearance, the Conway killing and Malik Martin's death. Yes, the dots were being connected, but I still didn't understand the configuration.

This was my second trip to a police station within roughly forty-eight hours. Previously, Jackie had gone into Captain John Matucci's office and had made her statement regarding the shooting. Before the police had arrived at the café I told her to say nothing of our conversation about Malika. Our cover was about African art. When she came out, shaking still from the shoot-out, I told her I would call her later. I also told her to go and stay with a friend, just in case.

For the hour since the attack I'd been a zombie. Emotionally I'd shut down and blocked out the carnage from the shooting. It was too much and reminded me of my family. Immediately after the attack I made sure that Jackie was all right; she was only dazed. I heard a sound and went over to one of the gunman's unintended victims, a young woman. She was moaning, obviously in pain from her wounds. The woman had been tossed beneath a chewed wooden table and splayed on the floor. As I slowly turned her over, I noticed that she had been shot in the chest; her shirt was drenched—soaked—with blood. I didn't want to touch her but she looked up at me with such pained eyes, eyes that were slowly being drained of life. I knelt down and brushed her hair away from her face. A small trickle of blood erupted from her mouth and went down her chin. She gripped my hand tightly and squeezed it, trying to hold onto someone else's pulse of life as hers slipped away.

She was on my mind until I saw those mechanical slots.

"Counselor," said Captain John Matucci, a smooth-faced man in his late forties, taut and trim like a naval commander. He offered me a seat and a stenographer was ready.

"I hope you don't mind Captain Kirby's presence."

I shrugged indifferently. "Nothing I could do about it if I did," I replied. Something was funny about him being here and this taking place in Matucci's office and not in an interrogation room.

"Well, let's start. Tell us what happened," said Matucci.

I related the chain of events: I met Miss Shandlin and we discussed some pieces of art that her gallery was selling. We were drinking coffee when I noticed a man wearing a duster who had a gun. We ducked and he fired. I stuck to the simplicity of that narrative and Matucci tried to peel away the layers.

"Was he aiming at you?" the captain asked. Kirby was looking intensely at me. I suspected that his interest in this matter hinged on my anticipated answer.

"I don't know, Captain Matucci," I said, shrugging my shoulders. "I've made enemies as a former D.A. It comes with the territory when you're a law enforcement official." Five-by-five wasn't happy with that. It wasn't definitive enough for him.

"Surely, a woman with your experience in the courts and on the street knows when she's being targeted," interjected Kirby.

Matucci looked over his shoulder at his midtown colleague.

"Sorry, John," said Kirby, not too apologetically.

I kept to my story. "I was speaking to Miss Shandlin...."

"About what, Ms. Halligan?" asked Matucci.

"African art, Captain. I'm interested in buying some large pieces and we were discussing them. Is there a problem?"

"We're just trying to establish a motive for the shooting, counselor—or is it, investigator?" Matucci knew I worked both sides of the street.

"Where is Veronica Martin?" asked Kirby.

I made eye contact with Matucci, then answered Kirby. "Don't know," I sighed. "I'm no longer on that case." It was the only completely truthful statement I made during the questioning.

"Then you shouldn't mind answering..." continued Kirby.

"Captain," I said to Matucci, "who's leading this investigation?" I invoked the turf imperative, aiming at Matucci, and hoping he'd block for me. Kirby, not too surprisingly, was beginning to annoy me.

Matucci was about to patiently explain, but Kirby broke in. "We're trying to see if the person who killed Conway was the same person who took a shot at you, Halligan!"

"What's the connection? The bullets used?"

"No, but Martin—"

"This isn't about Martin. It's about Paul Tower," I deflected.

"What about Paul Tower?" asked Matucci, smelling fresh meat.

"Paul Tower has been getting threats," I said. "Ralph Conway knew Paul Tower. Conway is dead. He was one of your people."

"A woman tried to kill the reverend!" Kirby spat back at me.

"And the person who rudely decorated the Peacock was a man," I replied. "And according to media accounts, it was a young woman who took a shot at Tower. Veronica Martin is middle-aged and ain't too swift on her feet. What's the connection? Huh, Captain Kirby?"

My instincts warned me that Kirby was trying to establish a "mad bitch" approach to Sister Ronnie and possibly have her shot on sight.

74

"Has anyone tried to establish a reason why anyone would want to harm Mr. Tower?" I asked.

"Yes. The New Nation," said Kirby. He already had that lined up, ready to be pulled: mad, ideologically-driven Negroes, the domestic version of Islamic fundamentalists.

"What?!" I said incredulously. My face felt as if it were Anna's, scrunching up.

"The New Nation, the black fascist group, has Reverend Tower marked for assassination."

"You got proof of this?"

"This is an intelligence matter, Mrs. Halligan," he snapped.

"And you're in homicide, Captain Kirby."

"Ah," said Matucci, attempting levity, "but Kirby knows these things. He's an old BOSS hand."

Kirby didn't like that slip of the tongue.

BOSS, I thought. Kirby was in BOSS? For five minutes or more—off the record, mind you—he spoke of the philosophy, methods, motives, agendas, and personalities of the "fanatically, racist Afrocentric agenda" of the New Nation. Nothing was mentioned about Malika Martin. Both Kirby and Tower used the same words, "fascist" and "Afrocentric agenda." Coincidental? But what was the connection with Towers? Conway?

"But why would they want to shoot Tower?" I asked.

"They consider him a collaborator with the so-called white racist ruling clique," answered the man with no neck.

No matter what I thought about the New Nation—and it seemed they were the kind of black rage group that was better at scaring white folks than doing something substantive—their take on Paul Tower as a collaborator was true. His rise to power and prominence had more to do with insinuating himself with *white power* than acting on black power. Or maybe it was a highly personalized version of black power which made him wealthy and famous. As the conservative's conservative, one who never missed a beat in extolling the virtue of free market capitalism, he was a living example of an idea, the principles of the Christian marketplace.

"Have you brought in any of them?"

"Mbooma Shaka has been brought in for questioning," answered Matucci.

"Then are we finished?" I stood up, indicating I was finished with my part.

"Yes, counselor," agreed 6th Precinct's CO.

I walked to the door and turned and looked back at Kirby. If he didn't have a badge, I thought, he'd be a killer. I shuddered and realized that he wasn't about the judicious application of the law.

Something was up, I thought. Something was dead up. What was also interesting was that within an hour's time Harold Kirby was informed on the shooting and was grilling me. Why was he so interested in what seemed to be two different shootings? My case—or cases—began with a mother looking for her daughter. Now, somehow the New Nation, Paul Tower, Ralph Conway, Sister Ronnie, and the late great Malik Martin were all tied together. But how? And why?

CHAPTER 14

Within half an hour I was rolling down my window to let the air buffet my face, fleeing Dodge City on Interstate 95 and heading to my brother's place in Connecticut. I had parked my car near the police station and made a beeline to it, drove up the West Side Highway until I got to Da Bronx, crossed it by using the Cross Bronx Expressway and then took the exit to reality, the Interstate 95. After that run-in with the hoodlum with no name, Anna, and that Mackie attack, I really needed to get out of the city. Before Jackie and I parted I got the number of the friend she said that she'd be staying with. I called to make sure she was all right.

I turned off the Interstate and began driving down the slight loop that led into a small township. The air was clean, crisp and sweet. The buds on the trees looked as if they needed many more days of warmth before they bloomed into flowers. I kept driving past suburban homes and lawns and headed into the interior of Connecticut. I then passed through a wooded area and up an access road, which led to my brother's turn-of-the-century Victorian house. The Butler home was once a Yankee merchant's mansion. This merchant had made millions during and after the Civil War from the railroads, steel, and oil. Things went so-so during the Depression; his progeny had neither invested nor spent as wisely as the founding patriarch. My brother, Gary, one of the few very successful black investment bankers, moved out here with Miriam and their three kids, Kareem, Monique, and Yolanda.

The place had acres of land surrounding it. Oak trees were placed around the mansion like sentinels, with a small barn and pond in the back. Spring had not quite set in and the earth was a dull gray brown that complemented the sky that day.

I honked my horn as I drove up and Gary stepped out on the front porch. He was five years older than me with a receding hairline. His still youthful face belied his age. He walked down the steps, his hands tucked into his suspenders.

"Miriam told me that you were coming," he informed me with a hug. "No bag, Nina?"

"I'm traveling light, Gary."

"What happened to your face?"

"Competition is fierce."

"Nina, you really ought to get back into law," he said, shaking his head.

"Technically, I never left."

"You know what I mean. Let's go in and see the tribe."

His statement about getting back into law made me think: instead of getting banged up front, I'd be stabbed in the back.

We walked up the pavement to the stairs and entered the house. When I closed the door I felt safe.

There was a small fire crackling in the fireplace, the last on a chilly spring afternoon. I sat down on the couch and looked around, trying to take notice of any new additions or subtractions. Still the same 24-inch television dominating the wall unit that housed an ultra-modern, sophisticated audio unit, including a souped-up CD player. Bookcases lined the living room wall, almost circling the room. Over the fireplace hung an original painting by the late Jean-Michel Basquiat, a notorious *enfant terrible* who died of a drug overdose.

"Nina!" Miriam entered the room. I got up and we hugged. She looked at my face. "Who did this to you?"

"I was sleuthing and had my back turned."

She just shook her head. "Girl..." she said skeptically. Miriam was a full-bodied woman who had a mass of black hair that cascaded down to her shoulders.

"Where are the kids?"

"The girls are out malling," she said. "Kareem's out back with the horse."

"A horse?"

"Yeah, he was getting into trouble in town, so we decided to get him a horse and some responsibility."

"An expensive form of responsibility," I added.

"Miriam shrugged her shoulders. "This whole life we lead is expensive. Let's go into command central."

I followed her down the hallway, past the dining room into the kitchen. The kitchen had a large work station with an overhead rack for pots and pans. Gary seated himself at the kitchen table near a window that looked into the back. His reading glasses were perched atop his head. From the back Kareem could be seen brushing a chestnut colored horse. I sat down across from Gary. "How's he taking to the horse?" I nodded in Kareem's direction.

"He loves it," he said, fatherly proud.

"Loves it?!" exclaimed Miriam. "The boy gets up early to take care of her."

"A feat in and of itself," added Gary. "You want some service, sis?" he asked, referring to a drink. I nodded.

"Babe?" he asked. "Miriam?"

"Sure, it's Saturday and the kids aren't around, more or less." She looked out the window. Gary and Miriam were very conscientious about what kind of habits they performed in front of the children. As a New York-based pediatrician, Miriam was ever mindful about how parents' good and bad habits influenced a child.

Gary handed me my drink. The ice in the glass rattled loudly: my hand was noticeably shaking.

"Trying to tell us something?" Gary was wearing the same concerned expression he'd inherited from our mother.

"Old age," I smiled.

The back door opened and Kareem walked in. He smiled when he saw me.

"Hey, Aunt Nina!" Kareem is a beautiful young man, lithe and graceful. He looks like his father but with a fuller head of hair. He came over and squeezed me as I sat and I wrapped my arms around his waist and responded in kind. When he was younger we used to have squeezing contests, trying to see who would give up first. The brother was getting stronger.

"Okay," I relented. "You got me in an awkward position."

"When did you get in?"

"Minutes ago," I answered. I sipped my drink; the warmth of the bourbon relaxed me.

Kareem sat down at the table and began telling me about the horse, Zulu, when the girls, Monique and Yolanda, walked in.

"Yo! Yo!," exclaimed the eldest, Monique. She and her twelve-year-old sister were baggy down and oversized to the max in denim, sweats, and barn coats. They dressed like the kind of kids I once prosecuted. Both girls wore turned-around baseball caps. At fifteen, Monique, called Neeky, was the leader of the pack; she pushed the boundaries of what wasn't permissible in the Butler household. She was also steadily budding into a cute *phat* sister whom all the young brothers would like a taste of her black puddin'.

"Yo! Homegirl," said Neeky. She came over and gave me a dutiful and very niece-like kiss.

"Monique, enough with those ghettocentric greetings," said her mother, who was preparing a late afternoon lunch for us all at the center counter.

Yolie, the baby of the family, gave a hug and a more traditional greeting. "Hi, Aunt Nina."

"Hi, baby," I said. Yolie was still wearing her "baby fat" which made her look like an extremely cute chubbette. She had hair like her mother's, but tightly coiled into long braids atop her head. The girls took off their outer garments and hung them up on a wall rack near the back door. When Neeky turned around she caught her father's eyes.

"What is that?" He placed the newspaper down and pointed to the inscription on her oversized sweatshirt: "Yo! Bitch..."

"Huh?" she feigned.

"Young lady, you're treading..." warned her father.

Smirking, Neeky said, "Then you'll love this...." She turned around and the back said: "Kiss this!" An arrow pointed down to her buttock.

"All right!" Gary rose from the table.

Neeky started laughing and darted away. "It's a goof, Daddy. Just goof! I'll take it off." She ran out the kitchen laughing all the way up the stairs to her room.

Kareem looked at me and said, "Monique is in her search for authenticity mode."

Yolie helped Miriam with preparing the food and Neeky returned without the shirt and sat down at the table. Gary looked across at her with a bemused skepticism.

Lunch was mainly the last of winter's beef stew and cold cut sandwiches. Gary had been reading the newspaper and only intermittently took part in family conversation. He was shaking his head in regard to something he was reading.

"What's wrong, Gary?" I asked.

"This stuff about Paul Tower. Someone took a shot at him," he answered in disbelief. "Tower is one of the very few genuine black leaders—"

A round of disapproval from the entire family, excluding Gary and myself, ushered forth.

"As you can see, I'm in the minority in regard to that opinion."

"He's just a businessman," said Miriam.

"And what's wrong with that?" asked her husband.

"He's using religion," said his wife. "I don't have anything against business, but anyone who knows anything about Paul Tower knows that BCN is not about God but about De Lawd."

Tower was derisively referred to as "De Lawd" for always invoking God's name and extemporaneously preaching about Him as a reply to almost every statement.

Miriam, who sat next to me, turned and said, "Gary's bank is considering loaning money to the Network for Tower's scheme—McChurch."

"It's not such an outlandish idea," Gary defended.

"What's the idea?" I wanted to know.

"Tower wants to start a church franchise," replied Gary.

My jaws dropped. "You're kidding?!"

The kids began singing, "You deserve a break today. Get on your knees and start to pray...At the Tow-er!"

Daddy shot them a very sharp glance and continued: "He's based his ideas on good sound business principles. He's planning to open brand new storefront churches instead of building traditional churches in every major city that has a sizable if not dominant black population. The idea is to attract the lower classes by offering them social services in a clean and wholesome environment."

The thought of a Ronald-McDonaldized Jesus Christ struck me as perversely logical. They have been doing everything else in Christ's name, why not this?

As Miriam began clearing away the dishes, the kids left, sensing we were going into adult-speak.

"Tower's merely trying to build himself a base in the Republican Party," said Miriam as I handed her some of the used plates and cups.

I thought that was an interesting angle. Tower does have ambition beyond being a mere black leader. He wants to be a "race transcending leader," as one of those postmodern black intellectuals put it. Hmmm. I believe the quote even came from Rudy Downs, as a matter of fact.

"And what's wrong with that?" asked my brother, the Republican patriarch of the Butler clan.

"Nothing, dear, but he's using the whole gamut of black power, Malik's theory of social capitalism, and today's current rhetoric about empowerment as a means to an end, the end being his black butt."

Hmmm, I thought. Miriam was doing better at divining motivation than the police department.

"The man's ambition knows no limits. He's more conniving than Reggie Baxter!"

"Well, the man isn't perfect," defended Gary. "But we ought give him our support when he proposes new ideas. I like his Christian marketplace theology. At least we ought to look at them." Gary had some reservations about De Lawd despite his ideas and power. "Baxter keeps preaching the same old welfare state shit."

Reggie Baxter was another MM alumnus. He positioned himself as a left-liberal, progressive social gospel activist. He ran for President on the Multicultural Coalition ticket, but never seriously thought of bucking the Democratic Party. Tower, on the other hand, did have the basis for being considered a serious player: a conservative ideology based on religion, millions of followers or television viewers (same difference), the attention of well-positioned white folks, and a powerful communication apparatus. Plus he was a nonthreatening Negro, a NTN; a very important quality when dealing with white folks.

As a black conservative, Tower, unlike black conservative intellectuals, was a chief *with* Indians, and was planning to bring more into the tent with his storefront church franchise. Yet he'd always been treated with a certain wariness by the black elite. It had only been during the years of Republican rule that his star began to rise. He began preaching, fulminating against what he considered the twin evils: rap and Afrocentrism. When BCN was featured as a Fortune 500 company, the black bourgeoisie became even more receptive to his jeremiads.

"Well, I don't care for either of them," added Miriam, referring to both Baxter and De Lawd. "And I'm not going to Tower's Gala Celebration. How tacky: that's the anniversary of Malik Martin's assassination."

"That's probably why he wants people to attend. He wants them to forget about the black prince," I said.

She looked at Gary. "You can do something else with those invitations, dear."

"I guess so," sighed Gary. He knew his wife; Miriam doesn't budge on principles. He settled back into his chair preparing to continue with the newspaper but looked at me. "You're not interested in them, are you? The invitations?"

"Why would Nina be interested in that?" asked Miriam. She placed the last plate in the dishwasher. The machine began to whir and hum. Finished, Miriam leaned against the counter and folded her arms. Her work was done.

"I don't know," said Gary. "It might help revive her law career."

Or help me figure out De Lawd's connection, if any, to the Martin mess.

"I'll take 'em," I said. A widow such as myself needed to get out, to meet new and exciting people, and hopefully not have to kill them.

CHAPTER

I spent Saturday night and Sunday morning with Gary, Miriam and the junior funk mob, missing church at St. Peters. When I arrived back in Manhattan Sunday afternoon, I discovered Donna and Anna seated at the table in the living room playing cards.

"She's back!" shouted Donna. "Mamou has returned." Mamou was her pet name for me, fake French for mother.

"Where the hell have you been?" demanded Anna.

"What the hell are you doing in my apartment?" I shot back.

"Okay, okay...Don't get fucky," said Anna.

I started to head down the hallway to my bedroom.

"She's in there," Donna informed me.

"Who's she?"

"Mrs. Martin, silly," said Anna, like I had forgotten that the girls had gotten together for a pajama party.

"What the hell is she doing in my bedroom?" I was annoyed. Pissed. Yes, becoming infamously fucky. I stood with my hands on my hips.

"Calm down, boss. Calm down," said Donna. "I found her at Tempus Fugit," she said, nodding her head toward the bedroom. "I went there to nose around some more and she was there askin' questions, making a nuisance of herself and blowin' my cover. Can't have two people there askin' the same question."

Good point, I thought. Even better was that she had gone back to the place on her own initiative. "Go on."

"Well, I told her that I knew Malika and she should come here with me and I'd fill her in."

"Donna then called me," added Anna. "She was fit to be tied— Mrs. Martin—but she finally calmed down. Where were you?"

"Connecticut," I said. "I needed some place to clear my head after the shooting."

"What shooting?" they both asked simultaneously.

I told them about the attack in Greenwich Village.

"Oh, my God," said Donna. She came over to me and gingerly touched me, getting worked up. "Are you okay, Nina?"

"Nina, people were—" Anna started. Her mouth was left opened.

"Killed," I finished for her. "Two."

Anna had been standing up but began to weaken, holding onto the back of the chair.

"Anna." I went over to her and she sat down, putting her hand over mine when I placed it on her shoulder. I guess the thought of her fresh transgression and me almost getting burned was a bit much for her. I turned to Donna. "First aid."

She went into the kitchen, returning with a bottle of Jim Beam and three glasses. She poured one for Anna, handed it to her and she kicked it back. Donna poured one for me and then herself as we silently toasted my good fortune.

"You're getting soft, Anna." I said. "You're used to be a toughie at the morgue."

"I didn't know them, Nina," she said. "This is different. It could have been you! You didn't say anything—you didn't leave a message! Anything! Jesus!" Anna's eyes were brimming with anger and tears.

Even Donna had a sad puppy look.

"Sorry, folks, but I just cleared out of Dodge and went to see my people in Connecticut," I said, trying to mollify them.

"And what are we supposed to be? Donna and me?"

"Girls, I'm sorry, but this is an occupational hazard. Bad people shoot at inquisitive ones for hire. I won't hold back the next time...you'll be duly informed in the event. Look, things are getting serious with the Martin case—and counselor, I'm willing to reactivate my contract," I interjected to let her know I was back on the case.

"Counsel accepts," responded Anna, wiping her eyes.

"I don't think it's merely about a mother and child reunion."

"Well, what do you think?" asked Anna.

"I've got some vague notions," I said.

"Let me help you make them clearer," said a voice from behind us.

We turned and Veronica Martin stood behind us in her stockinged feet. Her face was slack, her eyes even darker than before. She entered the room and sat down at the table.

"Malika is out to avenge her father," said the woman. "Months ago, before my release, she wrote and alluded to doing something."

"Do you think she shot Conway? Attempted to shoot Tower?" I asked. "No one has been identified in either shooting."

"I'm not sure. I'm only going by what she told me in the letter."

"What did she say?"

"She said it was time to do something about it. She was constantly talking about those men, those men she kept writing over and over. I was upset with that kind of talk...I destroyed the letters."

"What men? Who, Mrs. Martin?"

"Towers...Conway...Kirby."

"Kirby?" asked Anna. She looked at me. It was an "Oh, shit" look.

"Malika said she might not be around when I was released," continued Mrs. Martin. "I just want what's left of my family to survive," she said to no one in particular and to all of us in general. "Tower, I believe, is the ultimate target."

"Why him?" asked Donna.

"She's been raised by Roy Hakim and he believes that Tower

betrayed my husband."

"What did you learn on your second trip to Tempus Fugit?" I directed to Donna.

"I also went to For Art's Sake," she volunteered.

"Out with it, gal! Out with the 411!"

"She was seen there with Rudy Downs and Hakim last fall. Two or three times before she disappeared, and...."

"What?"

Donna gleefully rubbed her hands together. "There's an Afrocentric art racket going on."

"What?"

"There's a story going around that Rudy Downs siphons off some of the African art that's been supposedly liberated and sells it to private collectors. Guess who was makin' noises?"

"Malika?" I tossed out.

"Yes."

I nodded in silence, trying to sort this out. "Puzzle one: the anniversary of the assassination approaches, as well as the celebration of Tower's taking over the former Nation," I said aloud. "Conway was a security member of the late minister's entourage, but was in reality a police agent."

"Ralph Conway?" asked Mrs. Martin, shocked.

"Yes, ma'am," I answered. "Donna, get her the file on Conway."

"Okay." She went over to the desk and retrieved it, then handed it to Mrs. Martin.

As Mrs. Martin slowly opened the manila folder and began to read its contents, I continued: "Puzzle two: Malika may be involved with the New Nation. We've also heard rumors that she's a Black Art to Africa activist. The police suspect that the New Nation took a shot at Tower. And on top of all that, somebody rummaged through her apartment, then took some shots at me while I spoke to Jackie Shandlin. Rudy Downs seems to be the place to start. He may lead us to Hakim, and Hakim will lead us to Malika—hopefully."

Mrs. Martin closed the folder. "You'll have to stay put," I said to her. "There are nasty men folk looking for you, I believe."

"Is one of them bald-headed?"

"Yes."

"I saw him yesterday watching me from a car in front of the halfway house."

"A green Buick?"

"I'm not sure of the make, but the car was a dark green one."

Once I heard that, I went over to the window and peeked out. There was nothing suspicious, but that didn't mean anything. I turned back to her. "Don't worry," I said. "Anna is going to hide you in Chinatown."

"I am?" asked the former Miss Chinatown.

"Uh-huh. We'll work out the details later." I clasped my hands. "Girls' night in. Who's hungry?"

They all raised their hands. We were going to have a PJ party after all, I thought. Silly me.

The next morning we took Mrs. Martin up to the roof of the apartment building, crossed the rooftops, and spirited her down another building, out its back door and into a taxi. Donna went with her to a Chinatown location.

At my office I telephoned Jackie and made sure she was all right. She spent the rest of the weekend at a friend's and had no problems. I asked her about Rudy Downs and the secret market. Jackie said that she had heard rumors about it, but that they were only rumors. She also told me Malika had intimated something was wrong with BATA. I told her to put the word out that a Japanese collector loaded with "dead presidents," backed up with the "emperor's yen," was hot for some genuine African art. I hung up the phone and looked at my esteemed counselor.

"I'm not Japanese," corrected Anna.

"He won't know that," I countered.

"Do you know what they did in Nanking?" she asked, referring to the infamous raping, killing, and plundering Japanese soldiers committed during their occupation of her ancestral homeland.

"Do you know what your mother would do to you if she finds out...." I didn't have to finish.

"You ruthless bitch," she acidly smiled. She rose and told me she had an appointment at court, and she said it in Japanese.

After she left I phoned *Newstime* trying to connect with the reporter who wrote an article on Conway. Dexter Pierson was his name and he had written a profile a couple of years back.

"Pierson," said a very clipped but husky voice .

"Mr. Pierson, my name is Nina Halligan..." I began.

"*The* Nina Halligan?" he asked.

I wasn't aware that my name had been prefixed with a definite article. "Just Nina Halligan, Mr. Pierson. Have we met?" I thought about the legendary photograph of me on my knees in my children's blood, imploring to God.

"No, not really. You are the former Brooklyn A.D.A., right?"

It was the photograph. "That's me," I sighed.

"What can I do for you, sister?"

"I'm looking into a matter concerning the late Ralph Conway—"

"Late?" he answered back in a surprised tone of voice.

"Yes, he was murdered—shot."

"What?! When?!"

This really was news to him, and interesting that it had not been reported to the press. "He was murdered early Friday morning," I said.

"Jesus Christ," he said, sounding shocked. "I'm going to get on top of this. Thanks for the tip."

"Mr. Pierson, please, don't jump on this."

"Why not? You're familiar with who he was, right?"

"Yes, I am and I believe that's why the report of his death wasn't released by the police."

"Oh, really?"

"Let me buy you a drink... my brother."

CHAPTER 16

We planned to meet at a bar near Union Square early in the evening. Before meeting him I went to the library and checked all the newspapers; Conway's death wasn't mentioned in any of them. I went back to my office and called all my contacts at the local television and radio stations and obliquely inquired about the Conway killing and every other known killing, shooting, stabbing, bludgeoning, and strangling committed during the night of Conway's death and after. All were reported except for Conway's.

Pierson and I met at a bar off Park Avenue South. I had gotten to the bar a few minutes before him. I parked my ass in a booth, facing the door. I didn't have to give him a description of myself since I've been dubbed "the screaming Madonna"; he would be able to recognize me. But in case he didn't I told him I'd be wearing a red jacket over a white blouse and black slacks, my second standard ensemble after black on black. I was inspecting some carved inscription on the booth's wall when I heard him call my name.

"Nina Halligan?"

Dexter was a bronze complexioned man with closely cropped hair and salt-and-peppered beard. He wore dark wire-framed glasses and very casual clothes: a barn coat, a dress shirt with no tie, pleated gray trousers, and a nice pair of walking shoes. Probably in his late thirties. When we shook hands I noticed that he was wearing a leather cowrie bracelet. Nice, I thought. I could work with this after hours. Since it was my treat I went over to the bar and got us a pitcher of Bass Ale.

"At the risk of sounding conspiratorial," I said, after my first pouring, "did he know anything?"

"About Malik Martin? Only his guilt about the minister's death," answered Dexter. "He believed there was a conspiracy to kill Martin."

"What did he base that on?"

"He claimed he knew of or heard rumors of an impending hit, but the police were ordered to stand down."

"From what I remember the minister did not like the idea of the police protecting him."

"Could you blame him?" Dexter asked. "The cops and the Feds were making Martin's life miserable. Spying on him, trying to blackmail him about his affair with Eve Shandlin." He sipped his beer and then asked, "How did Conway get it?"

"Two shots, point blank to the chest." I also told him that Veronica Martin was found lying unconscious at Conway's feet.

"What the hell was she doing there?"

"He called her about some information regarding her husband's death."

I told him that I was helping her locate her daughter, and that Paul Tower's name kept popping up.

"Tower," he said contemptuously. "Now, if there's a guilty party behind Malik Martin's death, he would be my prime suspect."

"Really?" I said, warming to his suspicious nature.

"No, question, sister. No question," he answered emphatically. "The guy took over the Nation in one fell swoop. He took over the important assets, then locked out Hakim and Baxter. Tower was also the treasurer..."

"And?"

He stroked his beard. "You're a former prosecutor....Think about it. The problem was that you could never prove anything about Tower. But I think they—"

"They *who*?" I asked.

"The Feds. COINTELPRO. The CIA."

"You're beginning to sound like a conspiratorialist," I said as I poured him another one.

Dexter wiped his beard after he drank, then looked at me calmly with eyes that were a grayish brown. "Are you aware of the Phoenix Program?"

I shook my head "no." He then told me about the Agency's program during the war in Vietnam to assassinate the cadre leaders of the National Liberation Front, the South Vietnamese communists. Dexter believed that aspects of that program were imported for domestic purposes, particularly against popular black leaders who were perceived as a threat to the status quo: King, the X, the Panthers, MM.

"But there's no proof, like there is none with Tower," he repeated. "Conway went crazy trying to prove it."

"Maybe he did know something. He was in BOSS, wasn't he?" I offered. "Harold Kirby, too."

Dexter's eyes narrowed. "What about Kirby?"

"Kirby's in charge of homicide in the Conway murder."

Dexter mentioned that months before his death, Conway had begun to call him about the minister's assassination, telling him what to look for and what to check. Dexter wasn't investigating the Martin case and thought that Conway had gone off the deep end, suffering from the guilt that resulted from Martin's death and not being able to do anything about it.

"The man had tremendous guilt regarding Martin's death," reflected Dexter. "He lost his world over it: family, his job, his mind."

The reporter told me how Conway lived a lonely man's life in Hell's Kitchen. When he wasn't working as a security guard, he was combing through the New York Public Library, reading everything about the death of the minister.

"Funny how the press wasn't alerted about Conway's death. Just another dead black male, I guess," I said.

"Kirby," he said and repeated the name, as if saying it had an implication. "Kirby...."

He then muttered something inaudibly. "What?"

"Black Heat."

"What is that?" Whatever it was I felt it, or my version, stirring between my legs.

"Conway once said something about a code name for operations targeted at blacks, called Black Heat. It was part of the FBI's domestic operation against so-called black hate groups during the sixties and seventies. Switch around a couple of letters in hate and you get *heat*, and the Feds, the state and the local authorities did turn the heat on the Panthers, United Slaves, the Blackstone Rangers and anyone else they felt was a threat to the status quo."

"You think Tower is a target of Black Heat? After all, he is putting together a power base within the Republican Party."

"Naw," said Dexter, shaking his head. "Tower likes power, prestige, and money. He can always be bought, which means he's never considered a threat. He'll play by the rules. I would love to get close enough to whisper 'Black Heat' in his ears, see what his reaction would be."

I told him that I had invitations to De Lawd's forthcoming celebration and that he could attend as my escort.

"How'd you wrangle that? You have to be a member of Big Niggers Anonymous to get them."

"My brother gave them to me. He's an investment banker whose firm is considering BCN's church franchise."

He rolled his eyes and scoffed, "McChurch. I gotta hand it to Tower...the man is a genius. McChurch is so crass and vulgar that it stands a good chance of succeeding." He laughed.

I was less sure about its success in the black communities. Black folks put up with a lot of bull, and we also contribute our fair share, but this racket?

"You really think it'll go over?" I asked skeptically.

"Sister," he began confidently, "things are so bad for a third of us, that, in the words of W.E.B. Du Bois, black folks want to get on the train so bad, we don't even ask where it's going."

CHAPTER 17

While driving across the Brooklyn Bridge I thought of Dexter's remark about black folks wanting to get on the train. I was heading to a forum where some New Nation activists—the latest train pulling out of the station—were going to speak. Furthermore, according to what Donna told me, the New Nation was the up and coming group, winning new converts to its agenda every day.

Mbooma Shaka was the New Nation. A very charismatic former rapper, or raptivist, and very dynamic street leader, his street credentials were impeccable: thrown out of junior high school for assault; arrested for possession of a weapon; convicted for the possession of controlled substances (Anna busted him). He began rapping while in jail and produced a hit called *Nigga Notes from Da Underground*. That got him notice and play. But Mbooma was different. He heard the word "revolution" and began reading the works of Fanon, Guevara, the X, Kwame Toure, C.L.R. James, Amiri Baraka, Angela Davis, Nkrumah, Mandela and the late great Malik Martin. It was Martin's essay on social capitalism that inspired him to use rap and technology to build grassroots institutions in the urban Bantustans of what he called "apartheid America."

Only in his middle twenties, Mbooma was a very striking, handsome black man with a hot physique. (Donna and I would sometime get ripped and talk about what we would do if we had him restrained with no inhibitions. Bad girls are like that.) Some people claimed that he popularized the gleaming, shaved dome that has been sported by young and not so young black males and females. He also wore a goatee and had studs in his left ear and a nostril ring. His scowling visage has graced newspapers, magazines, TV talk shows, a few movies, and beer ads. ("I gotta reach the brothers wherever they may be—or whatever they be drinkin'," he replied when attacked by a PC squad.) Rap-listening liberals invited him to their parties, salons, and soirées where he spat on them and inflamed their postmodern musings.

Denounced as a racist by the white elite and scorned by the black middle class, yet loved by its children, Mbooma staked out a position as the leader of brothers on the corner.

Always dressed in street regulation baggies, Arabic or Islamic or African tunics and dashikis, carrying a carved ebony walking stick with a clenched fist, "the First Soldier of the Nation," as his followers called him, had been denouncing Paul Tower as a fraud and a traitor to the Black nation. Prior to the attempt on Tower's life, Mbooma's pronouncements were ignored by the police. But after the shooting, Mbooma's rantings about Tower received their full attention.

Though the police and the media focused on his inflammatory words, Mbooma spoke a certain truth to power about BCN's neo-colonization of black America's 'hoods via the storefront church project. Mbooma proclaimed that the black man's God was an African and not a Republican. Mbooma, however, totally disregarded the fact that black Christianity is a very conservative force and those not predisposed to the new churches are not likely to find Mbooma and his young warriors palatable.

I pulled up to a curb on Livingston Street and closed down my rambling mind. Downtown Brooklyn is a mixture of bargain basement stores, cut-rate discount venues selling cosmetics and other beauty enhancers. The area is also replete with social service agencies that would cause a Republican freebooter to have hives. Behind me were the courts, other city agencies like the Metropolitan Transit Authority, Brooklyn Law School and Borough Hall. The tallest building in Brooklyn is a sand-colored building formerly called the

Williamsburg Bank. A newer one in the vicinity is Metro Tech, evidence of downtown Brooklyn's so-called revitalization. But overall the area still appeared to be caught in a time lag with five-storied buildings that seemed to echo a far-gone era.

I got out of the car and began looking up and down the street for my objective: Timbuktu Books. I also noticed that the sky was rolling out potential rain clouds, preparing for a possible April shower. After walking a few feet I found Timbuktu Books and went inside. There was an older black man tending the cash register, I asked him about "the Egyptian Forum." He told me to go back out into the hallway I'd stepped through and take the stairs up to the second floor. The stairs creaked as I went up. I turned at the top of the stairs and headed for a door that had a pyramid in the outline of the mother continent. I opened the door and an intoxicating mixture of incense, Caribbean and West African dishes warmly flared my nostrils.

A sister seated near the door at a table handed me a brochure and I dropped five dollars into the collection box. The place was chock-full of black folks. They appeared to be the non-professional class: students, musicians, office support sisters, bohos (Bohemians), bus drivers, delivery men, bank tellers, a mostly 20-40 year old crowd. They appeared to be people who may or may not have a college degree, but who read and wanted to figure out what's going on from a black perspective. The Egyptian Forum was a series of lectures on Afrocentric ideas, themes and issues germane to the black community. It promoted a "black view," and as a black woman I had no problem with that.

However, my skepticism revolved around reducing everything to melanin or Africa as the "big concept." My main problem with the Afrocentric idea was making Egypt the high point of African civilization. If whites wanted it, they could have it. My people were west coast Africans. I'm more interested in the Yorubas than the pyramids. Besides, one has to be a little cool towards a philosophy that is rooted in the past glories of the Motherland yet silent about the iniquities of the present. I mean, what about a host of kleptocracies that are robbing the everyday Africans blind? And what about half a million dead Rwandans? Was that a reaction to a surfeit of melanin?

The room was large. At one end of it, near a window, was a small, slightly raised platform. The walls were covered with photographs of black political and cultural icons as well as with the nationalist colors of red, black and green. Kente cloth was also a prominent motif. People were milling about or seated, waiting for the forum to begin. Some sisters were selling refreshments, mainly Caribbean and African dishes. Children were also present: girls in braided hair like mine and boys with dreads, fades, and "shines," shaved heads that gleamed beautifully.

Up front near the platform Mbooma was speaking to a knot of men. My mamou senses felt the presence of someone behind me. I turned to find Donna. She looked as if she had intended to startle me. She wore a baseball cap (backwards, of course), a denim jacket and her street regulations. I left my red blazer in the car and had on an old tweed jacket of my late husband's. I slipped on some faded jeans and a denim workshirt at the bar after Dexter and I had finished our conversation and exchanged phone numbers for business, and hopefully for pleasure.

Looking around casually I asked, "What's up?"

"Nuthin much," she replied. "Things are warmin' up."

I continued looking around, trying to get a bead on things.

"What's the story? Heard anything?"

"Well...." She shrugged her shoulders which usually meant "no."

"Uh-oh," I said and quickly turned my head away from the platform.

"What?" asked Donna.

There was a tall light-skinned man speaking to Mbooma. I pulled Donna along with me, walking us both to one of the food tables. "What?" asked Donna again.

"See that tall brother?" I said, nodding my head back in his direction. "I prosecuted him sometime ago...for possession with intent to distribute."

"How come you were always bustin' brothers?" she said, looking back at him. "Dag...."

" 'Cause they were always fucking up!" I retorted, annoyed at what I believed to be an implied accusation. When I was a prosecutor my "black credentials" were always being challenged by black folks and by white defense attorneys who thought they were black solely because most of their clients were. It was questionable for me to bust the "brothers," but a "misunderstanding" if one of them threw his grandmother out of a building's sixth floor window or gunned a child in a cross fire. I felt it was my job to protect some of my people from those who weren't fit to live amongst us.

We stood at a table while a heavyset sister who smelled of jasmine served me a ginger beer and Donna a sorrel drink .

"You think he saw you?" she asked as we walked over to look at some books and get out of his range.

"I don't think so," I said. "I'm wearing my hair different from when I busted him." I sipped my ginger beer. I noticed that other people were still wearing shades. So I took out my super shades; it made me feel slightly more incognito.

A slight, wiry man went to the podium and began calling the forum to order. I decided that we should sit across from the door so we could see who was coming and going. The MC asked us all to stand, and bow our heads in praise and thanks to our ancestors and to the creator. He then gave the audience an African greeting in Swahili, to which most of the audience responded in kind.

"Black people of America," he said, "welcome to this evening's New Nation Forum, held in conjunction with the New Egyptian Forum. Tonight we have a special guest who will be introduced by Brother Mbooma." The man turned to Mbooma, who rose and strode to the podium like a proud warrior prince.

Donna whispered something deliciously salacious and I had to stifle myself.

Mbooma held his stick with both his hands while raising it over his head. "Blacker than black! Blacker than black!" he shouted.

"Blacker than black!" replied the audience.

He then ceremoniously placed the stick on the podium, his hands behind his back and jutted his chin into the air. "Tonight one of the elders of the Nation will address us. A man who was with the minister when he died. A brother who has been nurturing the return of the black revolution. A leader to expose the fraudulent and false usurper who claims to be the apostle of the last great black man. Brothers and sisters...Dr. Roy Hakim, the Elder of the New Nation!"

The audience enthusiastically applauded and began chant-ing, "MM! MM! MM! MM!" as the elder approached the podium.

Donna looked at me and winked, "Let's get wid da fever." We began chanting "MM" with the audience.

Dr. Hakim was about sixty years old. You could only guess his age by the snow-white hair that surrounded his face, combed back-wards in a longish natural. The whiteness of his hair accentuated his glowing brown skin which was without any deep wrinkles or creas-es. The doctor wore a west African kufi, a sports coat and one of those Indian shirts that ended just above his knees.

He turned to Mbooma who had returned to his seat. "Thank you, Brother Mbooma." He laid out his notes on the podium, put on some reading glasses and got down to dropping some "knowledge bombs."

"My people...my African people," he began proudly, reminding the audience of their common heritage and fate. "Today we are fac-ing, witnessing the final installment, the last phase of treachery in the annihilation, the plot to eradicate the memory and the work of Malik Martin!"

Dr. Hakim spoke in a very slow, measured way that betrayed a slight Caribbean lilt which had been tempered by his time in America. He was very precise and deliberate in his way of speaking, letting every word sink into the audience's mind and pores.

The "plot" he spoke of, and what Mbooma alluded to earlier in his introduction, was Tower's storefront church chain. Dr. Hakim went on to portray Tower in a lurid manner as the "most diabolical man that has ever lived."

"Don't think that this is merely a business opportunity!" exclaimed Hakim, who reminded me of professors I had in college. "No! This is the work of pure genius—evil genius! For what is being presented is a plan to wipe out the black church as we have known it! The church is one of the very few independent institutions in the black community and Tower's proposal is a sneak attack! A Pearl Harbor! A Trojan Horse!"

The audience seemed to agree and punctuated Hakim's remarks with "Uh-huh," "Tell it!," "Speaking truth to power!" Mbooma rapped the floor with his stick in the manner of a British Speaker of Parliament calling for order. The people clapped, whooped, and voiced approval of the doctor's denunciation of "the most dangerous so-called black man in America."

As I listened and looked around I thought of Kirby's statement about the New Nation "marking Tower for assassination." No one was advocating killing Tower; a fatwa had not been issued, but such a demonization usually meant a permanent corrective that only death could satisfy. No compromise.

Reaching back into the sixties—a period which represents to conservatives everything that went wrong in America and to the left, the only significant decade throughout the entire history of the United States—Hakim recounted the struggles of the black liberation movement from the March on Washington, to the Voting Rights Acts of 1964 and 1965, to Malcolm's death, to Black Power, to King's assassination, to the rise and fall of the Black Panthers and, finally, to the betrayal of Malik Martin.

"A man, my brothers and sisters, who sought to bridge the gap between integrationism and nationalism," the doctor said. "He had an economic agenda—social capitalism—that would put us in control of our own institutions and communities!" cried the late minister's former chief lieutenant, jabbing the air with an index finger.

"Just as Malcolm analyzed the power behind the March on Washington, how the white power clique sought to control the black revolution and turn it into an adjunct of the Democratic Party, Paul

Tower is trying to deliver us back into the Republican Party, a party that sold us down the river in 1877! Read your history books! Study your history! Read *The Betrayal of the Negro* by Rayford Logan," said Hakim, who could not resist a pedagogical point. "After the election of 1877, southern blacks suffered total disenfranchisement and terrorism, encouraged by the Party of Lincoln's indifference."

Donna pulled me over to her and whispered in my ear, "Is that true, Nina?"

I was going to answer her question but instead replied, "Go and read the book; it's on a shelf at home."

"None dare call it treason, but I do! Treason!" exhorted the doctor, who as a small man, bounced up and down when he became excited. "While young black men rampage and destroy themselves, while jobs are exported overseas, and the government conspires with international capital under the guise of the World Trade Organization to gut health, labor, and environmental regulations, the C.I.A. brings in drugs to our communities, what does Paul Tower preach against in his multi-billion dollar pulpit? What?!!"

"Rap and Afrocentrism!" roared the audience.

"Black people are dying and that's all he talks about," continued Hakim. "Rap music, which is a reflection of the situation—not the situation itself! Most of the people buying gangster rap are young white males! Do you hear the so-called Reverend Tower denouncing them and the recording industry, an industry that will be piping in recorded gospel music to his proposed churches! Don't take my word for it! Read the *Wall Street Journal*!"

"No!" the audience cried out in disbelief. I made a mental note to check the *Journal* reference.

"Yes! Yes! Capital never lies! It needs accurate information! Rap music is the living embodiment of Malik Martin's social capitalism," continued Hakim. "Jazz once was our people's music, but now the black bourgeoisie has got it locked up at the Lincoln Center. Now these elitist, pompous jazz musicians and white critics fight over who'll control it, but does it represent the seat of and creative juice of black America? No! Now it's *American* music and that means whites have got to control it! We ought to thank Mbooma and Enemies of the State for spreading the word about Malik Martin and the X. Thank them I say, for working to build our own institutions, to stop depending on white welfarism. This is why rap and Afrocentrism is a threat, because it springs up from the people or it is developed as a tool to equip us to get our minds right!"

They began chanting again and there was an unmistakable black energy, another form of black heat in the room.

Hakim went on for a few more minutes but he didn't specify how this corruption was to be dealt with. When he ended his presentation I looked at my watch and realized that he had spoken for a little over an hour. The audience was on its feet applauding him.

CHAPTER 18

A surge of people went up to the small platform after Hakim finished his lecture. That's when yours truly noticed the doctor's "muscle": a quartet of football player-sized young black men. They were dressed in some sort of uniform: red shirts, black cotton "Ike" waist jackets, sharply creased olive drab trousers and black combat boots. The brothers were clean.

I pressed the temple activator to reveal what my eyes couldn't see. They were carrying automatic pistols, holstered under their jackets. They were constantly on the alert. Somebody had trained them very well. It was time to consider my next move. Switching off the x-ray shades, I turned to my ace field operative.

"Donna, I want you to hang around and try to join the New Nation," I said in her ear after I blew in it first.

"Yeah? I'm down with that," she said, eyes on the First Soldier of the Nation. "What about Mbooma?"

"What about him?" I whispered.

Donna was licking her lips. "He's deep...Nina." She sighed and said, "I don't know...."

"Steady, girl. We're on duty. There's a thin line between flirting and infiltration. It can get tricky."

"Or sticky," she added. She looked at me and smiled. Donna is a very pretty young woman with a hot body that wasn't worth shit a couple of years ago when she was strung out. Now it was a deadly weapon. I just hope I had adequately prepared her mind as well. I was sending her to deal with a very strong brother. To be honest, if he stuck his fine black self in my face, I wasn't sure if I could keep my legs closed. This was a tricky and sticky business.

I pointed to the target. "Go get him."

Donna growled like a tigress and walked on.

"Save some for me," I said wistfully.

"You got it, Mamou." She approached the platform slowly, swiveling gracefully through the crowd, dropping the kind of bombs that turned men's heads.

I watched Hakim speak to a few people. He was very courteous to all the well-wishers who approached him as his muscle detail moved him towards the exit. As they left I looked up at the platform, there was Donna and Mbooma engaging in conversation. She winked at me as I headed out the door.

By the time I reached the bottom of the stairs it had started to rain. The sky was broodingly dark. I stuck my head into the bookstore to see if the doctor had taken shelter there. Negative. I went to the doorway of the building. The rain, a fierce storm, was chasing people to shelter. Hakim and his detail were briskly stepping, trying to walk between the raindrops. They stopped at a blue van and entered. Seated behind my steering wheel I watched them in my rear view mirror and waited for them. They were parked behind me and would have to pass me if they didn't make a "U" turn. As I waited for their move, they pulled out and drove past my car. I followed them for a short distance over to the Fort Greene area, mainly a residential neighborhood. As a neighborhood it doesn't have the same panache as Park Slope, but it's home to a slew of black businesses, black buppies, and a somewhat controversial black film maker. The blue van stopped in front of a West African restaurant. All the occupants of the van went into the restaurant. Watching from my car as they settled and placed their orders, I waited, then went to a Jamaican carry-out and returned to the car with my own dinner.

The rain had slowed traffic down as we drove on the Brooklyn-Queens Expressway. I followed the van as it exited into Greenpoint, the most northern tip of Brooklyn. Greenpoint is a curious area. It's home to a predominantly Polish community, but also has Hispanics and immigrants from the Indian subcontinent. If it weren't for the Manhattan skyline across the East River, one would think that the area wasn't a neighborhood in New York City. It's a drab and colorless section with mostly working class and lower middle-class people; the housing stock of mostly two or three storied row houses gives it a very non-Manhattan look.

Along the East River are some of the remaining manufacturing companies, albeit small ones, with lofts and storage houses. Hakim's van drove into this secluded commercial area, and finally made a stop outside a five-storied red brick building. The area's isolation made it perfect for male cruising, but the night's downpour made that an unlikely activity. But then some people are dangerous when wet. I passed the parked van and turned a corner and slowed to a stop. Two of Hakim's bodyguards remained in the vehicle; the other two accompanied the doctor into the building. I noticed that the building was completely unmarked, no signs or placards.

The weather had been chilly a couple of days ago and tonight's April shower was not enhancing any enthusiasm on my part for night surveillance. Because of the rain it took me several jumps to get a firm grip on the metal bar of the fire escape; my fingers kept slipping on the cold metal bars. Finally, I hoisted myself up and climbed the rest of the ladder. Cursing myself for not bringing gloves, I pulled up the ladder behind me and crept up the fire escape looking for a point of entry. Both the second and third floor's windows were secured, but the fourth floor window was cracked open enough for me to jimmy it further with the chisel I had brought along.

Once inside I immediately put on my x-ray shades, switching on the infrared night vision scope to scan the room. It was filled with crates and boxes and I had barely enough room to move around. I slowly opened the door, trying to muffle the sound of any possible creaking.

It wasn't until I was creeping down the hall that I realized that the soles of my shoes were squeaking, the kind of noise that occurs when water, rubber, and a dry surface meet. I knelt down and removed my shoes, placing each one in the jacket's pockets. Before I made another step I listened for any approaching sound and moved on when I heard nothing. Slowly, I began walking downstairs and on to the third floor where I found three doors. I reached inside my coat pocket and extracted an 'electronic' stethoscope and placed the 'ear' against the first door and slowly increased the volume. I heard nothing, proceeded to another door and had better luck: there were voices coming from behind the second door. I stepped back to the first door and gingerly opened it, inching my way though a room that was up to my tush in crates and boxes.

The scope's ear went to the wall and I cranked up the volume. One of the voices was Hakim's. I pressed the button on the tape recorder and began recording.

"What do you expect me to do?!! She's almost my own daughter," said Hakim, sounding troubled.

Somebody was walking around the room, pacing; either Hakim or the other person.

"She knows the deal, Hakim." said the other voice. "Something *has* to be done."

"Something has been done. I got her where I can keep an eye on her. She's not going to go anywhere," replied Hakim.

"But for how long?" the other voice wanted to know. "You're making money off this, too!"

Hakim said nothing for a few seconds.

"I suggest then, that we close down this operation, Rudy."

Rudy? Rudy Downs? I thought. Eureka!

"What?! This is a gold mine, Hakim! You can't be serious! Just get rid of her!" the Rudeboy demanded.

"You seem to be forcing me to make a choice: either continue with this or discontinue with Malika's life! And I will do no such thing in regard to the latter! Martin was betrayed once. I won't betray him a second time!"

"Martin is dead, Hakim!" snorted Downs.

"You have two months, two months to close this down..." the elder of the Nation informed his associate.

"Just who do you think you are giving orders to?" Downs sounded hot, angry. "You're a pathetic old man trying to live out the days of the black revolution! These hip-hop poseurs trot you out like an old museum piece and you suck it up!" said Rudy Downs. "You don't get it, old man: your revolution is passe!"

"You're right, I don't get it. I'm not a cynical member of your postmodern generation, masking greed under theoretical pretensions. My biggest mistake was getting involved with you! Instead of two months, I want this closed down in two weeks or else!"

"Or else what?!"

"Or the choice will be death—yours!"

"Don't threaten me, Hakim!"

"My dear brother," said Hakim with a sublime iciness to his tone, "that wasn't a threat. I meant what I said. Omar!"

The door to the room opened and another set of footsteps entered the room. "I told this Negro that he has two weeks to close this operation down and if it hasn't been done, it will be your responsibility to correct the situation. Is that understood?"

"Yes," replied Omar.

"Now wait a minute—" interjected the intended target, Downs.

"The subject is closed, Negro!" The door opened and Hakim then popped my ears by slamming the door.

Hakim's and his bodyguard's footsteps passed the room I was hiding in, fading away as they walked down the stairs. The door opened a second time and Downs left, also passing by the room. I cracked my door to listen as they both headed to the ground floor. Doors were opening and closing, voices faded from the premises. The soundlessness of the building told me that they had all left. I went back into the room, closed the door, and jimmied open a crate. I pushed away plastic wrapping paper and held an ivory chest mask that was from the kingdom of "Benin, circa 1600," read the tag. The other crates were also chock full of gold, silver, bronze, and non-metallic treasures. BATA output, I surmised.

It wasn't hard to put together what happened. Malika found out that Downs wasn't repatriating the patrimony back to Africa's original owners and complained to Hakim who wasn't in any position to do anything about it since he was in league with Downs. But why was he doing it? Obviously for money, but Hakim was an ideologue, not a scumbag intellectual like Downs. Money for Hakim was for a purpose. What was the purpose? I put everything back, left the room and headed back upstairs to my point of entry and departure.

I was about to leave that room when I decided to take a look at the crates up here. I angled one around and saw the lettering on the side of one that would have given BATF agents a fit: PROPERTY OF THE UNITED STATES ARMY. I jimmied one open. Hmmm. A spanking new M-16 assault rifle. This wasn't the sort of item that would be offered at a Kwanzaa Expo.

My trip out of the building was easier than going in except for the landing. I took off the latch that kept the fire escape's ladder up and climbed down. By now, the rain had become torrential. My primary goal was to get home and out of my wet clothes. But there was a change of plans, for when I hit the ground I heard a sudden rush of movement behind me, followed by a blow against my temple.

CHAPTER 19

A pair of mournful brown eyes looked down at me. The eyes didn't blink but only gazed benevolently; they were large and told a story of sorrow, tragedy, triumph, and redemption. As my eyes began to focus more clearly I realized that I was looking up into the face of a black Christ. His head was wearing a crown of thorns and a small trickle of blood anointed his black skin. His arms were stretched before Him in a welcoming gesture that offered comfort and salvation. Come unto me...baby.

"Mrs. Halligan?" A man's voice from further down the end of a long conference table called out to me. I had been propped up in a very plush chair in the recline position. The light was so dim I could not make out the face of the person who addressed me. The person was sitting beneath the portrait of the black messiah.

"Mrs. Halligan?"

The voice was calling me again. I was shivering. My clothes were wet and the room's air was cold.

"Is there anything I can get you?"

My throat felt sore, raw, and scratchy, but I was able to croak out, "Yes. Turn off the chill."

A man rose and went over to a wall and turned a dial. The effect was immediate. "Is that better, Mrs. Halligan?" he asked solicitously.

"That'll do for a start." I began rubbing my right temple and recalled being hit, slammed.

"I'm sorry about how Ganga and Hess handled this...the way they brought you here."

"Who are they?"

"Men who work for me. Ganga and Hess. I asked them to bring you here," he said. The man began moving away from the shadow and walked in my direction. By the outline of the room's low light I could tell he was a heavyset man. He stopped at a credenza and poured a glass of water, then began walking toward me again. It wasn't until he handed me the glass that I recognized him. It was Paul Tower, the head of the Black Christian Network, arguably the most wealthy and powerful black man in the United States. De Lawd himself.

As I drank he stood over me watching me intensely. He was wearing a very dark, double-breasted suit. I couldn't make out the exact color. In photographs and on television, Tower appeared to be a ruggedly handsome man in his middle sixties. His skin was a bright cardboard-box brown. He would have made a fine leading man in an Oscar Micheaux film during the thirties and forties, with his square jaw and trimmed mustache. He had very piercing eyes that sought to extirpate the sin of a fallen miscreant, but wasn't interested in redeeming him or her.

"Feeling any better?" he asked.

"I'll feel better when I'm in my own bed," I replied.

De Lawd smiled, pulled out a chair from the table and sat next to me. He began scutinizing my face for something: weakness, strength, character defects, virtue, vice, all which I gainfully employ.

I gulped down the last of the water and stated, "No, I'm not wearing any lipstick or eyeliner. So we can dispense with the physical examination and get on with the reason why you had me abducted."

I thought it was best to go on the offensive since in fact I was a captive. I saw no reason to act like one.

"Mrs. Halligan," he began, clearing his throat, "I've been following your career for quite sometime."

Uh-oh. He's one of those secret admiration freaks. The

higher up on the social scale, the deeper the freakishness.

"Oh?" innocently peeped out of me.

"Yes." He leaned back, reflecting. "I remember the tragic account of your family's slaying...I also know of your efforts in the MacKenzie kidnapping, the affair regarding Ambassador Slocum and your efforts in apprehending the murderer of Warren Tate."

I wasn't sure where all this was going. It sounded like a power play, as though he wanted me to know that he had information about me; none of those cases had ever been reported in the media. After all, I am a private investigator and my credibility as such is based on being discreet.

"And the commendable work you do by teaching at the borough's community college..."

This was getting boring. Time to funk it up, I figured.

"And now you want me to investigate the death of Ralph Conway," I said.

"Uh...no," he replied, thrown off the track by the power of female unpredictability. He wasn't expecting that.

"I was saddened by the death of Brother Conway. When I read about it...." He wearily shook his head.

"It wasn't reported in the newspapers, reverend."

The man's eyes didn't betray one glint of compromise.

"As a matter of fact, it has been kept rather quiet and out of all media outlets," I explained. My arched eyebrow implied the use of illicit influence.

De Lawd's face broke into a beneficent smile and explained that the police had informed him of Conway's departure when he had called and complained of death threats. Conway was a possible suspect in the issuance of such death threats.

"I'm a man of position and as such I use it to achieve things..."

"For yourself..." I interjected.

"For the benefit of my—*our*—people, Mrs. Halligan!" he indignantly thundered. "I detect a certain tone in your voice, young lady. Unwarranted disdain."

I just looked at him, quite sure my facial expression read: Excuse me. "My tone, reverend?"

"Yes. Your generation acts as if it were the first to demand our people's rights. You all seem to forget who organized the sit-ins, the freedom marches and sat down with presidents and senators and carved out progressive legislation! Nooo! Yours is quick to point a finger and accuse someone of not being black enough! Just let me remind you that the only true black power is green power! I've made damn sure that BCN is the flagship of black entrepreneurialism! The true role model of achievement and greater glory to come."

Oh, God, I thought: Booker T. on a testosterone trip.

"The nationalists created nothing! A bunch of dick-waving hoodlums who left nothing but preposterous stories about the glory of Africa! I'm sorry but our destiny is here! The Negro mainstream saved the black struggle and returned it to a righteous and corrective path."

"That may be the case, but even some of the consensus brothers think that your project—"

"Intellectual faggots," he sneered. "They work for me! I own them! Celebrities! Market intellectuals! Some flatter themselves by using the term "policy entrepreneurials." But let me tell you, there hasn't been an original idea since Harold Cruse's *The Crisis of the Negro Intellectual*—and I made sure that didn't receive wider circulation. I open doors, Mrs. Halligan. I get them onto the pages of the *New York Times*, have them sound-biting on CNN, give an influential nod in regard to a grant or position. Who do you think okayed the freelancing of Dr. Grant Hopkins at *The New Yorker*? Do you think it's about ideas? This generation of scholars, the niggerati, doesn't have any original ideas. The only one who does is me."

Market intellectuals? Niggerati? Those were terms coined by Lee, my now-dead husband. It became clear to me what Tower had been reading and by whom.

"I have the ideas and the will and the power to use it. I make things happen; they only comment and interpret," he continued, working up a small fire of resentment, pleasurably stoking it. "I don't do theory. They think they're doing important political work, but I'm my own movement...unstoppable and formidable."

As much as he hated rap, he would howl if he knew that he had a great deal in common with those whom he derided as dickwavers. I became flushed with a perverse mixture of skepticism, awe, fright, and pleasure at seeing a first rate power-mad Negro in action.

"I put Grant Hopkin's Frederick Douglass Center at Harvard on the map. I funded it."

Skeesa Hopkins, a new jack star and the chair of the FDC, was putting together a team of intellectual media stars, with a strong multicultural bent, to become the focal point of what was called "policy pimping" by some. He recruited the vacuous Conrad Eastbrook, author of *Beyond Blackness*, a postmodern preacher from Princeton. Conrad was a consensus builder who sounded like a bad imitation of Richard Pryor doing a preacher. From Chicago, Hopkins plucked Gerald Foster, a noted sociologist who made a splash with a tome called *The Unimportance of Race*. That book inspired New Democrats to begin slapping black folks around.

To round out his feminist credentials, he hired a critical race theorist by the name of (nellie marcos). (nellie), who had decoded herself in homage to matriphilia, was considered a paradigmatic genius for constructing a language out of key words and concepts from the obscurantist text of identity politics. The buzz was that De Lawd was going to front her a show on a non-Christian network of his so she could critique his patriarchial gonads. Mind you, this went beyond being bedfellows.

Hopkins, according to Lee, was trying to set up a social policy network to either funnel ideas to the discredited Democratic regime of President Jeff Benton or to the Republican presidency of Paul Tower.

"None of them took on rap!" he pontificated, snapping me out of my mental backfiling. "Instead, they interpreted it! I saw it as the glorification of antisocial ghetto tendencies. I had to set the tone of the debate with the other media companies who insisted on producing that garbage! I was the shield and the sword...."

"And the bank," I added.

"That's how power is wielded in America," he replied with a confidence which bespoke that he indeed was a player and a winner who took all. Tower had no respect for the rentier class of intellectuals who pimped policy and theory, artiste types and their ilk, because he could buy them. Buying and selling was an act of aggression for him, a masculine terrain, and thinking was considered passive and feminine. He was a classic American: he knew the price of something but not its value—if indeed it had value.

"Reggie Baxter couldn't do it," said Tower as he continued with his tongue streaking. "His run for the presidency was a joke and he only succeeded in making whites nervous. Too black. Too hungry. The fact is that Reggie is just a hustler and has been one ever since the day the minister died. He smeared himself with our teacher's blood and tried to anoint himself as the heir apparent. Always talking that social democratic bullshit and hasn't done squat in twenty-five years. Did you know that nigger preacher ain't never had a home church? Never pastored a church? And these fools who shout 'Reggie! Reggie! Run, Reggie, run!'"

De Lawd oozed venom and scorn for the man who would be MM, a former member of their teacher's inner council. A brother. His nostrils quivered as he contained his rage. He finally began to breathe slowly and heavily, letting the anger subside. "America needs a race... transcending...healer."

I'd tired of his performance moments ago, but when he started quoting Eastbrook's line from his embarrassingly anemic book, I knew the last thirty years of so-called black progress was an illusion. It was time to book a flight.

"Reverand Tower, you didn't have me brought here to listen to a disquisition on power or the lack thereof."

"No, I didn't," he said. He tugged on his shirt's French cuffs.

"So?" I quirked an eyebrow and then winced. That headwhipping I received in Brooklyn was settling in.

"I'm aware that you're looking for Malika Martin and that your investigation may lead you into the affairs of Roy Hakim."

"You seem to think that the road will lead to Hakim. If so, what does it matter to you?"

"Are you aware of the threats being made against me?"

I thought about the speech of Dr. Hakim's heard earlier. It was short of an explicit threat—with an emphasis on the word *short*. I rotated the empty glass's bottom on the table. "Reverend, some people are unhappy with the McChurch idea—"

The man's palm slammed the table and my ears popped for the second time tonight.

"I don't care what other people think, Mrs. Halligan," he said between the whitest pair of clenched teeth I've ever seen on anyone, black or white, north or south, male or female. "When they have contributed as much as I have to the black community, then they can inform me of their opinions! It's people such as Hakim who are misrepresenting this project!"

Obviously the "project" was his baby and big daddy wanted to get to the source of the maligning, but I figured if he knew about my business he must have known about Hakim's, and that Hakim knew about Tower's. I'm quite sure that both were setting up—had set up—intelligence and counter-intelligence...Shit! It hit me...*That's it.* The showdown, twenty goddamn odd years later. Hakim just wasn't amassing an army for nothing, he was coming after Tower. Why? Everyone had always thought that the Malik Martin assassination was an inside job. The fact that none of the killers had ever been caught, in addition to Tower grabbing the assets and closing out everyone else...Add to the mix that Conway was BOSS and the man with no neck, Kirby, was also BOSS.

BCN had its own security force, Sword of Christ, and I had seen some of Hakim's security apparatus around him. De Lawd had mentioned two names, Ganga and Hess, and without seeing either of them, I would bet my last "dead president" that they were the tag team I'd been running into lately: Malika's apartment, the shooting at The Peacock Cafe, dodging Veronica, whacking me.

"Was it one of your people, Ganga or Hess, who viciously redecorated the cafe over the weekend?" I asked, playing on my instincts.

He smiled, slightly embarrassed, "That was a tragic, tragic misunderstanding, Mrs. Halligan."

"To the cost of two lives," I replied. "Do your contacts in the police department know about that?"

"Mrs. Halligan..."

"Ms." I corrected.

"Ms. Halligan, our people have been dying for years in the wars of Uncle Sam and around the world..." he said calmly.

"Meaning what?"

He turned a hand over to show it was empty and turned it back over. "Two dead Caucasians in a black family feud isn't very much."

Miriam was right: he is a businessman. No, I thought: he's a death merchant, a man who calmly factors in the death of two other humans as a small price for a "black family feud." Granted, two deaths are nothing compared to those who suffered the slave trade, slavery, and Jim Crow lynchings, but that kind of callous and casual calculation by one human being in regard to another has always made me uneasy. If he was blithe about them, then I reasoned he could be even more so in regard to black lives.

"Sorry, Mr. Tower, I'm booked. I got enough clients."

"Drop them," he commanded. "I'll make it worth your while."

"I don't want your money," I informed him. I wanted to tell him more, but I was also interested in getting out of his building in one piece.

Sighing, he sat back, drumming the table with well manicured fingers. "I know you have suffered the loss of your family, but do you think it's wise to, uh, jeopardize others so close to you. Your assistant, Miss Taylor...your brother and his family...such lovely and beautiful young black people...very positive."

Tower must have noticed my fingers gripping the empty water glass. I was even beginning to notice a slight twitch in my left eye.

"Now don't get me wrong, dear lady. I'm not threatening them, but there is someone who might. I can help you." He reached into his inside breast pocket and withdrew an envelope, then slid it across the table to me. I opened it and discovered a picture of Nate Ford, the man of my nightmares.

"I know where he can be located. All I'm proposing is an exchange of information. You tell me about Hakim and I'll tell you about Ford."

De Lawd's remark was an epiphany. I could imagine twenty years ago a crew-cut FBI agent approaching him, the two sitting down, and the agent passing over to a young Paul Tower either a compromising photograph of Malik Martin or a damaging bit of information about Tower himself. The agent tells him: *All I'm proposing is an exchange of information. You tell us about Martin and we'll keep this from being....*

I crumbled the photograph. "Ford is my business, Tower, and I'll take care of him when I get around to it. Don't get in my way." I pushed myself from the table and he grabbed my hand closest to him, my left one, which left my good arm free and still holding the empty water glass. I saw his eyes shift in that direction. He wasn't Ford but he would do. My rage would not discriminate; it began the countdown...two...one....

He released my arm and sighed. "Mrs.—Ms. Halligan, I wish...I'm asking you to reconsider. I need your help."

A peal of laughter blurted out of me. "You don't need my help, reverend. You may want me as a decoy, but you don't need my help." I couldn't help but laugh. This man was going to launch a nationwide scheme that could make him the leading black Republican and yet he was trying to act as if he were afraid of a man he had politically emasculated a generation ago. "Sorry. I'm not interested." I stood up.

"Very well." He rose and walked down to his end of the table. He reached down and pushed a button."

"Security. Escort Ms. Halligan out of the building."

As I rode down the elevator, sandwiched between two huge Sword of Christ securitrons, I could see the lights of Manhattan from the glass empaneled elevator. It was a spectacular view. The building itself was built by a consortium of law firms that bellied up during the recession of the late eighties and early nineties. Tower purchased the building, a postmodern pastiche of black marble and smoky glass, and placed a black cross of onyx atop the building. In the center of the cross was a monitor that allowed Tower to preach to the public and air Christian marketplace infosermons 24/7.

The securitrons handed me my car keys and a clear plastic bag with my personal effects and my tools. I inspected my car that was driven up from the garage of BCN for explosives and listening devices. By the time I arrived home it was one o'clock in the morning. Too tired to take off my damp clothes, I crashed onto my bed.

CHAPTER 20

The following morning I had a fever that was unrelenting. Donna and Anna took turns watching me. They fed me soup, vitamins, and orange juice, and everything else that witch of a doctor ordered.

I kept asking about the status of the case, but all they did was shove chicken soup down my throat. My body and mind had collapsed due to stress. The night in the rain and the constant assaults I'd received hadn't helped. It wasn't until Friday that I recovered. Anna was making sure that I was eating properly and dutifully taking my medicine.

"How's Mrs. Martin?" I asked Anna.

"She wants to be around people who speak English. I said I'd ask the skipper—you," she said pointing to me, "about a change of venue. What do you think?"

"She hasn't tried to break?" I asked.

"She's been a good mommy," Anna confirmed.

"Okay, I'll figure a new place. I think I'll ask the pastor of my church to hold her."

Donna entered the room with the newspapers. She wore a very un-Donna-like expression on her face.

"What's wrong, Donna?" I asked.

"Nuthin'. How you be?"

"I'm okay. Thanks for taking care of me."

Donna absent-mindedly nodded.

Okay, I sighed to myself. I ain't the easiest person to take care of when sick. "What's happening with the Nation?"

"Mbooma seems to be recruiting brothers who are former bangers," she reported without her usual elan.

"For what, Donna?" I already knew; I'd seen the weapons, but I was trying to put all the pieces together.

"Dunno," she shrugged.

"Are they staying in the city or what?"

"There's talk about some retreat—"

"Where?!" I almost screamed, starting to rise.

"I don't know, Nina," she answered defensively.

"Will you please go and find out! I need to know, Donna."

"Okay, okay," she said sulkingly. "Don't have a baby." She took the tray away and left the room. Anna and I both cranked our ears and listened to the sounds of Donna putting away things in the kitchen, going into her room to get her belongings and then leaving the apartment. "Bye," she yelled out to us.

"What the fuck is her problem?" I asked Anna, cocking my head at the recently departed gloomy gal Taylor.

"Don't be too hard on her. She's in love," Anna counseled.

"Who the hell with?" I demanded, acting as if she had no right to be.

"The First Soldier of the Nation."

I may have adequately prepared her mind, but I forgot about her heart. "You mean in lust—the man's got a hot physique but the mind is weak. This isn't the right time for her to fall in love, but I need her. Some serious shit may go down. Damn."

Anna shifted her right arm, placed it over my leg and leaned on it forming an arc over me. "Don't get fucky."

We sat in silence for a moment. We had unfinished business regarding our relationship.

"Feeling better, Nina?" She stroked my face. It was a nice touch and made me purr appreciatively.

"I'm ready to get out of here."

"I have to talk to you."

"Shoot."

She withdrew her arm and held both my hands. Uh-oh, I thought. I knew her moves. She looked at me and dipped her head.

She sighed. "I've been thinking about that night. I'm really sorry about the way it happened. I...uh...was scared. I used you to sort out my own feelings about my sexuality."

"Which is?"

"I'm definitely going over the hill, to the other side." she said. "I'm a dyke. Listen to me. Listen to me," she said in a very intense voice.

"Okay, okay," said I like a little girl.

"This is very hard for me, Nina," she sighed. "I don't want to dishonor my family, but I'm tired of living a lie!" Anna was trying not to drop some big tears. I pulled her to me and held her, patting her back, soothing her shoulders.

"I'm sorry, Nina. I just can't help the way I feel."

"You don't have to apologize, Anna, for being you."

"I've been trying and trying to deny my feelings, but I love her," she said.

I felt my brows furrowing. "Her...who?"

"Shinyun," said Anna, "Ming Shinyun."

"A woman?" I asked, relieved that it wasn't me.

"Yes. I met her some time ago, and we were immediately attracted to one another. But I couldn't deal with it. Once she came over from work—she works at MOMA, that's where we met—and we were talking and she just abruptly kissed me."

"What happened?"

"I freaked. She dropped a bomb on me. I liked it, I wanted her, but it was too much for me to deal with...my feelings...I realized that

I wasn't in love with Winston."

"Oh, Anna...Anna. I'm so happy for you." I was, and secretly relieved.

She, instead, had a look of complete and utter terror on her face. "What am I going to do about my family? I'm Chinese. I'm the eldest daughter. Everybody looks to me."

"Honey, You're a grown woman, too. All thirty-three years of you. How old is Shinyun?"

"Twenty-five."

"Cradle robber," I teased.

"She pursued me!" protested the former Miss Chinatown.

"Sounds like a woman who knows what she wants," I said approvingly. "Do you?"

Anna's eyes began welling up. Her lower lip quivered.

"This might make you implausible for the office of mayor, though, " I cautioned. "The city can barely deal with white dykes. A chink dyke would cause the city's bond rating to plummet—unless you're Japanese."

The former Miss Chinatown groaned and fell back against me.

"Look," I said, comforting her, "the two of you have a right to your own private business, but as lesbians..."

Anna cringed and withdrew at the mentioning of that L- word.

"I'm not a lesbian!" she protested. "I'm not a lesbian!"

"Anna Gong, you yourself used the word dyke!"

"That's different! That's an attitude...lesbians are a condition!"

I looked at her." Girl, you got a problem called reality," I informed her. "You can't have your clit and eat it, too. You, you..." I was searching for a term. "You chuppy punk!"

"What?" Anna's face scrunched up when I dropped that term on her.

"Chinese urban professional! You want this woman, but you don't want your love for her or hers for you to disturb your nice lit- tle comfortable world—a phony one. You don't want to deal with the possible implications and ramifications of being a lesbian—a lezzie! Have some backbone, Anna! Go out and get a real life—your own! What about her?"

Anna looked contrite. "Her family disowned her. They called her sick."

I swerved my legs out from under the covers, placing them on the floor. I pulled my robe tighter around my waist. Anna was sitting on the edge of the bed, her head hanging: she had "lost face."

"Anna, I don't care about you being a dyke lesbo...I'm more concerned about your integrity—which appears to be in short supply."

"You left out chink," she said.

I stood up, feeling kind of woozy. "Cut the crybaby stuff. You knew the love was dangerous when you took it."

"I'm not strong like you, Nina!" snapped Anna.

"Look at me! Look at me!" I said, thumping my chest. "I'm warped! I get shakes just thinking about killing the nigger who iced my children. I'm not strong, Anna! If I had been, you wouldn't have caught me at what I was doing. Most of my professional black women friends won't have anything to do with me! Why? Because I'm downwardly mobile! I'm no longer the plausible black woman who could be the city's first viable black female candidate for the office of mayor. All my girlfriends, except for you and a few others, have ignored me since I've gone PI. I'm déclassé. I'm no longer on the career track. Now men spend more time beating me than trying to get into my pants! It ain't about being strong; it's more like being too stupid to lie down and die!"

Anna continued sitting on the bed, trying to figure out who she was and what part belonged to her family. I couldn't tell her that she had no familial obligation. I felt I had some to the one I'd lost and that was to either bring their killer to justice or mete it out myself.

I left the bedroom to take a shower and thought about trying to reunite one family that had been deprived of its right to exist.

CHAPTER 21

After I dressed and gulped down juice and some vitamins, Anna and I left the apartment and walked to my office on West 14th Street. After a hard winter with a record 15 or 16 snowfalls, people were on the street soaking up the sun's vitamin Ds, hanging out on stoops, and slowly breaking out warm weather clothes. It was still a tad nippy, as they say, but some of my elderly neighbors were taking their first excursions outside their abodes, testing the weather and keeping their eyes out for marauding thugs. The street denizens were back to congregating on corners abandoned during the winter, the sounds of salsa or hip-hop demarcating or specifying corners or crews. The sticks that were rumored to be trees were budding and a few more showers and bursts of heat would cause them to sprout what little greenery they had to offer.

Anna and I parted when we reached the stoop of my office. She caught a cab, heading down to Chinatown. I climbed the stairs to enter the building.

I hadn't been in here since I came down with the flu. Donna looked as if she had been running the office efficiently. I thought about my attitude toward her supposedly being in love and felt that I ought to slap myself. After all, she just works for me. Plus I did place her in that situation. I should talk to her about it and her feelings. She never had an easy life and she's entitled to whatever happiness she can grab for herself—after the case is finished.

I plopped myself down in my chair and looked at the mail. I switched on the answering machine. A couple of messages were about jobs. I sat back in the chair and closed my eyes.

"Mrs. Halligan, I'm calling in hopes that we could meet again and discuss a certain matter that I presented before you a few nights ago."

The message ended; it was Paul Tower. He was going to be a problem, the kind who would throw money around or use violence to achieve his ends.

"Nina," began a cheery voice that I didn't recognize until he stated his name. *"Pierson. I've been asking some questions down in D.C. and elsewhere. I got some info you may find interesting. Give a call."*

Dexter's call reminded me that I had to call Chuck Murchison at Midtown Homicide. Tower admitted that his goons tried to smoke me and that they were the ones who killed Conway. I reached Murch, relayed to him what I knew, and how Tower had me kidnapped. I also filled him in on what Tower said to me in his office. Of course, I left out my breaking and entering, the stolen artwork, and the spare parts of the American arsenal. I gave a rough description of the two men and the car they drove. Rather than following up with any detailed questioning he only said "Uh-huh," "Yeah," and "Hmmm."

Then silence.

"Murch, are you going to follow up or make a move on this?" I asked.

"These two guys..." he began.

"Ganga and Hess," I said. I could hear his chair restlessly squeaking over the phone.

"Yeah," he sighed. "We got a couple of bodies in the morgue that fit your description of these dudes. Found them in a green Buick, no plates."

"Dead?"

"Baby," he chuckled, "you know any other reason that someone would be laid out in stiffsville?"

"Are you sure it's them?"

"Well, no, counsel, that's where you come in. We want you to come on down and ID them. Gamed?"

"Sure." I haven't been too keen at looking at dead bodies since the death of Lee and the children. "What about fingerprints?"

"Well...that's going to be difficult."

"Why so?"

"Because besides having neat little black holes in their skulls, their hands have been removed."

"What?"

"Somebody cut off their hands. You still coming?"

"Yeah." I hung up the phone and heard myself mutter aloud, "De Lawd."

"You want to take a closer look, counsel?" asked Murch with a slight glee breaking through his professional mien. He was bent over one of the bodies we came to examine at the morgue. I knew what he was trying to do: get me to play chicken. This is where the female is challenged in the male domain. If a guy could keep his dick hard while looking into the cold face of death then he was tough. In all honesty I didn't want to get any closer. I could see the black and blood-encrusted hole in the left side of the decedent, and the ruptured side of his head where the bullet exited.

Murch took out a collapsible pointer and placed it beneath the wrist and lifted it. "See this?"

I looked at the dried stump and it was clinically severed. The end was smooth but revealing the marrow of bone. "Unnnh," was all I could and did reply. I began thinking about my hacked children...my viciously punctured man.

"Somebody was serious about not I D'ing these suckers," said Murch.

I wanted to leave but the man's face had morphed into someone else's: Nate Ford. Slowly any sense of revulsion became a small, perverse and rewarding pleasure in seeing my foe laid out on a slab. I moved closer and examined him. His sneering smile and West Indian, pseudo-Oxford countenance had vanished, extirpated.

"Is this one of the dudes, Nina?" Murch pulled away the pointer and the wrist slammed the metal as it came down. The sound snapped me out of my revenge fantasy.

"Yeah. It's him."

124

"Do you want to see the other body, Lieutenant?" asked the attendant, a woman.

"You want to see the other bookend, Nina?"

"Sure," I slowly breathed out. Maybe the other would remain Nate Ford.

Half an hour later Murch and I sat in a lower Manhattan diner. It was an hour after the 12-to-2 lunch period and we were two of the very few remaining diners. Hungry, Murch wolfed down a double burger, fries, onion rings, and a cup of coffee. I kept to tea and honey, mindful of my recuperation.

"So what's this stuff about Tower? I thought you said you were looking for Martin's daughter?" Murch asked between bites, his jaws a black grinding machine.

"I am. Tower seems to think that my search for her will lead me to Roy Hakim," I answered.

"Who's he?" he asked before sinking his teeth into another bite of his burger.

Kirby, I thought, knows about Hakim and the New Nation. Why doesn't Murchison? "Ah...a former associate of Malik Martin and Malika Martin's guardian. Hopefully, when I locate him he may be able to shed some light on finding Malika."

I watched Murch closely, looking for some clue or sign, of what I wasn't sure, but he seemed less interested in what I said and more concerned with his appetite.

"So what does Tower want from you?" Murch asked perfunctorily. "He wanted information on Hakim?" he said, answering his own question while I sipped my tea.

"Yeah..."

"And those two handless stiffs worked for him?"

"If they were once Ganga and Hess, they did."

"Loose, very loose connection, counselor..."

"Tell me about it, lieutenant."

"You wanna swear out a complaint against Tower?"

I let out a rueful laugh. "There's nothing. Nada. Two dead head-moes and Tower will either say I wasn't at his office or that I was sexually harassing him."

Murch nodded his head, conceding my point and placed another french fry into his mouth. "What's the deal with Ha...?"

"Hakim."

"Yeah—and Tower?"

"Hakim has been badmouthing Tower's McChurch idea and Tower wanted to challenge him on that point. Both Hakim and Tower were associates of Malik Martin."

"Uh-hmmm," responded a disinterested Chuck Murchison. None of this sounded particularly homicidal to him and wasn't worth his mental energy. "So, Nina, what are you *really* working on?" He popped in another fry and eyed me intensely.

I listlessly shrugged my shoulders. "Like I said, just looking for Veronica Martin's daughter, Malika Martin." I was aimlessly stirring my tea, thinking about things: being slugged, Donna, Nate Ford, Tower, missed classes, Mrs. Martin, Anna, my brother's family...Dexter Pierson.

"C'mon. What do you have on Kirby?"

That pulled me back from my internal trip. "Kirby?"

"Yeah, my boss." Murch settled back into the corner of the booth's seat. He wiped his face and tossed his napkin onto the ketchup smeared plate.

I slowly shook my head, *no comprende*.

"You got something on that no-neck motherfucker—excuse me—fatherfucker. He thinks you do."

Now this was weird, I thought. Why would Kirby think that? "Do you think I have something on the man with no neck?"

"The man's been getting agitated when your name is mentioned or Mrs. Martin's. We've been discussing the Conway murder and your client's name has come up. The man becomes really annoyed..."

I shrugged my shoulders again. "Beats me, Chuck. I do know that he was front and center at Matucci's precinct when I was questioned about the Greenwich shooting. Why was he there?"

"I don't know, Nina. Maybe he was trying to find out what you knew."

This was beginning to annoy me. I looked him squarely in the eye. "Are you trying to find out what I know?"

"Baby," he crooned nigger smooth, "I'm trying to find out anything that'll get me his job."

"Ahh sooo," I intoned like an American stereotype of a Japanese caricature. Murchison was interested in anything that pertained to inter-office politics within the police department. There was a new commissioner in town and he was shaking things up.

"So you don't know anything, Nina?" he asked again.

"Nothing that'll be of interest to you, Murch. I'm merely a widowed woman trying to make a living."

"Okay." He didn't quite believe my feigned ignorance and looked at me while he tooled around with his left baby finger, trying remove a bit of food from between his teeth. "So how's your love life?"

That was a change of subject, I thought. "I'm working on something," I said, thinking about Dexter Pierson, my interest in sex precipitated by the tryst with Anna.

"What? He doesn't know?"

"I just met the dude, Murch. We women take our time and then zero in. I'll see him again."

"When?"

Where this was coming from and going to perplexed me. Murch and I were "professional friends," that is, we have gone out for drinks and dinner during the course of our professional relationship, pre-and post-Ford. He was very supportive during my "crisis" period, but I couldn't make out the line of his questioning. He's a very attractive but married man.

"Why?" I smiled. "You interested?"

"What if I were?"

"Not if you're married," I said shaking my head. "I'd be flattered, but I'm not a home wrecker. I remember the bitch who almost wrecked mine."

Murch silently nodded his head. I looked at his face which was a mask of stolidity but his eyes briefly flashed loss and emptiness. I placed my hand over his that rested along the edge of the table.

"What's wrong? Is there something going on between you and Erika—"

Murch snatched his hand away as if I were a contemporary leper, a person with AIDS.

"Nothing! There's nothing wrong," he snapped. His eyes flashed annoyance. I wasn't interested in sex but friendship; he wasn't interested in friendship but was possibly interested in sex. That precluded or excluded any emotional connection that wasn't based on an exchange of fluids.

I'd be lying if I didn't admit that his abrupt rejection of my concern wounded me. However, I wasn't going to beg to be his friend. "Sorry, you feel that way, Chuck," I whistled.

He just looked at me, embarrassed at his overreaction. We sat in silence for a few more seconds until I announced that I wasn't good at reading minds. I gathered my purse, looked at the bill that had been placed on the table, and was figuring out my portion.

"Nina..."

"Hmmm?" I said while reading the bill.

"Look...I'm sorry," he finally said and sighed. Murch placed his elbows on the table and cradled his face in his cupped hands, rubbing his eyes.

"Let me take care of this," I said, referring to the bill. "And we can talk, if you want to." He nodded his head and I went up to the cash register and paid for our meal. The brother was getting a good deal: lunch and my ear.

I walked back to the booth and Murch was gone. I was mentally reading him the black riot act in absentia when I turned and noticed him speaking on the telephone in the back of the diner. He wasn't on the phone long when he returned to me.

"Nina, I have to git...Kirby wants me back uptown."

"Another body?"

"Sister, there's always another dead body in this city," he said while he buttoned up his collar and adjusted his tie. "Thanks." He

128

held out a hand and we shook.

"I didn't do anything except buy you lunch."

"You tried," he smiled.

We walked out the diner together and I got into my car and he entered his and we drove off to our different destinations.

CHAPTER 22

That flu kept me out of the loop. Meanwhile, De Lawd had gotten rid of Ganga and Hess, in what we in the D.A. office used to call a "community beneficial homicide." Such a homicide removed a person who was a menace to the community. By taking Ganga and Hess out, Tower "avenged" the two women who lost their lives in the cafe, but not due to justice, just expediency. De Lawd was definitely somebody who wanted things done—and done to people. He had "peeked my shit" and that made me wonder about the security of my home and office. Added to the mix was Kirby and his police power.

I decided that it was time for tactical back-up. Mustapha Kincaid was a Muslim brother who operated an electronic equipment store on Canal Street. I met him while working as an Assistant District Attorney. At the time he was living in Crown Heights and he and some other Muslim brothers—Sunni, not NOI—had gotten into a turf war with the NYPD. They, the Muslims, were patrolling their neighborhood ferreting out the drug dealers, and doing a better job than the police.

Of course, they weren't doing it under the eyes or the procedures of the law. Some of them had unregistered firearms. Reverend

Mel Farmington was trying to organize a protest march demanding that the charges be dropped. But a small delegation of Sunni brothers sought me out. They remembered me as the "sister D.A." who came to their Islamic schools and talked to their students about the law, their rights and responsibilities as citizens.

The delegation was led by Mustapha. He wanted to set up some sort of joint patrol and/or coordination with the authorities. Unlike Mel Farmington who didn't live in the 'hood, Mustapha was interested in results. He also wanted to get rid of the drugs, to stabilize the community in order to get on with the real business, nation building. After some hemming and hawing from the police department—and bad press about cold shouldering citizens who wanted to protect their neighborhood, leaked by you know who--Plaza One decided to work out an arrangement with Mustapha and his community. The brothers and the Blues began joint patrols. In return the Muslims would inform the police of known or suspected drug houses. I've often thought that people such as Mustapha were the real heroes, the genuine leaders in contrast to the flamboyant mouths who are not interested in the real problems of everyday black people when television cameras aren't available.

Mustapha further endeared himself to me when he offered himself and a detail to watch over me after the killings at my former home. He always made sure, discreetly, mind you, that someone was watching my back after I returned from my "sabbatical." It was later that I found out that he was a former U.S. Army officer, intelligence division.

I drove to the store on Canal Street, the cut-rate discount strip of Manhattan where goods are placed on the street in front of the stores: clothes, stereos, surplus military equipment, Chinese seafood and vegetable stands, and X-rated video store refugees from 42nd street. Canal dissects Little Italy from Chinatown. The place is lively—too lively.

"Aslaam Aleikum, Sister Nina," said Yusef, the young man who greeted me. He was the store's manager.

"Wa Aleikum Salaam, Brother Yusef," I replied. I looked around the store; they sold consumer electrical goods and electronic equipment for a more selective and professional market. Those items were in another room and arrayed on matte black industrial shelves.

"Is Brother Mustapha in?"

"Yes." Yusef was looking over a videocassette player at the counter space. "He's in his office, in the back. Go right ahead," he said and pointed down a passageway behind the counter. I stepped around him and followed his direction down the hallway until I came across a solitary door. I rapped my hand against it and remembered that it was reinforced steel.

"Come in," said Mustapha's voice from inside.

I opened the door and entered. It was a large room, half office space with a large wooden desk, chairs, file cabinets and cannibalized computers. The other half housed many electrical and electronic pieces and components, in various stages of preparation, compilation, or abandonment. To me, terminally computer illiterate and electronically deprived, everything looked as if it were either a box, a monitor, or a computer. Mustapha, with his prayer cap on and jeweler's eyepiece in his right eye, was working on something that resembled a diskette. He swung an overhead lamp over his intended repair and tooled around with a finely pointed instrument. He finally looked at me and smiled.

"I knew Allah was sending me someone special," he said. "Let me take care of this and I'll be with you in a moment."

"Go ahead," I said. I continued looking around and saw equipment that could be used for surveillance.

"Awk!" said Mustapha, giving up on what he was working on. He pushed himself away from the bench and off the stool. He quickly walked over to me and held both my hands. This gave him the leverage needed to push himself upward on his toes to touch both my cheeks with his, offering me the traditional Islamic greeting. He whipped off his gray work smock and placed it on a coat rack near me.

"It's good to see you, my sister. How're you doing? How are sister Donna and sister Anna?" he asked in a rush of words.

Mustapha led me into another area of the room where a small armchair and a maroon leather couch created a comfy niche. A coffee table was in front of the couch. It held the companion book edition of the television documentary on Malcolm X, *Make it Plain,* the Koran, and several picture books on Africa. I sat on the couch while Mustapha placed himself in the armchair.

"What can I do for you?" asked Mustapha as his right hand stroked his beard.

"I'm up against a heavy this time: Paul Tower."

Mustapha's eyebrows rose and his beautiful smoky gray cat, Astrud, jumped up into his lap.

"What's the assignment?" He stroked the cat but kept his eyes on me.

I told him that I'd been hired by Veronica Martin to look for her daughter. Mustapha let the cat down, stood up, and went over to a small table in another corner behind the chair. He began preparing some Turkish coffee. "What does Tower have to do with this?" he asked over his shoulder.

"Malika's guardian is Roy Hakim."

"Brother Hakim..." said Mustapha, while he placed the small brass pot that held the aromatic coffee on a burner.

"Do you know him?"

"Slightly. We met at some forums."

"New Nation?" I asked.

"No. Not my cup of coffee," he said. "Those young brothers are into wild west shoot 'em up stuff. I do approve of the idea of building up black institutions, but this Mbooma..." Mustapha shook his head. "Wild west—or he likes to talk wild west."

Mustapha poured the coffee into two demi-tasse cups. It had kick and the coriander seeds nicely spiced it.

"Anyway, to make a long story short, Tower and Hakim are planning to put a hit on each other..."

"No," said Mustapha in disbelief.

"Yes. I think this is the payback....You know, the old suspicion about Tower being behind Martin's death and then swiping the assets of the Nation."

Mustapha nodded his head. He was old enough to have been a young man back during the days of "the struggle."

"Tower," I continued, "had me abducted and brought back to the Black Cross. He wanted an exchange of information. I tell him about Hakim and he would tell me about Nate Ford."

"Does he have information about Ford?"

"I doubt it, but Tower probably had one man killed and then his goons shot up the cafe I was sitting in last weekend."

"You were there?"

"The target," I grimly replied, thinking about the two dead women. I also thought about the men with the severed hands. "The men who did the shooting are dead."

"Tower?"

I sipped my coffee and nodded.

Mustapha stroked his beard, shook his head. "This man is a fraud! A swine with a Bible! It's disgusting how he's ruining the name of Christian ministers. What do you need from me? How many men do you need? What kind of weapons?"

Mustapha was ready to declare jihad but I only needed some sophisticated equipment that could detect hearing devices. I had to make sure that my home and office were secured. Clean.

"Tower knew things about my business that hadn't been part of the public record, so I suspect my places have been bugged."

"You're in need of a detector?"

"Yes, sir."

Mustapha put his cup down and left the room. He hadn't been gone very long when he returned with a black aluminum case. He placed the case on the coffee table, opened it and revealed a panel with a series of dials, switches, and buttons. He pressed one that activated it and a small square-framed monitor slowly angled itself up for viewing. Mustapha switched a dial and the monitor went from dead gray to active blue. He then took out took cables, cords, with suction or attachment cups and placed them on the back and the side of a standard AT & T telephone. A line appeared on the monitor bisecting the screen. He turned up the volume and the line widened but not by much.

"That means the telephone is clean," he said, indicating the straight line.

"And if it were dirty?"

"Then the line would have been broken, jagged like the Dow's Index of October 1987." He took the wires off the phone, then opened a side compartment and extracted what looked like a microphone with a windscreen. Mustapha pulled out one more black metal rod, screwed it into the back of the first one and attached a cord from the panel into the twenty-four inch pole. To make the thing easier to handle, he attached a pistol grip about three-quarters of the way down the extension.

"This will allow you to sweep your rooms or over and under objects for plants," he informed me as he picked up the case, detaching the cover from the rest of the body. "You can look down at the monitor and take a reading. This device will also emit a sound when it nears a bug or plant. Since a bug or a plant is taking in sound it will emit sound that's on a different frequency. Make sure your other equipment is off—computer, answering machine."

We negotiated a price for the rental and walked out of the store together. Mustapha, ever the Muslim gentleman, saw me to my car.

"Remember," he began, as I opened the door and looked with annoyance at a parking ticket I had acquired, "don't hesitate to call upon me if you need assistance."

"Thanks. I might need to if Tower is as dangerous and persistent as I think he is."

Mustapha closed the door of the car after me. "Peace."

23
CHAPTER

For about an hour I'd methodically gone over the windows of the outer office, sweeping down to the floor and over to the visitors' chairs and table, on to the desk, and around the file cabinets. Donna walked in and watched as I extended and swept the detection rod around the room, aiming it at objects and watching the monitor's response. She closed the door and just gazed at the mamou in her hi-tech splendor.

"Kinky! What's up?"

"Just checking to see if we've been bugged," I replied. I had already checked her phone and found it clean. "Talk to me," I said while I worked.

Donna stepped around me and sat down at her desk.

"What's with the Nation and Mbooma?"

Donna didn't immediately answer. She busied herself at her desk, and policed the coffee area.

"I haven't seen him in a couple of days," she said as she offered me a cup of coffee. "He hasn't called me in a couple of days."

"Donna..." I began, "that is important." I took the coffee and placed it on her desk.

"I'm sorry but I don't know where he's at," she began defensively.

"Are you two...uh...uh...?"

"Skinning?" She nodded her head.

"What does he say?"

"Baby," she answered in a deep voice, "You got the finest ass I've ever licked—"

135

"Not that! Later! About the New Nation?!"

"The black man has got to rise up and prepare for the next—"

"Donna! I don't want the rhetoric!! I want the 411!" I snapped. I caught myself, clicked off the unit and placed it on her desk. "Don't play with me, young lady. This is serious. What's the deal?"

She lowered her head, went around me and sat down in her chair at the desk. "Nina, I want out of this 'signment... I feel like I'm caught in the middle."

"In the middle of what, Donna?"

"In the middle of you and Mbooma."

"Honey," I said, "you've got to understand that this is an assignment and he's a second level target insofar that getting next to him might allow us to find Malika Martin."

She pouted. "I feel like a traitor."

"To what?"

"To the street."

"The street?"

"Yeah. We're both from the street, me and Mbooma. We've gone through the same shit."

"And?"

"That makes us alike...blood. I'm not like you, Nina."

"Meaning what?" I asked, arching my eyebrow.

"Bougie," she said quietly, not sure whether it would hurt or insult me, or both.

"You picked a hell of a time to become class conscious," I said evenly. "Don't do this shit to me, not now!"

"I'm not doing anything, Mamou...I'm just telling you my feelin's."

"You're chumping out on me, girl. I need you, Donna. I need you in there. I don't want Mbooma. I just want to know if there's any information about Malika. She might be in danger and we've been hired to help. You got a job to do!"

"I've got a fuckin' life!" she spat at me.

"And we got a real problem, don't we?" I picked up the coffee and began sipping it.

"Well, what do you expect? I'm an addict—a recoverin' one—and you've placed before me a dude whose love is like dope."

I groaned, shaking my head at hearing her street version of a New Age inner child.

"Nina, Mbooma likes me. He thinks I have a mind..."

"Of course you have a mind," I interjected. "Why do you think I send you out on these assignments? You're quick witted and inventive." I needed to let her know that I treasured her talents, but I also knew that as a female my influence in this department—love—was going to mean less than a smooth talking dude or an adoring male.

"But he really 'preciates me," she said, awed that somebody actually would see her as a wonderful person.

The telephone rang. "You're on," I said. Donna picked up the phone.

"Halligan and Associates," she answered. "She's here, Anna." She placed her hand over the mouthpiece. "It's Anna."

"We'll continue this very important conversation after I finish talking." I picked up the detection unit, hauled it into my office and closed the door. I placed down the case on the desk and grabbed the phone. "Shoot!"

"What's wrong?" asked Anna over the phone.

It was either the tone of my voice or the word shoot, which I have a tendency to use in tense moments. "Donna's fallen for this Mbooma dude. She's coming up short on me," I informed her in a low voice. "I don't need this, Anna. I really don't. I can feel Tower's hot breath on my neck. He already eliminated the guys who've been punching and shooting at me."

"Well, that ought to take a load off your mind, sweetie," she said in a very chipper but annoying voice. Hours ago this gal was a sobbing sister.

"I know you didn't call me to cheer me up, Ms. Gong. What can I do for you?"

"Uh oh, I know your fucky tone. Chill, girl. I got a tip. Rudy Downs is going to be at a Soho soiree."

"Yeah? Who dropped this 411?"

"Shinyun."

My mind tried to click onto the name but.... "Who's that?"

"You've such a short memory, number-one girlfriend. She's the woman I'm seeing—in love with," she replied with great emphasis, especially on the word *love*. This must be the season, I ruminated.

"Well, you seem more sure of that than earlier today."

"I have you to thank, and Shinyun wants to meet you. I told her that you were a strong, progressive black woman—with postmodern and multicultural credentials."

I ignored the empowerment endorsement and cut to the chase. "How does she know that Downs is going to be there?"

Shinyun's boss, a sub-curator at MOMA, Anna informed me, held monthly get-togethers and usually invited the hottest item of the moment, month, day, nanosecond, to discourse—bullshit—informally on art and politics. Downs was this moment's star and tonight's featured attraction. I wrote down the address, a West Broadway number.

"So we'll see you there, huh?" asked Anna.

"We?"

"Yes, Shinyun and I will be at the party."

"Going public?"

"Sweetie, we'll be in an artistic and intellectual environ. People there won't care."

"Okay. I gotta go and straighten out my gal wonder..."

"Don't be too hard on her. She's young and in love," cooed Anna. "Ciao."

Young and in heat seemed to be the case. Her version of black heat. I got up, opened the door and found the outer office empty. I went over her desk to see if Donna left a note or something. Nothing. Maybe she went out on a quick errand.

An hour passed and still no Donna. No phone call. I was sitting in my office speculating when it dawned on me that I had been running my mouth in a room and on a phone that were possibly dirty. I activated the unit and placed the wires on the phone: it was hot, hot, hot, as the Mighty Sparrow, the calypso king, once sang. I pulled opened my desk's side drawer, took out a screwdriver and worked off the body of the phone. There was nothing inside so I unscrewed the mouthpiece and found a Law Enforcement Research Products—known in the trade as LERP—transmitter, the kind that only works when the phone is off the hook. LERP products are restricted to the police and other such authorities.

Violated, I waved my magic wand and found nothing until I lowered it at a corner of my desk. The monitor zipped up and radically downward. I reached underneath and yanked off another transmitter. More LERP equipment. I figured it was Tower who could easily have people with this kind of equipment, restrictions notwithstanding. But I recalled my conversation with Murchison about Kirby's thinking that I had something on him. Perhaps I did but I didn't know it. The only thing I was sure about was not getting sucked into Hakim's and Tower's personal shooting war.

For good measure I scoured the rest of the room until I was sure it was clean, then I called Anna. She was neither at her office or at home. I punched in her beeper number and waited. The phone rang ina few minutes.

"Anna?"

"Nina?"

"Listen, my office has been bugged," I said.

"What? Are you serious?"

"Dead serious. Somebody bugged my phone. I also just ripped out another from my desk. So listen, be careful...watch your back. Don't use your phones for any sensitive conversations until we can check them. I'll speak to you at the party."

"Okay. Who do you think did it? Tower?"

"Or Kirby."

"Kirby? What does he have to do with this? Why does he keep popping up? I don't know, girl. This is spooking me, Nina. Really beginning to spook me."

"Tell me about it, honey. Listen, we're going to have to initiate some serious protocols," I said, thinking about ways to protect all involved. "We'll discuss that later. Bye—Oh! Check this out. Donna skipped out on me."

"What did you say to her?" my friend asked me accusingly.

"I hadn't gotten around to releasing both barrels of my mouth," I told her.

"Oh, a preemptive run, huh?"

"Later, Anna."

"Ciao, girlfriend."

I returned the phone to its cradle, closed up the black case and decided it was time to check my apartment.

I found two more. Another on a phone and one near my bed. I left my apartment and went downstairs to the first floor and knocked on Mrs. Lupino's door. She's an elderly woman who spends a great deal of her time looking out of windows, a buttinski when not wanted, but the neighborhood's eyes when needed.

She barely cracked opened the door. An eye suspiciously focused on me until she recognized who it was. "Nina?"

"Evening, Mrs. Lupino. Can I speak to you for a few minutes?"

"Sure, hon." She opened the door and stepped out into the hallway, drying her hands on what I used to call a Betty Crocker apron. Mrs. Lupino placed the eyeglasses dangling from her neck.

"Did you buzz in a repairman recently?"

"Yes. This morning after you and your friend Miss Gong left."

"Did he show you any identification?"

"Oh, yes," she nodded. She was a short woman with gray hair knotted in bun, a very warm and open Sicilian face that could easily shift into an old world mask of *omerta* when necessary. "Nobody gets in here, past me without an ID, Nina. You know that. I've lived on this street for...."

"Yes, ma'am," I nodded. She was about to go into the rise and fall of the neighborhood. "What was he exactly?"

"He was from a cable company and needed to check the wiring from above."

140

I asked her what he looked like and she described him as white, around thirty, fair complexion, roughly six feet with a stocky build and dark hair. NYPD material, I speculated as I retreated back upstairs.

CHAPTER 24

The water felt good streaming down my face, creating streamlets down my shoulders and breasts. I slowly rotated my head to let the water into my face. Usually I do my best speculating in the shower but I was trying to think of what Dexter's body would feel and taste like, my tongue lapping at the water on his skin...my teeth teasing and biting his shoulder, neck, and ears...My nipples hardening to the delectable combination of water and thought of his fingers. Unfortunately my fantasy was interrupted by the intrusive thoughts of listening devices, guns, severed hands, Tower, Kirby...the kind of things and people that a woman can really work up a fit of passion over; they crowded out what little pleasure I was building in my mind. I turned off the shower, stepped out and dried myself and reached for my forest green terry cloth robe and padded out.

I stood in the kitchen in my bare feet with a cup of tea in my hand and gazed out the kitchen's window. Down in the square patch of New York earth Mrs. Lupino was tending her garden, trying to get it ready for planting. I looked at the old woman with her tools and gloved hands clearing away the old growth and weeds, her back bent, on her knees digging away at the earth.

Watching her made me think that I wasn't getting closer to finding Malika. Tower had taken shots at me. Kirby I suspected of bugging my home and office; Donna was wimping out on me and Miss Chinatown. I gulped the last of my Earl Grey and walked back towards the bedroom.

I was getting pushed around and now somebody had to be pushed by me. I had to shake up something, get something going. I wanted to retreat to bed and pull up the covers but instead found myself walking in front of the bed pounding my fist into my open hand, enjoying the sound of my skin slapping into my palm. I shoved my hands into the robe's pockets and wheeled around on my heels, trying to figure out who to step on, push, mess with, fuck up.

My mind was whirring with possibilities when I glanced at a desk calendar and realized that it was the first day of May. That meant that April had slipped by while I'd been sick. Next week was Tower's celebration. Wouldn't Hakim strike then? And if so, how? The telephone rang. I walked over and picked it up, still mulling over next week.

"Hello?" I immediately smiled: it was Dexter.

"Where have you been?"

"Sick," I said as I sat down on the bed.

"Feeling better?"

"Some."

"Doing anything tonight?"

I told him that I had to make a connection in Soho but nothing prior to that. He let me know that he had some information he wanted to share with me. The man wanted me to come over to his place in the Village for dinner.

"Want me to bring anything?"

"No...Just your fine brown frame."

"Uh-oh..."

Dexter was surprised when he saw me with the black case. I thought I should bring it along to see how far the infestation had reached. As he closed the door behind me, I reached up to his ear and whispered that my office and apartment had been bugged. I wanted to see if he had been under electronic surveillance, too. He looked at me skeptically.

"Sure. Knock yourself out. Want a drink?"

"Water."

He left me in the living room of his basement apartment. The room had several cartons in a corner. I got to work. I popped up the case and directed myself to his living room phone and attached the wire and flipped the switch. Dexter reentered the room and handed me a glass of water.

"What's the diagnosis?" he asked. I could tell he was amused at what he perceived as professional overreaction. I lifted his phone to unscrew the mouthpiece and pulled out another LERP performance item.

"You've been hit, brother." I held up the item.

"What the fu..." He took the transmitter and examined it.

"Any other phones?"

I found another in the bedroom. The rest of apartment was clean. We walked back into the front room, I packed the case, he put on a Betty Carter CD and we sat on his couch. Dexter was still fingering the transmitter.

"Got any candidates?" he inquired of me.

I sighed and let out what I thought I knew. "This is supposed to be a restricted item, only in use by the police or the Feds."

Instead of saying anything, he furrowed his eyebrows into a deep and angry V.

"Kirby," I continued. "I had lunch with a Lt. Chuck Murchison and he wanted to know what I had on Kirby. It appears that either myself or Veronica Martin make him nervous."

Dexter leaned forward to place the transmitter on the coffee table. I looked around the living room and asked, "Moving in or out?"

"Uh..in. Moving in. I was up in Harlem for a while." The question caught him off guard. One minute, he was pondering the implication of his home being under electronic surveillance and the next minute I'm questioning him about his personal life. After all, a woman has to make certain inquiries. While checking for plants I noticed a framed portrait of Dexter and a woman, both dressed in wedding clothes. The apartment looked as if it were a habitat for one.

"Look...uh...," he began. "This is not definitive, but there are stories going around about Tower. I spoke to some people in Washington..."

"When and on what phone?" I interrupted. "Here?"

He stared at me. "At the office...last couple of days. Our phones are secured."

I nodded for him to continue.

"Years ago Malik Martin had called in an outside accounting firm to audit the Nation's books—this firm usually didn't do their bookkeeping or accounting. The firm did an audit and issued a report which, according to my sources, implicated Paul Tower in skimming money. Tower was the treasurer."

"Do you mind?" I asked. My feet were raised and I was about to place them on the top of the table.

"No, go ahead."

"Thanks. What made Dr. Martin so suspicious that he wanted the books checked?" I asked.

"Well, another firm had been doing it before—one that had been selected by Tower—but Martin, now this is hearsay, Nina, had become suspicious that money that the organization had been taking in wasn't going to the projects the movement had been trying to implement. Also, things weren't being purchased, bills weren't being paid on time. Supposedly Tower was living beyond his means. The officials of the Nation sort of took a vow of poverty, eschewed material goods and that was making things rough for some of them who had families."

"And I suppose Martin was resented because his wife, an actress, could make up for the lack a vow of poverty entailed?"

Smiling, he said, "I like how your mind works. Yes. So there was tension, resentment, and jealousy going on in the Nation."

"The perfect condition for outside manipulation."

"Right!" Dexter poured himself another glass of wine from the bottle he brought in from the kitchen when he'd handed me the water. "Also, Martin was preparing a major speech that was to initiate his program of social capitalism and pick up from where the X left off."

"Meaning what?"

"He was going to implement X's idea of having the United States brought up on charges of human rights violations, plus he was also going to clear the deck of some of the Nation hierarchy."

"What about the firm, the one that did the report?" The background story was interesting but I wanted to know if there was a paper trail that could lead to a smoking gun.

"I'm working on that," he said. "This stuff is from people who know people in the intelligence community. But check this out, Nina...." Dexter leaned closer to me. "The firm's report was never shown to Martin, or rather, a bogus one was issued that said everything was okay."

"Who blocked it?"

Dexter shrugged his shoulders. "Someone or something who wanted to protect Tower. Keep him in in a place where he could be useful."

"The Bureau?"

"It would be my guess. Look, they spied on King and Malcolm, Martin was on the way to uniting the integrationists and the nationalists. 'This nigger is dangerous.' Boom!"

I shook my head. "But Malik Martin wasn't dangerous. He wasn't a rifle-toting, rabble rousing guy."

"No, he wasn't. He was even more dangerous than the Panthers," countered Dexter. "He was a brother who had thought through the dualities and the dichotomies of black politics. He had a plan that was about organizing black folks, and independently organized black folks are more of a threat than disorganized black folks. Think about what happened after MM was gone."

The Black Panthers were on the scene, snapping to attention, throwing dap—power fist salutes—and talking about "offing the pigs", preaching revolutionary black nationalism. Huey, Bobby, Eldridge...Kathleen, Ellen, Erika, and Angela...Fred Hampton and Mark Clark. Think about what happened, I heard Dexter say again. What did happen? The knuckleheads had stepped in and believed that nonsense about power growing out of the barrel of a gun. They read Fanon but forgot his most important chapter, "The Pitfalls of National Consciousness."

"Yeah, I guess you're right...." I drained the remainder of my glass and sighed.

"The black left helped in wiping itself out. The Bureau had them shooting at one another while Hoover and his boys laughed. Now, we have Tower who's ready to be the race man to end all race men."

"Where's the report?"

"Two possible places: The FBI's files, or with the firm that did the audit."

"Are you going to file a—"

"A Freedom of Information Act request?" he finished. He shook his head. "And give the sucker the jump? They would probably stonewall or excise the document or destroy it, if they haven't done that already. I'm trying to do some backtracking, to find the firm and the guy who wrote the original report. If that isn't successful, I'll do some back channel document production."

"Meaning what?"

"You don't want to know," he said emphatically. "As an officer of the court you probably wouldn't want to be privy to my means."

That meant he probably was going to have somebody feed him stolen documents.

"Okay, why do you think it's Kirby?" he said, not quite changing the subject but switching the players.

"He's got a motive—fear. What he fears I'm not sure. Except this....Suppose as a member of BOSS Kirby knew of the hit on Martin?"

"So," said Dexter. "What's his connection, if any, to Tower?"

"Suppose the Bureau was blackmailing Tower and Kirby knew of it...knew the reason and the history. Conway was a low level agent, but Kirby was perhaps a handler and may have handled Tower."

"I don't know, Nina," Dexter said skeptically. "The Feds and the locals jealously guard their...."

I looked at him. "But if it's about keeping the niggers in line?"

"You may have a blurring of jurisdictional prerogatives," Dexter reconsidered after I threw in the smack of the black. "So what's stuck up Tower's and Kirby's asses?"

"Veronica Martin shows up at the feet of a dead Ralph Conway, and some people knew that he'd always felt that something wasn't right about the Martin case. Sister Ronnie showing up was a coincidence that unnerved them."

"Who do you think killed Conway?"

"I suspect Tower. He's trying to make out that others are behind it, particularly those who were connected with Martin and want to carry on his legacy. He knows that Roy Hakim and his boys are planning something."

"Like what?" he asked, his eyebrows furrowing again.

I told him about the cache of weapons and art I had discovered in storage at the building in Greenpoint.

"Wha-at?" he said, the word expanding into incredulity.

"Yeah," I said, nodding my head. "The return of the cult of the gun..."

CHAPTER

The Soho soiree was being held in a loft apartment on West Broadway. It was definitely the abode of a sub-curator: it was a cross between a performance art stage and a retailer's showroom of contemporary designer kitsch. The place was decked out in dark colored drapes and white classical columns. It was filled with an expensive odd-lot assortment of furniture. Multicultural art pieces abounded that spoke of blackness, gayness, lesbianness, Asianness, Latinness, but nothing that signified the people of pallor, whites. Except perhaps the white columns.

I edged my way into the dim but crowded living space and caught a whiff of marijuana wafting through the air. I began checking out the occupants: the under-thirties were more casually and indifferently dressed, while my cohort, the above-thirties, was more stylishly turned out. I moved through the crowd alternating between a smile and a grimace.

"Nina!"

I saw a beaming Asian face coming my way. "Hey, girl," said Anna, slightly sloshed. "Glad you made it."

I smiled and pecked her on the cheek, my eyes constantly on the move for my pushee. "Seen Downs?"

"Oh, yeah. He's here....Relax. He ain't going anywhere. Want a drink?"

"Sure."

Anna grabbed me by my hand, almost yanking my arm out of the shoulder socket as she led me through the crowd and over to a table where the evening's poisons were being kept. She was in her element. Obviously, she was a great deal freer here than in the rigid world of law and family.

"Here," she said in an almost singing voice. "Glad you made it." She handed me a white wine and we clicked our glasses.

"You missed the lecture," she informed me.

"How was it?"

"I don't know. I don't speak postmodernese. Damn, I thought we lawyers talked shit. Hey! I didn't know that Downs was a swirl."

Shrugging my shoulders I let on that I wasn't privy to that, either. A swirl was a black who dated white and if he or she did so exclusively, they were a double swirl. This also applied to whites, but they were called zebras.

"Where is he?" I was ready to make a hit or at least get a bead on my target.

"Forget about him," she said, hooking an arm around my shoulder. "Here's my sweetie."

Shinyun walked through the crowd towards us. She had a thick, thick mane of black hair that framed her high cheekbones and round face. The woman had a chunky but sexy build; voluptuous, her width and roundness accentuated Anna's slimness and fair complexion. Shinyun's complexion was darker, which isn't prized in Chinese culture and may have indicated that she was from peasant stock. She also had a very nice smile.

"Shinyun," began her lover, "Nina Halligan. Nina, this is Shinyun Ming," said Anna, switching around the order of her name, for Chinese names begin with the surname first.

"Hel-lo," she said haltingly. "Ah...It's a pleasure to...meet you." Her accent was a little thick but she could communicate with us natives. We shook hands and I thought she was very sweet and shy. She also seemed nervous and awkward. Maybe she thought I had dibs on Anna.

"Are you enjoying the party, Shinyun?" I asked.

"Yes. Yes...very nice. My boss likes to do this often."

"Who is your boss?"

"Nancy Pallindin," she replied.

I was about to ask when had she arrived in the States, but something diverted my attention. I noticed some slinky but hefty-teated body wearing a gold lamé dress a few feet away. The bald head convinced me that it was Donna—wearing my dress.

"Is that Donna?" I asked Anna, trying to get a witness.

"Oh...yeah," she smiled. "She's here with Mbooma."

I must've looked like murder. Anna pulled me aside, away from Shinyun who she said something to in Chinese. "Chill, Nina."

"That twerp walked out on me! " I told Anna.

"Shhh," she cautioned.

I guess I was becoming loud, but I was pissed!

"Look, Downs may know where Malika is," I told Anna. "Hakim and Downs are doing business, Downs is the target of the night." I also told her that Downs wanted to get rid of Malika and that I had taped the conversation. "I'm going to make a move tonight that might require back-up. Are you down or what?"

"Of course, Nina. This is our case. I'm going to see this through. What are you going to do about Donna?"

"She's fired." I was about to leave but Anna held me back.

"Don't tell her that now," counsel advised.

"Why not?"

"Because you're getting fucky and you don't think clearly when you're in that frame of mind, my dear. Besides, you tell her that and she might say something to Mbooma about her former employer—you."

Anna was right, but that was another kind of push or shove that could be used. Suppose she did tell him? Would she risk alienating herself from him? If she exposed me that might make it easier for me to get what I needed from Mbooma, namely access to Hakim. Yes, somebody was going to get slapped.

"Talk to me," said Anna.

"Donna is fired," I reiterated.

Anna shook her head. "If you're going to do that, don't do it while you're angry."

"I'm not angry," I smilingly lied. "Let's go and get a drink." We returned to Shinyun who was talking to another woman.

"We're back," said Anna. I got us all a drink and watched the room. Anna more than nudged my arm and caused my wine to create a mid-air arc. "There's Rudy."

Downs entered the room with two blondes flanking him. He was about average height and had a Nosferatu frame. He wore his hair in a modified Afro and wore thick glasses. For tonight's soiree he was dressed in a teal-colored double breasted Armani knock-off with a black mock turtleneck. Downs had gained a reputation as the intellectual of the moment, a man whose depth could be measured by the glibness of his pronouncements on the "racial space as a societal construction of binary opposites." His book *Race Space* was on the best-sellers list and he gave the impression, at least to whites, that he knew what was going on in the 'hoods of "Amerikkka." He was the link between Tower and Mbooma; he could easily speak about Christian marketplace theology as well as knowing what jams the kids were kickin'. As a leading member of the theoretical bourgeoisie, he was the best representative of the hot air sector of the economy. He talked black, but loved as a swirl, which he attributed to the age of multiculturalism. "I have to be fair to all the races," he replied when his black credentials were challenged by Brother Saddiq Farquhar of the Society of Muslims.

"Professor Downs?" I said, squeezing myself in between him and his two friends.

"Yes, sister?" The man had really bad teeth.

"Hi, I'm Nina Halligan. I'd like to have a word with you."

"Oh, look," he began, "my friends and I are having a really wicked discourse on the representivity of cunnilingus. You'll have to wait your turn."

"This really won't take long, Dr. Downs."

"I don't think you heard Rudy," interjected one of the blondes. "We're in the middle of a serious discourse."

I ignored her, figuring that she's the type who would write some pretentious treatise on the political implication of Madonna's mode of identities. I looked at him earnestly. "I really must speak to you."

"Sister," he sighed. "I'm here with my two friends...."

Being nice was getting me a double swirl brush-off. I decided that I had to be a representation of a forceful and demanding black woman. In other words, an unapologetic black bitch. I suggestively placed my hand on his coat's lapel and began brushing away some crumbs. "Nice suit. Yugo Bossinato?"

"Armani," he insisted and whispered something into the other blonde's ear.

My fingers curled underneath the fabric and I yanked him within inches of my face.

"Hey!" he yelped.

"I really don't like doing this, but you really do have to pay attention to me. I'm representative of street knowledge. Real primordial fire."

"Get your hands—" he began to squeak.

"This stuff is a gold mine, Hakim," interrupted my tape recorder. I snapped it off and released my grip. His eyes nervously registered compromise, not of negotiation but of exposure.

"You got one minute to get your ass over to me and talk." I walked away and stood across the room in a corner, my arms folded and my foot impatiently tapping out the seconds. People were passing back and forth before my view of him. Downs was excusing himself from the two blondes and making his way over to me. If it weren't for his reputation as a cool intellect, he would have scampered over to me panting.

"What do you want?" he said icily.

"Malika Martin."

He stiffened and his eyes darted around, checking out the immediate area around him. "Who are you?"

I sighed annoyance and said again, "Nina Halligan. I'm a private investigator. Dum de dum dum."

He began nervously rubbing his hands. "What?"

I held up the tape recorder. "You want me to refresh your memory bank?" My finger was poised over the play button.

"Look, I don't know where she's at!"

"But you know the man who does—Hakim!" I poked his chest with my index finger. "You get word to Hakim that I'm looking for him and that I want to see Malika Martin!" I flipped out a card and slid it into his pseudo Armani's breast pocket. "I want to hear from you by 10 a.m. or from Hakim! But one of you better call by then!"

I quickly turned away and got lost in the surge of bodies. I suddenly felt a familiar hand on my arm and turned to see Anna.

"Are you on your period?"

I was too busy looking for my second hit of the night to answer. "Have you seen that trifling bitch, Donna?"

"You *are* on your period, aren't you?"

Donna was standing with Mbooma who was wearing a white collar tunic and a neo-Afrique kufi. His back was to me as I approached them. She was smiling, talking to Mbooma but all that vanished when I came into view. Donna turned Mbooma around and he smiled at me.

"Nina, what are you doing here?" she asked. Donna wore a very faint but unwelcoming smile.

"You're wearing my dress," I answered.

"Oh." She looked at me. "I needed somethin'...special." She looked at Mbooma and held his hand. "Nina, this is Mbooma Shaka. Mbooma, this is my aunt, Nina Halligan." Being her "aunt" was our cover in public.

The First Soldier of the Nation held out his hand and we shook. "Hello. Donna has told me a great deal about you," he said in a mellifluous voice that I hadn't detected at the Forum. Donna looked embarrassed and nervous. He looked at us and smiled.

"I'll leave you sisters to talk." He held up her hand and kissed it and left. She turned to me and I discharged.

"What the hell is going—"

"Mbooma asked me to marry him," she fired off.

Talk about a slap. I guided her by the elbow over to a deeper corner. "What the fuck are you talking about, Donna?! Marry him?!"

"Yes!" She was clearly excited. She threw her arms around my neck. "Hold me, Nina! I'm in love!"

My arms went limp momentarily and then I unclasped her hands from around me. "Donna, what about...?"

"I'm sorry, Mamou...I love him. He wants to marry me."

"Donna, you've only known this dude for a couple of weeks," I argued.

"Things happen that quickly, Nina. Aren't you happy for me?"

I heard her and didn't. She began talking about wedding plans, me being her maid-of-honor, a shower, Mustapha giving her away....

"Donna, what about Malika Martin?" I interjected. "We have to find her," I blurted out, pushing aside her dreams and happiness. Donna looked at me and then swerved around the purse that hung over her shoulder. She opened it and pulled out the keys to my apartment—our home—and the office and handed them to me.

"I love him, Nina, and you're not going to take this away from me. He's my man."

The keys added extra weight to my fist as I swung it upward to her jaw. The thud she made hitting the floor, knocking over some art objects, caused people to turn in our direction. Standing over Donna who was unceremoniously laid out, her—my dress—hiked up over her thighs, I slowly turned around and my glowering eyes dared anyone to come near us, or me. Mbooma came though the knot of on-lookers.

I dramatically raised my finger and voice at him. "You! You tell the Elder that I want Malika Martin! He has until ten fifteen to talk to me! Tell him to check with his boy Downs!"

I thundered past him and everyone gave me a wide berth. I was running down the steps of the building when I heard Anna calling my name, but I didn't stop. I kept running down the stairs and soon found myself outside, bent over, and vomiting. Anna stepped to my side, then behind me to keep from getting hit by my involuntary geyser.

"God, Nina...are you alright?" She placed me up against a wall. I felt hot but the coolness of the bricks felt good against my head and skin. Anna pulled out a handkerchief and wiped my mouth.

"You didn't have to whack her 'cause she skipped out—"

"She's marrying Mbooma, Anna," I gasped.

"What?!!" Anna stopped in mid-stroke. I took the cloth from her and continued wiping my face.

"She told me that she and that first nation nitwit are getting married." I continued wiping my mouth and tasted the aftermath of the dinner that Dexter had prepared for me earlier. "I gotta sit down somewhere, Anna." At first I didn't know why I felt weak. Granted, I did knock the cowboy shit out of Donna, but I've expended more energy on more formidable opponents. In seconds I remembered that I had been sick and that my anger had pushed me over the limits. Anna held me steady on one side and then Shinyun was holding me up on my other side.

I smiled weakly at her. "Sorry to be coming into your life like this."

We sat in a Soho bar on Prince Street. I hadn't said much. I just kept to my ginger ale and listened to Anna explain to Shinyun, in Chinese, what had transpired between Donna and myself. Shinyun at first thought it was a lover's quarrel.

"Ah. She...she like daughter to you?" Shinyun asked me.

"Was," I said, feeling sorry for myself and betrayed. "He's my man," was the kicker, the 1990s version of "Bess, you is my woman."

"So now what?" said Anna. "What's next?"

"Tomorrow, go and get Mrs. Martin, bring her up north 'round eleven o'clock to Father Dave's church. By ten or so I should have heard from either Downs or Hakim, maybe both."

Anna nodded at my instructions, I told them that I was going home. I placed some crumpled dollars on the table and said my good-byes.

Both the car and I were on automatic pilot. Instead of heading home I found myself driving back to Dexter's neighborhood. I got a parking spot and was "clubbing" my steering wheel when I asked myself, What am I doing here? I wished I had been intoxicated so I could blame it on a Jim Beam or a Jack Daniels, but I felt alone and needed someone.

Since Dexter lived in the basement apartment, I could see that the lights were still on. He was bare chested, his hairs flecked with gray.

He saw me through a window and opened the door. "Nina.... Come in. How was the party?" he asked as he held the door open and I passed through.

"So-so."

"You want a nightcap or something?" He had closed the door and stood with his hands in the pocket of his sweat pants.

I nodded yes. "Ginger ale or anything that's non-alcoholic."

He left and returned with a drink and a shirt on. He handed me a glass and we sat down on the couch. I studied my drink.

"Are you alright?" He gently touched my shoulder and I sipped my drink. After a moment I placed the glass down on the table and looked at him. "Something on your mind?"

"I just need to be with someone..." I began to blubber. He brushed my face with his hand. "I'm sorry to intrude...."

"You don't have to explain. I know how that feels. We don't have to do anything but hold one another. Come."

We both stood up and went around the apartment turning off all the lights and walked into his room and closed the door. It was what my mother and father did nightly. They held each other's hand and went around the house and turned off all the lights, blew out the candles, and made sure that their children were peaceful in their sleep.

CHAPTER

By nine o'clock the next morning I had parked my car and was changing my clothes in the office. I showered at Dexter's but decided to go straight to my office to get a jump on things. Dexter and I went through what I called "the preliminaries," heavy foreplay. Neither of us were quite ready to do the nasty...give up some "skin," as the kids say. I thought his reluctance stemmed more from his connection to the woman in the picture than skittishness about intimate contact in the age of AIDS. It wasn't until later while lying in bed, with me resting my head on his chest and playing with his chest hairs, that he told me his wife had been an uptown murder victim.

"She didn't hand over her purse quick enough to the fourteen-year-old who shot her," he sighed.

Two scarred people, I thought, needed to take their time.

I kept a black pants suit at the office in a garment bag. I pulled out fresh panties and a bra, slipped into them and snatched out an oatmeal-colored tee shirt, pulled it over my head and then slipped into the suit. Then I walked into the outer office and looked around.

The place would be empty without Donna. Sure, it was nice and easier to have someone to answer your mail and do your keyboarding for you, but that was over. Dead. The time had come to start pushing things and getting results, and she had pushed my button, Miss Persona Non Grata.

Sometimes a woman just has to be a Madam Nhu, I philosophized, thinking about Anna's model of a "strong but not progressive Asian woman." Madam Nhu was the bad girl of South Vietnam during the Ngo Dinh Diem regime. She was thought to be more ruthless than her husband, Ngo Dinh Nhu, Diem's brother, the oriental Richelieu. She even had an all-girl militia back in Vietnam. My kind of woman....

I checked my phone again by unpacking Mustapha's electronic surveillance unit.

At nine-fifty the phone rang. I switched on my office tape recorder.

"Halligan and Associates," I said. "Nina Halligan speaking."

"Hello, Ms. Halligan...This is Roy Hakim. You wanted to speak to me," said the Elder, in his faint Caribbean accent.

"Yes, doctor, I need to discuss something with you."

"I haven't seen Malika, Ms. Halligan," he said, quite unconvincingly.

"Doctor, I didn't call you. Downs must have delivered my message and he—"

"Yes! He did!" He sounded annoyed.

"Didn't he tell you that I recorded a conversation between you two, discussing your commitment to Dr. Martin?"

"That's illegal!" he snapped. The pot calling the kettle....

"So is kidnapping," I reminded him. He said nothing for a few seconds. I wasn't going to push him too quickly. "Doctor?" I finally asked when I thought the pause had become too pregnant.

"What is it that you want?" he asked.

"Veronica Martin wants her daughter back, doctor." The Elder sighed and I heard the door of the outer office opening and closing. The door to my office was open and I could see only a portion of the outer area from my desk. My hand went over the mouthpiece and I called out, "Who's there?" No one answered.

I returned my attention to the caller. "Doctor Hakim?" He didn't answer yet he hadn't ended the call, the line was still active. He was waiting for something to happen....

My knee pressed a plate built into the right side of the desk and a panel flipped over. I quickly switched the phone to my left shoulder and reached underneath with my right hand and gripped the other 9 mm gun, a bad boy stopper.

"Well, doctor, I think we can arrange something that's mutually beneficial to both parties..." I blabbed while I kept an eye on the door...waiting...sensing something.

A figure with a shotgun appeared in the door. I immediately raised my gun, fired and ducked behind the desk, to the floor. A wild and wide shotgun blast tore up my desk and ripped my chair. I scrambled around on the floor then flattened my back against a wall and fired again when my assailant peeked his head into the door, trying to assess my status.

"Aaagghh!!" I heard the weapon discharge as it hit the floor in the outer office. I slowly got up and edged myself around the office, knocking things over in the process, back still to the wall, the butt of my gun-hand braced in my left palm. I heard the door open again and quickly stepped into the room scanning it with my eyes and gun. The shotgun was on the floor and it had riddled Donna's desk. The departed had also left some blood on the floor and I saw more of it as I walked to the door and cautiously left the office.

Outside, down on the steps and on the pavement was a trail of blood. Drops, droplets, and splotches. I put the gun in my coat pocket and quickly followed the trail. I kept moving with my eyes on the red spots, but when I reached the corner of West 14th Street and Seventh Avenue the trail ended. Instinctively, I reached into my coat and gripped the pistol.

"Halligan!"

I spun around on my heels and was about to withdraw my gun but saw Carla McDaniels, a police officer who was walking her morning beat.

"What's going on? I've been watching you from across the street."

"Somebody took a shot at me!" I said breathlessly. "I didn't see who it was. I got off a few rounds."

"Hit the perp?" she asked while she reached for her walkie-talkie.

"Yeah. You're almost standing in his trail."

She looked down at her feet and began calling for assistance. "Are you alright?"

"Yeah...I'm cool." I was standing near a newsstand and decided that the chase had ended with the cessation of blood. I sighed and was about to pick up a newspaper when I noticed that one had blood on it. "Carla!"

"What?"

I pointed to the newspaper. The newsie was a middle-aged Pakistani man. Carla tried to get him to remember and identify the blood donor, but the man's English was very rudimentary. He undoubtedly paid more attention to customers' hands than their faces. I looked at the bloodstained copy of *The New York Times* and surmised that if a previous copy had been bought, it may have been used to soak up blood. Carla confiscated the paper and I purchased another copy, noticing that it was a very cool and sweet smelling morning.

"Again?" said Anna.

I was pacing the floor of her office. The police had come and asked questions, picked up the shotgun, scraped up or soaked up some more blood, told me to come over to the station later and make a statement.

"I'm really getting concerned about you, dear," she said. "Suppose we call this quits, huh?"

I looked at her. "What about Malika Martin?"

Anna clasped her hands over the desk. "I don't know her," said "Madam Nhu." "I'm beginning to regret ever hearing about that goddamn committee!"

"It's too late to stop now," I said.

Anna asked, "Have you spoken to Donna?"

"No. I got too much to think about right now—such as people trying to kill me!"

"So, let's drop this case then! Shit, it's not worth getting people killed over. Besides, if they're holding Malika to keep her silent about Downs' and Hakim's dealings, then perhaps we should call in the Feds! This is heavyweight stuff, Nina. Kidnapping...stolen arms...God knows what other state and Federal laws they are breaking besides trafficking in stolen art objects."

"Hakim isn't going to allow anything to happen to her. I can bust this case!"

"Don't get *femo* on me!" shouted Anna. "Femo" was Anna's term, a conflation of feminine and machismo; it meant trying to act like a tough guy, a reckless, tough bitch, and not wanting to admit defeat in a so-called man's world or game.

"I'm not being femo!" I protested

"Yes, you are," said Anna. She sat in her chair, eyeing me, arms folded across her chest.

"It's called determination. If I were acting femo I'd be coming on like gangbusters, as they used to say in the old days."

"Nina, you manhandled Downs and then fuckin' whacked Donna! That isn't femo?!"

"I had to push Downs! He's the link to Hakim, and Hakim has been keeping himself out of sight!" I said in my own defense.

"But you don't want to deal with your feelings about Donna! You feel as if she's betrayed you!"

"Goddamn it, Anna! What else would you call it? I'm sitting on top of this mess, getting slapped around and shot at, some girl's life in possible danger, and this girl is talking about the legend of the streets, blood, my fatherfuckin' man..." I replied. "I'm taking Mrs. Martin back uptown with me, Anna. Father Dave said she could stay with him and the Mrs. at the rectory."

Anna unfolded her arms and steely looked at me. "If this wild west shit happens again, all the bets are off. I'm calling in the Feds."

"Anna..." I started.

"No, you listen! You listen!" She bolted up from her desk and walked over to me. "I know you, Nina. You're working out your race woman, sister black thang on this! She's not Sister Ronnie who needs to get her man back! The revolution is over! She's a woman who wants her daughter. Nothing more, nothing less. Hakim and Tower are two knuckleheads—like most men, excuse my reverse sexism—who can't settle an ideological dispute without resorting to arms! This isn't a race mission! Let's drop it!"

"What do you know about this?" I threw out.

"It's the same thing, Nina. I'm from Chinatown, sister. I know about gang warfare. I lost my father and a brother to a gang war! Yeah, it's more ideologically based, but it is still a testosterone shootout!"

"Okay," I conceded, "it's a dick thing, but two women are in the cross fire. What about them?"

"Close the book! Let the big boys handle it!" she countered. "That's what we pay them for!"

"Uh-uh. I'm not going to give Kirby, Tower, and the Feds the go 'head sign to have them come in and shoot up a bunch of black folks who are now being portrayed as the biggest threat to domestic security since the Branch Davidians. Hakim is not going to harm Malika. He cares about her."

"Be for real, Nina! The guy tried to ice you!"

"He probably thinks I'm shilling for that onyx faker, Tower! He doesn't know me!" I reasoned.

"And Tower? He tried to smoke you at least once, as far as you know, it still could have been him!"

"Tower is expecting me to lead him to Hakim—and then he'll try to kill me."

Anna warily shook her head. "This is getting too big for us. Some more people are going to die."

Asian fatalism or a logical conclusion based on already known evidence? Anna was right: it was getting too big. I went around her to the desk, picked up the phone and began dialing.

"Who are you calling?"

"Colonel Mustapha Kincaid, U.S. Army, Retired," I told her. "Aslaam aleikum," I said into the phone.

CHAPTER 27

Veronica was very quiet, pensive, as we drove uptown. I told her that she'd be staying at the rectory of my church and that we, Father Dave and I, decided that she should wear a dark dress and scarf over her head to give the impression that she was the member of a holy order. She calmly nodded her head in agreement. While waiting for a change of traffic lights she turned to me.

"Miss—Ms. Gong said that somebody tried to kill you again."

I smiled wanly. "Trade secret. You weren't supposed to know that."

"And you fired Ms. Taylor, your assistant."

"Miss Taylor," I corrected. Donna had her sisterhood privileges revoked by me. She ain't no Ms. "Couldn't keep her mind on business. She wasn't there when I really needed her..." I said as I shrugged my shoulders. "I don't want to sound like a refugee from a film noir, but betrayal and bullets are part of the business, unfortunately." I geared the Dodge and passed other New Yorkers on Sixth Avenue, Avenue of the Americas to the non-natives.

"Betrayal and bullets," she intoned, gazing out the car's side windows.

"What's wrong, Mrs. Martin?" She looked very sad. The poor woman had only been back in the world a month or so. In that brief time she'd been subjected to viewing a murder victim, hearing about other killings, cooped up with non-English speakers, and had men shadowing her. And now my friend—her attorney—was probably

163

guilt tripping her into canceling the assignment.

"This is all coming back..." she said, not finishing her thought. "The ballot or the bullet."

"Betrayal and bullets," I attempted to correct.

"Same difference...the jealousy...the petty sniping and jealousies.... Now they're lethal....Now my daughter and I are caught in the middle...again."

I patted her left shoulder with my right hand as I kept an eye on the flow of traffic we were in. "Don't worry, Mrs. Martin."

"Call me Veronica or Ronnie."

"Ronnie," I winked. "Don't worry. We're gonna get you and Malika back together. To paraphrase Enemies of the State, the brothers and sisters are definitely gonna make it work."

"I just wish I could retire like Eve Shandlin to some bucolic estate...."

"Eve Shandlin?" I thought it was an odd choice, but maybe she was comparing the fates of the women of MM.

"Yes. Malika said she has a really nice life. She went down to the family's estate with Jackie Shandlin a few times," she continued.

I had to keep my eyes on the road but I quickly looked at Veronica. I guess I had a quizzical expression on my face.

"Dear, I'm Hollywood. I'm not shocked. After all, Jackie is my daughter's half-sister. They do have something in common...the last great black man."

No...what was running through my mind but not revealed by my glance was a previous statement of Jackie's: "She wasn't coming to visit my mother." She implied animosity, hostility on Malika's part.

"Some people can do what they like, Veronica..." I said ruefully.

"Yeah, and Eve Shandlin always did what she wanted to do," answered Veronica, her mouth tightening a bit. "She always put me down for being petty bourgeois. I guess she had a point. Her money was from real wealth—stolen. I had to work for mine and in some circles being an actress was a cover for tricking."

As we turned a corner and swerved to avoid hitting a homeless man clad in dirty rags. Veronica caught sight of him and looked back at him over her shoulder.

"Looks like a brother I did time with," she mused. "Now Eve's great-grandfather got all his money from selling defective arms and other merchandise during the Civil War. That was kind of a family secret. Remember, the Great Emancipator was also the first Republican president," she smiled. Veronica shook her head. "Eve was a wacko even back then."

"Yeah?"

"Uh-huh. She was working on this theory called Euro-Africaneity."

"Euro-Africaneity?"

"She claimed that since she had some African blood in her family's background it gave her rights and privileges. In essence, she believed that blood made her as black as me, even blacker because she had a *black* attitude."

Veronica began to laugh, a moment to treasure. She hadn't smiled or laughed since she'd been up here. "Eve was always trying to prove that she was a hot-blooded, thirty-second Madinka mama by fucking." Her mouth turned downward. "I was counterfeit and she was authentic; I was cruising and she was working for the black revolution...."

"White is black?" I said.

"And black is white," Veronica answered.

I could imagine J. Edgar Hoover salivating and instigating with that kind of carrying-on, but there was something else that was beginning to make sense. "So...uh...Malika visited her place?"

"Yes...somewhere in Pennsylvania."

Click. The train stubs?

"Eve runs a summer camp where she teaches African American history and self-esteem to so-called lost young Africans in the inner cities."

The New Nation? Click-click.

"Malika, months ago, wrote to me about visiting Jackie. She said

165

they talked about some new project."

Click-click-click. Hakim and Mbooma's headmoe recruitment from the 'hoods? I made a sudden stop and fished around in my purse for my notebook. I got out of the car and went directly to a corner phone and called the House of Olodumare. I asked for Jackie. Gone, and had been for the last week.

I deposited Veronica at Father Dave's, then drove across town to the East Village, where Jackie resided. She lived in a tenement walk-up on Second Avenue blocks below St. Mark's Street, the main drag of the East Village. I buzzed her intercom, got no answer, turned to the super's, and got a fuzzy voice over the intercom.

"Whatdaya want?"

"Is Jackie Shandlin still at this address?" I said into the grill.

"No...she moved out a week ago. You interested in the apartment?"

"Yeah." I was buzzed in and walked to the apartment that was located in the back on the first floor. The door opened and a portly, graying Hispanic man in his fifties stepped out. He led me up to the third floor and into Jackie's old apartment. Nothing. Nada. Clean.

"Did Jackie Shandlin leave a forwarding address?"

The man quickly began scrutinizing me as the enemy, someone who might make his life difficult. "Are you interested in the apartment or what? I ain't got time for—"

"I'm interested in the person who last lived here," I said, and pulled out my credentials, a twenty dollar bill.

He smiled at that. "Oh, yeah...Well, she left no forwarding address, but I know the guy who moved her stuff..."

I smiled.

Back at my office and over the phone, the hauler said that Jackie didn't have a great deal of stuff to move, but that she had a ways to take it: a four-hour drive to her mother's estate in Astonia, Pennsylvania. He also told me that he stopped in Brooklyn to pick up some crates.

Finally, I thought, we were getting somewhere. I was very pleased until the Darth Vader of TV evangelism, De Lawd, called and wanted to talk. I let him know I was busy and didn't wish to continue an association with him at the present time. Then he became very solicitous, inviting me to his forthcoming gala celebration. I didn't let him know if I was an RSVP. I was going to keep him guessing, then walk in with Dexter.

CHAPTER

Donna was waiting for me at the bottom of the stairs that led up to the office. She sat at the foot of the steps watching the traffic, human and vehicular, pass. I was stymied for a moment. Should I just quietly go back into my office and wait her out? Or should I quickly walk down the stairs past her? Sighing, I walked down the stairs and stood on the step above her.

"Waiting for someone?"

She turned, looked up, and then rose. "Hi, Nina." She handed me a plastic bag.

"What's this?" I didn't want any gift as a peace offering.

"It's your dress...Exhibit A," she replied. "Can we talk?"

I took the bag. "Well...there's nothing to say, except that I am sorry that I hit you. Of course, with all those witnesses you could have my ass hauled to court...."

"Nina," she sucked in her breath. "You're the closest I ever had to any real family, like a mother. Why would I take you to court?"

I looked at her face and saw my work from the previous night. Her face, her jaw, was slightly swollen, bruised. "Are you okay?"

She nodded. "Yeah. You really packed a wallop, Mamou."

We stood on the steps and looked at each other. Almost two

years ago she had robbed my office and months later I was trying to help her kick her habit, and now this....

"I would like to go somewhere and talk," she said.

"About what?"

"Us."

I stepped down to her level. "Okay."

We walked over to a coffee shop near 8th Avenue and sat in a booth. I gazed out the window as Donna tried to formulate what she wanted to say. Her lips moved as she rehearsed mentally. Just as she was about to speak, our coffee arrived. Sipping it gave her time to gather her thoughts.

"Nina, you were the best thing that had ever happened to me...until Mbooma," she began. "I never had anybody who cared about me the way you did. I stopped feelin' like I had nothin' going for me. With you, I started my life again...goin' to school...doin' 'signments for you—with you." She kept stirring her coffee as she spoke. "But I met somebody, somebody who's deep for me...."

"Sure it's not lust?" I asked, sipping my coffee.

"It's not like that. He respects the black woman."

"The black woman" concept. That bothered me: Women were a sexual concept to some nationalists and didn't exist as individuals.

"I'm sorry if I hurt you," she said, sighing deeply.

"You didn't hurt me," I lied. "You disappointed me. I didn't turn my back on you when you were getting slapped around on the street. I could have let you contract pneumonia or...or die from the bad shit you had taken, but I didn't. The point I'm trying to make is that we all have responsibilities to others that sometimes impinge upon our personal lives. We have a job—or had a job to do, together. There's another person in possible danger. You fall in love, and then decide that nothing else matters. You just can't do that."

Donna was about to speak but I stopped her.

"Let me continue," I said, holding up a finger. "You walked out on me, showed up with Mbooma and handed me the keys. How do I know you haven't said anything to him?"

"I told him," she began, "I was workin' for you.... I didn't tell him anything else. He wanted to know what was goin' on. He told me what you said to him after I woke up. "

I looked at her closely.

"Honest," she said defensively. "I don't like being in the middle, Nina. It's drivin' me crazy. Fuckin' with my mind. I...I love you.... You're like a mom, a big sister...but I want to be with him."

"The First Soldier of the Nation," I said with undisguised contempt.

"Aren't you even happy that I'm gettin' married?"

"Donna, do you really want to know what I think? Do you really want to know what I feel?"

"Yes."

"It won't last. He's a stud brother. He'll be steadily humping you until you balloon up and produce a child—preferably a male one—to feed his ego."

"He ain't like that," she said as she shook her head. "He's a new black man."

I almost spat out my coffee. "A new black man?!"

My ears could not believe what they were receiving. Donna obviously, unbeknownst to me, had been influenced—infected—by that New Nation bull, and partially it was my fault. I sent her up against a charismatic street rapper and now she was spouting his new black line.

"Are you a new black woman?" I asked her.

"Yes, I am—but you're not!" she countered. "Mbooma says that some people like you belong to the dead world and cannot be reached with the Word."

I let out a groan; my face went into the palm of an upright hand. The corner of my left eye caught a shadow falling across our table. I looked up quickly. A man standing outside the window was looking in.

"Donna!" I cried as I reached over the table and pulled her to the floor with me. We were on the floor until the waitress came over.

"Are you two alright?" she asked, standing over us.

False alarm, and bad nerves. I stood up wearily, brushing off my clothes and tried not to catch the eyes of the other customers. We sat back down.

"What was that about?" Donna wanted to know.

"Someone tried to burn me earlier this morning...at the office."

"Tower! That motherfu—"

"It was Hakim, Donna," I interjected.

Donna stopped. She slowly shook her head. "No...Nina...no...the Elder wouldn't do that."

"Yeah...you go ahead and think that, baby. It might even have been Mbooma who pulled the trigger or directed the sucker who did!"

"He's not a killer! Why do you keep tryin' to make him out something that he ain't?" she cried out.

" 'Cause he may be Hakim's hatchet man."

"He ain't like that, Nina! God, you're so fuckin' programmed! You just believe that every brother is fucked up! You can't relate to real black men!"

The conversation was degenerating; I had to remember that I was speaking to a confused young woman who had let men punch her for years.

"Look," I said, "we're finished, but I'm just going to say this: you're in the middle whether you like it or not, admit it or not. They are going to ask you about me because I'm not dead!"

"I'm not sayin' shit about you—"

"They are going to ask you about me, Donna," I reiterated.

"I'm not going to say a fuckin' word," she protested.

"You're really in the middle now, girl. How do you know they aren't watching you? Aren't they going to want to test your loyalty—see if you're a bona fide *new* black woman?" I asked.

Donna wore an openly blank face, as if she did not know what I was talking about.

"You're committed aren't you, to him? To Mbooma and the New Nation?" I pressed. "They are going to want proof. After all, you were once a dead woman. Usually there's a ritual...."

"What are you talkin' about?" Donna demanded. "What are you

tryin' to say, Nina? Don't fuck with me!"

I looked around the restaurant, then leaned over to her. "They might tell you to kill me."

"They wouldn't ask me to do that!"

"Don't be too sure," I said as I rose from the table. "Let me know when you want to come by and get your things."

When I passed by the coffe shop's window, Donna was still in the booth, looking confused and lonely...not exactly the image of a new black woman in love.

CHAPTER 29

When I returned to my apartment, there was a message from Dexter on the answering machine. I called him at the newsroom. He wanted to get together. "Business or pleasure," I asked.

"Both. How'd your day go, babe?" said Dexter.

I thought about the shooting. "I'll tell you about it when I see you. Your place?"

"Sure. Bye."

I went into my bedroom, threw the bag with the dress onto the bed and went to Donna's room. The door was ajar. I pushed it open and looked in: a mess, the same way that Andy and Ayesha had kept their rooms. There were clothes jumbled and strewn across her futon. Donna had put up pictures of rappers selling malt liquor, politicos offering Afrotopia, and gorgeous black divas representing hot pussy on the walls. One corner of her desk held her school books. She was enrolled in an alternative adult education program and I wondered if she would stay in school now that I wouldn't be playing mama. Mama. That was my former occupation. Mbooma did us both a favor. He was a reality check. I was no more her mother than she was my daughter. I had no daughter, no children. I was demothered, trying to act out some role that no longer applied to me. Donna was at least grabbing or grasping for something that was flawed but real, a relationship. I closed the door thinking that I could shut out two previous chapters of my life.

Dexter paced the room of his apartment. He was mentally digesting the news that I could've been permanently delayed from ever seeing him again.

"Nina..?"

"Hmmm?" I was reading some very interesting documents that he had dropped on me when I arrived at his abode.

"Nina, I'm not going to tell you how to handle your business..."

"But?" I glanced up at his fine brown frame.

"You're not safe!" he sputtered.

"No shit, Sherlock," I said. "Worried about me? Hmmm?"

"Yeah. I like you... I like your company."

That made me purr. I began getting a warm, moist feeling between my legs.

"You got to go somewhere, I mean," he continued.

"To a safe house?" I offered.

"Exactly!"

I shook my head. "Can't do that. I have to be on the move. I have to find the daughter of the last great black man, Malika Martin. I'm zeroing in on her."

"You located her?"

"I think so. She may be in Astonia, Pennsylvania."

"What's down there?" Dexter seated himself beside me on his couch and I threw a leg over his.

"Euro-Africans," I whispered conspiratorially, and tried to keep from laughing at the silliness of the concept. I also felt a flush of lust as he ran a hand over my thigh.

"What the hell is that?"

I was about to answer him when my eyes zeroed in on a passage that he had circled on a photocopy of an August 25, 1967, FBI memo to the Bureau's field offices. It was the kick-off letter that initiated the Bureau's counterintelligence program, better known as COINTELPRO. The passage that caught my eye read:

THROUGH YOUR INVESTIGATIONS OF KEY AGITATORS, YOU SHOULD ENDEAVOR TO ESTABLISH THEIR UNSAVORY BACKGROUNDS. BE ALERT TO DETERMINE EVIDENCE OF MISAPPROPRIATION OF FUNDS OR OTHER TYPES OF PERSONNEL MISCONDUCT ON THE PART OF MILITANT NATIONALIST LEADERS SO ANY PRACTICAL OR WARRANTED COUNTER INTELLIGENCE MAY BE INSTITUTED.

"Is this how they got De Lawd?" I asked as I pointed to the passage in the memo.

"Maybe. That's the methodology. We just need to know if an audit was done and then subsequently squelched just after it was dangled before the good reverend's eyes. I'm still trying to track down the accountant who did the audit."

I began thinking about the team that was being assembled: myself, Mustapha, and Anna. Dexter would more than make up for the loss of Donna. "Look, Dex," I began, "I'm working with some people and we're setting up a task force to handle this case."

One of his eyebrows rose. "A task force?"

"Yeah, I have a man who does work for me, a former army officer."

"Intelligence?"

I nodded yes. "We're putting together a back-up system to deal with the cross-currents of information and agenda. I'm trying to find Malika but I have to deal with Hakim, Tower, and I don't know what the hell Kirby is about or up to. So this brother, the former officer, is setting up a command center for me."

"And?"

"Well...would you be interested in working with us?"

"I don't know...As a reporter I have to keep a certain distance...objectivity."

"Is your editor interested in the Conway angle?"

Dexter shrugged his shoulders. "Conway's a nobody—was a nobody."

"Haven't sold him on the Malik Martin assassination, huh?"

"No. And most people are scared to death of dealing with any-thing that smacks of criticism of Tower."

"So why are you still hot on the trail?"

"I got my own ideas about this story. I want to know who flipped the switch, set the killing machine in motion to get Dr. Martin. You know, do the right thing."

"Do the black thing," I cooed, pulling him closer to me and lick-ing his neck. My hand reached down to his crotch, felt his swelling. Yes, he was ready and I was willing.

"Nina, we have to talk," he said in a tone that usually meant that the male of the species was resisting the female's initiative.

"About what?" I asked. I was concentrating on his implement and I could tell that he was betwixt and between pleasure and business.

"About your security."

"I'll be okay," I said continuing my massage. I was about to pull down his zipper when he stopped me. He raised my hand and kissed my finger tips. Hmmm.

"We really should talk before we get into anything deep."

I raised my hands in surrender and removed my thigh from over his. "Okay...okay. You want to mess with mood control? Be my guest."

"Look, why are you getting an attitude? I'm concerned about you getting shot."

"It's more like you're acting the male role of being the defend-er," I retorted. "I can handle myself." I got up and went over to an armchair where I had plopped down my purse and withdrews my hardware. "See, I'm packing. Satisfied?" I held up my 9mm.

Dexter froze, only his jaws moved. "Get that out of here."

"What?" I looked around trying to see what he was referring to.

"That fucking gun! Get it out of my house!"

"Dexter, it's my protection." I moved towards him and he quickly stood up. I suddenly realized what he was reacting to—his wife's murder.

"Get it out of here," he said again, sounding like a desperate man backed into a corner or breaking down from too much stress. "I want you and it out of here!"

"I'm sorry," I apologized and put the gun back in my bag, preparing to leave. "I'll call you tomorrow."

I looked at the documents I had been reading and picked them up. "May I borrow these? I'll return them."

"Take them. They're copies," he said, trying to get me out of his house, away from his presence, perhaps out of his life.

As I crossed the room I noticed that Dexter had a searing look in his eyes. *What kind of animal are you?*

CHAPTER 30

I didn't exactly remember my trip from Dexter's apartment to the car to Mustapha's. I must have entered the zombie zone, that space where one goes on automatic pilot. It's a familiar terrain. I first encountered it when Lee and the children were killed. It's an odd and unnerving combination of being conscious yet being asleep, not in control of one's faculties but not entirely surrendering them to an alien force. Dexter's reaction underscored my current state of being: an inability to connect with people. I have especially felt that way since I'd been violently disconnected from my loved ones. How could I be so careless as to flaunt a gun in front of a man whose wife had been a victim of a shooting when my own family had been viciously executed? I was so intent on being a macho mama that I'd begun to intrude into other people's space, insensitive to their pain and grief.

Somehow I arrived at Mustapha's store. I floated down from the basement to the sub-basement and, mysteriously, the access card key was in my hand. I had arrived.

The situation room, unoffically called "the Womb," wasn't a high-tech center of cold video monitors and computers surrounding a round table. It was an open space where video and computer monitors sat on dark cherry shelves or desks. The walls were lined with tall book cases which housed my late husband's voluminous library. (After the killings I needed a place to store his books and Mustapha allowed me to use his basement.) Street maps of Manhattan, Brooklyn, Queens, the Bronx, Staten Island, the U.S., and the world covered the walls in between bookcases.

As I entered the room, Mustapha sat at one of the computers. He spun around to greet me in Arabic, but I didn't respond to him. My mind kept flashing on the preceding fifteen minutes: Dexter, the gun, his reaction, and my stupidity. Instead, I just sat down, staring at one of the walls. Mustapha walked over to me; mechanically I handed him the documents I'd been reading at Dexter's. "Scan these," I said flatly. Mustapha looked at me. "Please," I remembered to add. He took them without questioning me. Then the kind man passed them to an assistant, a young black woman wearing a scarf. With maximum efficiency, she fed them into a scanner. The machine electronically reproduced the data onto a disk. I didn't know that I was stranded in the ozone until Anna appeared. I hadn't seen her when I entered; she must have been sitting in the area that we have turned into a lounge, with furniture from my Brooklyn home.

"What's wrong?" She sat down next to me at the table, then looked up at Mustapha, who threw up his hands. "Are you listening to me?" I finally heard her say.

"Wha..?" was my reply.

"What's wrong, Nina?"

"Huh? Nothing is wrong."

"Then why are you crying? You got tears streaming down your face," she informed me.

I wiped my face, she was right: there were tears on my cheeks. "Stress," I weakly smiled. Embarrassed, I wiped my face with my sleeve. Anna looked at me, not convinced.

"Okay...okay..." Anna said, nodded knowingly. "This operation is shutting down!"

"On whose order?" I demanded.

"You're flipping out, Nina! You were crying and didn't even know it!" she charged.

"I'm just stressed. No big deal!"

Anna looked at Mustapha, then pointed at me. "Did she tell you that someone tried to shoot her this morning at her office?!"

"Anna!" I snapped. Mustapha looked at me.

"With a shotgun!" she continued.

Mustapha walked over to me, his arms behind his back. "Is this true, my sister?"

"Mustapha, that is the nature of my profession," I said indifferently.

"You didn't answer him," said Anna. Her arms were folded and she was tapping her foot.

I looked at Mustapha who was waiting patiently. "Yes. Somebody with a shotgun entered the office and tried to, but I got him! I winged him or her—

"She doesn't even know who it was," Anna threw in, like a child giving a parent more justification to punish a sibling.

"Nina...Nina," sighed Mustapha. He closed his eyes then slowly shook his head. I imagined the pictures in his head of yours truly splattered across the office walls.

"You're cracking, Nina. I want this operation closed down!!" said Anna.

Anna's Madam Nhu persona was beginning to annoy me. I jumped in her face and read her my version of the riot act. "Look, you pulled this shit when I was messing up in Brooklyn, but this is different!"

"No, it's not, Nina! You're doing it again! You're falling apart, but you deny reality by trying to get on with the mission at any cost!" Anna looked at Mustapha. "She punched Donna last night at a party, then fired her."

"I didn't punch her," I denied. "I energetically slapped her!"

"Girlfriend, get with your own program. You knocked her off her feet. It was the scene of the evening! You punched that girl, Nina! I saw it! All of fucking Soho saw it!!"

That put a deep, incriminating furrow in Mustapha's brow as he stared at me.

"Stop getting emotional, Anna! We're on the way to breaking this case! I may know where—"

"Nina, this case is closed!! This is it, sister!" Anna turned to Mustapha. "Shut it down."

"He's only taking orders from me," I reminded her.

"I'm the attorney on this case. I hired you, Ms. Halligan!" she threw down.

"I run this operation in here, Miss Gong, and as of this second, your ass is 86'd!" I grabbed her by the arm, yanking her to the door. Anna began struggling, pulling away.

"Nina, get your hands off me!" she snarled. A major cat fight was brewing. Anna broke my grip at the door where we began pushing, shoving, and trying to block each other's attempts at a decisive blow. Mustapha snapped his fingers and the young woman, whom I then realized was his daughter Zee, came up behind Anna and clasped her arms around her in what looked like a very tight and effective bear hug. Anna Gong was null and void. She grunted and fumed but to no avail.

Mustapha was following a policy of never getting involved in "womenfolk's matters," particularly a woman-to-woman brawl. He always thought it was better to let the women iron out their differences without an intervening male dynamic.

"We will sit and discuss this as civilized people," he announced.

"There is no need for you sisters to be beating up on one another. It is obvious that you two care a great deal about each other. It's just that you are going about this thing the wrong way. Please, no more arguing."

He nodded and Zee released Anna. Zee was dark like her father but taller with a slim build. She seemed somewhat androgynous looking, neither male or female features dominated, yet she was a striking looking woman of twenty-five, more or less.

Zee left the room, soon returning with a tray of tea. Mustapha gestured at the table for us to sit.

"We will leave you two to discuss your differences and await your decision." The door slid open and father and daughter left. Anna and I stood looking at each other, embarrassed that we had come to blows after so many years on the trail of life together.

"I'm sorry, Anna," I started. "But you have got to stop acting as if I'm always reacting to my family's murder."

Anna nodded her head slightly. "I apologize. I guess Mama doesn't need a mama."

"I was a mother, Anna. *Was*." That was the reality that Donna had dropped on me earlier.

Anna nodded her head while reaching over to the tea pot. "But what happened? Something got to you."

I sighed and told her about my conversation with Donna. Then recounted what happened with the new man in my life, Dexter, just prior to my arrival at Mustapha's.

"Donna's a lost cause, but this thing with Dexter sounds promising," she reflected. "I'm glad you're starting to take a non-professional interest in people again."

"I'm beginning to realize that I'm not very good at it...relationships...I lost my family, the stuff with Donna, and now Dexter. I thought things could be worked out with him. I was becoming interested in men again. But I was totally insensitive about his personal tragedy. Mine has almost made me...femo! There, I said it. Femo!"

"The road to recovery is always rocky, my dear. Drink your tea and let's get this goddamn case over with," she said, adding a few other choice words in Chinese.

Half an hour had passed when Mustapha and Zee returned. "Have we come to an amiable conclusion?" asked Mustapha.

"Yes," said Anna. "The mission continues."

"Splendid!" said Mustapha. The two of them sat down at the table and we got down to cases: Malika in Astonia, Donna's defection, Rudy Downs, Kirby, Hakim, and Paul Tower. A plateful of contingencies.

We theorized, strategized, and developed scenarios based on what we knew or what we thought we knew. I was quite surprised and impressed at the depth of Zee's knowledge in regard to intelligence matters and tactics.

"She knows her stuff, Mustapha," I said to him. "I'm impressed."

"Good," he said with a smile. "I'm assigning her to you as your bodyguard."

"I don't need a bodyguard, Mustapha."

"Yes, you do," chimed in Anna. I cocked her an evil look.

"Sister Nina," began the colonel, "you need an assistant and my daughter is the best. She's very good. You even said so yourself."

I looked at Zee, who smiled shyly and looked down at the ground as if she was being betrothed to me. "Mustapha, these suckers came at me with both barrels blasting."

"And this young woman is," he said as he presented her to me, "a force unto herself. She is the equal of ten Fruit of Islam."

Zee said, "I will protect you with my life, Sister Nina, *Inshallah.*" There was a simple earnestness in her voice that Muslims have a tendency to use, for they know—*they know*—that God is on their side.

CHAPTER 31

As soon as we arrived at my apartment Zee got to work. She checked all the rooms before I entered. She looked under the beds, into closets, searched for bombs and re-checked everywhere for listening devices. I wanted her to make use of Donna's old room, but she insisted on sleeping on the couch.

"The first line of defense," she said.

The following morning she had installed a miniature video camera with a wide-angled lens. This meant the entire living room would be monitored from the Womb. Zee wore slacks and had a shoulder holster with a 9mm pistol over her white blouse.

While I read the newspaper at the table she read the *Koran*. Zee appeared to be a very serious young woman with an infectious smile. I asked her about herself and learned that she was a doctoral candidate at CUNY in African and Arabic studies.

"Any men in your life?" I knew I was asking a sensitive question; Muslims can sometime be very puritanical, but she was in my house and I felt like being nosey.

She shook her head "no." "Not that I'm not interested. I'm looking for a special man...a progressive Muslim."

"Progressive Muslim?" I intoned.

"Yes." She closed her Holy Book. "A man who's a Muslim but has a more expansive interpretation of the *Koran* and shira, Islamic law. Some of the brothers I know and have dated..." she trailed off. "Islam means submission to God, not to man. It is very hard to be a

181

good Muslim and a modern woman. So, I'm looking for a progressive Muslim man, perhaps a contradiction."

"Someone like your father?" I queried.

She smiled. "No woman should ever marry a man like her father. A husband should have the qualities that would make a good father, but one father in a woman's life is enough. *Inshallah.*"

I liked this girl, I thought. She's her own woman. Rare in a world full of pseudo-feminists. "I like your style, sister...you got funk."

Her response was interrupted by the telephone.

"Good Morning," I said brightly.

"Good morning, Nina. This is Dexter."

My watch read eight-ten. Hmmm. "Hello, Dexter."

He sighed. "I...uh...want to apologize for my behavior last night...I was reacting to the gun, not you."

"And to your wife's death..." I added. "I was being callous, Dexter. I'm sorry. I wasn't thinking."

The rest of the conversation danced around our "relationship." We agreed to hook up later. I hung up, then dialed the rectory and spoke to Father Dave and then Veronica.

"Like your accommodations, lady?" I said.

"I like the fact that everyone speaks English," she replied over the phone. "Being here is getting me in touch with my spiritual needs."

"Well, look out. Father Dave is a subtle recruiter for the Anglican faith. I'll come by later."

"Nina?"

"Yeah?"

"Take care of yourself. I know this has been a great deal of trouble..."

"Don't worry. I got a new sidekick and she comes highly recommended." I looked at Zee and winked. "You take care and think positive thoughts."

"I'll light a candle for you," offered Veronica.

"Ave Maria. Bye." I hung up and clasped my hands. "Alright

Ms. Zee, let's saddle up."

Our first stop was my office. While I oversaw the removal of the damaged furniture and the installation of the new, Zee hooked up more camera equipment around the inner and outer offices. They would also be monitored from the Womb. Mustapha had contacted an associate of his who was checking out Astonia for us. I was planning to go down there in a day or so and wanted to know the set-up. I knew that Hakim, Tower, and the man with no neck, Kirby, were all buzzing around me for their own reasons, none of which were going to do me any good. My first objective was to find Rudy Downs. I was sitting on the edge of my desk trying to conjure up the miscreant when the phone rang. Zee, who immediately assumed Donna's former position without me asking her, answered the phone.

"Halligan and Associates...Who's calling? Please hold." She pressed down a button and looked at me. "A Jackie Shandlin."

Inshallah, I thought and picked up the phone. "Jackie!"

"Nina!" she almost screamed. "You gotta help me! People are trying to kill me!"

I quickly circled around my desk, sat down and grabbed a pen and pad. "Hold on! What's the deal?"

"They are trying to kill me!"

"Who is? Who's trying to kill you?"

"Downs! He's been threatening me! He says he's going to get Tower's people to take care of me!" She began crying over the phone.

"Where are you?"

"I'm at West 46th Street, Hotel Fairmont, between 7th and 8th Avenues. I'm in room 3D. Please help me!"

"Okay, I'll be there."

I wasn't going to walk into a possible set-up unarmed. I reached underneath the desk and pressed the plate and pulled out the office gun. From inside the top side drawer I pulled out a clip-on holster and secured it inside the back waistband of my slacks. When I looked up Zee was standing in the doorway with her jacket on and her purse slung over her shoulder.

"Are the cameras operational?" I asked, searching for my gun permit and placing it in my wallet.

"Yes. All you have to do is dial the number, enter the code and the cameras will go on when we leave."

I dialed the number, entered the code, and we were gone.

As Zee and I arrived at the Fairmont Hotel, paramedics were wheeling out a body. The police were blocking the street and holding back the on-lookers. I stepped up to a police officer and flashed my ID.

"Is Lieutenant Murchison here?" I asked.

"Yeah," answered the officer. "Third floor."

We passed into the lobby and I was hoping that the body being placed on a gurney was that of some businessman who'd OD on potent China Cat heroin. But when we arrived at the third floor there was a knot of police people standing in front of room 3D. It was a very short distance but it still turned out to be a very slow walk to face a reality that I dreaded.

Murch was looking around the room, then turned to look over his shoulder when he heard me identifying myself to the police officer at the door. "What are you doing here? One of yours?"

"Yes," I sighed. I looked around the mauve colored room. The bed was unkempt and there was an outline of Jackie's body between the door and the bed, with blood stains on the carpet. One of the detectives was placing her personal effects in a plastic bag.

"So?" Murch was ready for me to give him a rundown on what I knew about her. He informed me that she had been shot twice. I told him what I knew and as I did so Captain Harold Kirby walked in.

He looked at me, Murch, and then at Zee. "Who's she?" he directed at me, cocking his head in Zee's direction.

"Zee Kincaid. My assistant," I said.

"Another one of your welfare cases?" He was referring to Donna's less than illustrious past. "What was the other one's name?"

184

"Donna Taylor."

"Bald head and wears a stud in her nose?"

"Yeah—What's the interest in her, captain?"

"Oh, nothing 'cept she happens to fit the description of the woman who was seen coming up here to this floor prior to the killing. I also know she's been hanging with that New Nation crowd. Where is she?" Kirby's eyes were becoming his trademark slots with ball bearings.

I told him that I didn't know. "She no longer works for me. She quit."

"When was the last time you saw her?" he demanded.

"Yesterday. We talked about her leaving."

"Why did she leave?"

I didn't answer that, and I didn't like the way the questioning was going. I felt he already knew the answer.

"You want to come down to the station and answer some questions, Mrs. Halligan?" Kirby threateningly inched his five-by-five stump towards me.

"Nina," said Murch, becoming disgusted, "tell him what he wants to know."

"Yeah, listen to the *brother*," Kirby sneered.

"She left because there was a conflict of interest regarding the Malik Martin—Veronica Martin case. She was becoming emotionally involved with one of the targets of observation."

"Emotionally involved? Emotionally involved?" he repeated contemptuously. He looked around the room, signifying to the other men. I then realized that I too had mocked Donna.

"I hope your mind isn't as lascivious as J. Edgar Hoover's, captain," I said. "You make the words sound as is if it were a sex crime."

"I don't give a fuck what you think, counselor! You better not be harboring, aiding or abetting a murder suspect?!"

"Donna Taylor? What's the motive?"

"Motive?" he responded as if that didn't matter.

"Yes. You know, the reason why a person might kill another? Or don't you know who the dead person was?"

"Should I?"

"She was Malik Martin's other daughter...and a member of the New Nation."

"What are you basing that on?" Kirby asked.

"A hunch," I informed him.

"I think you're a lying bitch, Halligan!"

"Now wait a minute, Captain..." said Murchison.

No-neck swiveled himself towards Murch and pointed a stub of a finger. "No, you wait, son! I'm asking questions!"

"Disrespectfully, sir!" countered his subordinate.

"Look, I don't have time for fairy tales! I just better not catch her or that chink lawyer harboring these New Nation scumbags."

"Well, Captain Kirby, if you think that I'm doing something illegal...."

"You? The Screaming Madonna? God forbid!" he laughed for a hot second, then continued in heat. "I remember during the early seventies how you radical attorneys were slobbering over the Panthers. Everybody thought it was so chic and hip to be defending those criminals who called themselves revolutionaries! A bunch of sociopaths! The same vermin who are the mothers and fathers of these rappers and afroshittists!"

"Who's writing your material? Newt Gingrich?" I swear if it weren't for the fact he had a pension he needed to protect, the man would have tried to throttle me. Then I could see Zee withdrawing her gun...and then others drawing theirs....

"Get outta here!" he shouted, almost hitting me with his spittle.

Zee and I made our way out of the hotel in a state of grim, angry silence. During the drive downtown I filled her in on the brief history of the Veronica Martin case, my hunch as to who killed Ralph Conway and who took a shot at Tower.

"Jackie Shandlin," I told her as we sped by a red Maxima.

"The murder victim?" Zee asked.

"Yep. I neglected to see Jackie as a possible candidate for icing Conway. It wasn't until Veronica Martin mentioned that both Jackie and Malika had been to visit her and that Malika had visited the Shandlin estate that it hit me. Jackie was somewhat contemptuous of Malika and Veronica. When she moved the crates from the warehouse to Astonia, I knew she was a member of the Nation, for sure."

"What was at Greenpoint?"

"Arms—M16 rifles—and African art," I said. "I stumbled on to them while snooping on Hakim and Downs."

"What about this Rudy Downs?"

"I think that bastard is playing both sides of the street. My suspicion is that Jackie was in on the last art heist...."

"Art heist?"

"Sorry. There is another group that is repatriating African art back to the motherland. Rudy was siphoning some of those profits into his own pocket. Hakim was in on it for a nobler purpose. He was using the money for weapons. He's planning to kill Paul Tower. I think Jackie was killed because she sent the art back to Astonia that Rudy wanted to hold on to. She did say over the phone that Rudy Downs threatened to get Tower's people on her."

"You think that's why she called you?"

"She called me because she wanted protection. The world was closing in on her, Tower and Kirby."

"He's the police, Nina."

"Believe me. Kirby is somehow connected."

As we rode downtown to her father's place, I told her about BOSS, COINTELPRO, and Black Heat. "I think Kirby is extorting money from Tower. Tower is trying to make himself the plausible black candidate on the Republican ticket. Kirby may be doing a freelance cleaning operation. He's my prime suspect for bugging my office."

Zee placed her card key into the slot and the door opened. We walked in and Mustapha greeted us.

"Well, what do you think?" he asked. He was referring to the crystal sharp images of both my apartment and office on two video monitors. I stepped over and peered at them.

"No activity?"

"None thus far."

"Then I like it." I told him to place a call to Astonia, Pennsylvania. I had to inform a mother about her murdered daughter.

Before the connection was made I sat at the table thinking about what I was going to say to Eve Shandlin. It was important to sound sympathetic, to wrangle my way onto her estate. My feelings of sympathy would be genuine but they veiled an ulterior motive: I instinctively knew Malika was being held at the estate.

"We're ready, Nina," said Mustapha. The call would be monitored and recorded. We waited for someone to answer. Someone finally picked up. "The Shandlin residence."

I slowly sighed and got to work. "Professor Eve Shandlin, please."

"Whom may I say is calling?"

"Nina Halligan...It's in regard to her daughter, Jackie Shandlin."

"Please hold."

"Thank you." I quickly moistened my lips with a sip of water as the line began to click, indicating that I was being transferred from one phone to another.

"Eve Shandlin speaking."

"Professor Shandlin, I'm Nina Halligan. I'm a private investigator hired by your daughter, Jackie."

"Yes?"

"Yes, ma'am," I continued. "Have you been contacted by the New York City Police Department?"

"No. Why?" Her voice went up to the parental concern level.

"Professor Shandlin, I regret to have to inform you that Jackie is dead...."

The woman gasped and became silent.

"I'm sorry that I have to be the one to tell you. I'm also sorry that I have to tell you that she was shot."

"Oh, my God...My Jackie..."

I gave her a few seconds to let the news sink in. "Professor Shandlin, is it possible for me to speak to you in person...Jackie had hired me..."

"For what?"

"Well, it's a delicate matter. I would rather discuss it in person. It's very important that I see you as soon as possible. It's in regard to her father, Malik Martin," I lied.

"Yes...Oh, God...When would you arrive?"

"Tomorrow?"

"Very well," she said flatly. "I'll be expecting you around 11 in the morning. Goodbye."

She hung up and I felt like one of those pushy, predatory media vultures that circled around me when Lee and the children were killed. I wasn't vulgar but I was encroaching upon her grief. I sat quietly for a moment, trying to figure out my conflicting emotions.

"Lunch time!" announced Anna as she entered with two large brown shopping bags. She placed them on the table and began emptying them of their contents: pint-sized and quart-sized white cartons.

My face must have been close to a death mask, for Anna stared and asked "Who died *now*?"

"Jackie Shandlin," I informed her.

Anna sat down heavily in a chair. Her elan dissipated into the air with the food's aroma. She pushed the food away like a child refusing her meal. "I don't like this case...God, I hate it!!"

Lunch was a very quiet and somber affair.

Afterward, we went over a diagram and photographs of the Shandlin estate which had been faxed to us by an operative of Mustapha's. The estate was situated on two hundred acres of land. The mansion was an Italianate villa, two stories high, complete with a Tuscan tower and circular turrets.

"See what money can buy," I said to Anna.

"What's the plan?" replied Anna.

I turned to Mustapha. "Colonel."

He pulled down a screen attached to the ceiling while Zee rolled over a slide projector and dimmed the lights.

The projector showed a photograph of the villa. The next slide was an aerial shot of the two hundred acres. Mustapha advanced the projector and the next slide was a barn and some other buildings.

"The usual bucolic buildings," intoned the colonel. "But this…" he advanced the projector and another aerial shot came up. This was a woodland area that covered a great deal of the estate; the other half was cleared land. There was a cluster of buildings in the middle of one quadrant of the cleared area.

"What's that?" asked Anna. The place was dotted with small structures around the building.

"The headquarters and the training camp of the New Nation," answered Mustapha.

"Uh-huh," snorted Anna in the dark.

"Of course it operates under the cover of being a philanthropic organization dedicated to helping wayward young black males," Mustapha informed us.

"That's where I suspect Malika is being kept," I said.

The lights went back on and Zee rolled away the projector. "You asked about the plan," I said, turning to Anna. "I'm heading down tomorrow to see Eve Shandlin, meanwhile someone will creep around the estate and find Malika."

"And if she's there?" queried Anna.

"We'll go in and get her." I then turned to Mustapha. "Who do you have for this kind of work. I only need one person."

"The candidate I have in mind is a U.S. Army officer, in the reserves."

"Who is he?" asked Anna.

"Captain Zee Kincaid," replied her father.

Zee joined us, placing two black canvas bags on the table. "Ready when you are, skipper," she said to me.

Suddenly I understood why she needed a progressive Muslim brother for a mate.

CHAPTER 32

Zee and I decided to leave New York that afternoon in order to arrive in Astonia around four or five p.m. This gave us time to get a room and plan for the next day. I didn't want to break my date with Dexter, but duty and the thrill of adventure called.

Coincidentally, Dexter was heading out of town to Washington. There was an organization called the Domestic Security Archives that specialized in monitoring the surveillance of U.S. citizens by various levels of government—local, state, and federal agencies. Dexter was hot on the trail of the accountant who wrote the original audit report that implicated Tower in misappropriating the Nation's funds. This necessitated him being in Washington. We said our goodbyes over the phone and promised to rendezvous back in New York and put the heat on Tower.

Mustapha's contact in Philadelphia informed us that Astonia did indeed have some hotels and a few quaint bed and breakfast inns.

It was refreshing to be in a land of trees, ferns and fresh air. Flowers were blooming alongside the roads that led in and out of small towns. God's critters were darting across the roads as well.

At roughly four-thirty we arrived in Astonia, located in Pennsylvania "Dutch" country. We cruised around for a hotel and discovered the Astonia Inn. I parked the car and we gathered our bags and walked up the stairs to the Victorian-style house. The hotel looked as if it had an extension or annex built on. The annex complemented the original structure, but it was definitely built later and towered over the former.

Inside, the parlor had been turned into the front desk and lobby area. The place was filled with old polished wood as well as antique Shaker tables and chairs.

"Welcome," beamed a woman who looked like the matron of the establishment. She was in her mid-forties and appeared to be of German-American stock.

"Hi," I said. "A room with two singles, please."

She turned and took down a key. I signed the registry and spun it back around to her. She read our names, then came from around the counter to lead us down the hall to an elevator. As we rode up to the fourth floor, the woman made small talk. I told her that I was an attorney, Zee was my legal assistant and that we were here to attend to some business at the Shandlin estate.

"The Shandlins are an old family in these parts," the woman told us as she led us to our room. "They used to own everything. Steel mills out further west. Local farm lands. Manufacturing."

"And now?"

"Well, mostly they engage in philanthropic and educational work now. Here we are."

She unlocked the door and we entered a room decked in kente cloth, iconic wooden statues, and prints of nubile African princesses. It looked like a bad version of a Kwanzaa set on a Hollywood studio lot. Kwanzaa kitsch. Zee and I weren't shocked, but we were surprised.

"We're trying to get with the times and be multicultural," she explained. Her eyes eagerly searched our faces for positive or negative responses.

Being a former thespian I clamped on a nonchalant face and said very innocuously, "Oh."

Zee looked around the room and said archly, "Just like home."

The woman's face brightened. A connection. "Oh! Are you from Africa?"

"I meant New York," said Zee putting her bags down on a desk near a window.

"Well, I'm Dorie Brucker. But please call me Dorie. We serve dinner at eight. Enjoy the room and your stay in Astonia. Call if you need anything."

Both Zee and I said thank you and I closed the door after she left. I listened for Dorie's footsteps to recede, then cracked the door open and saw her enter the elevator. When I turned around Zee had brought out the map, then handed me a cellular phone.

"Girl, you are quick—and silent."

She smiled. "U.S. Army. Killing people is our profession."

"Hmmm," was all I could say and dialed the Womb. "Nina here. We've situated ourselves at the Astonia Inn...Uh-huh...Will contact you tomorrow before we meet Shandlin and after... Okay... Bye."

I handed the phone back to Zee. I looked around the room and began unpacking. "Multiculturalism...what a racket."

We went down to dinner at eight and were the only guests; it was the middle of the week. Dinner was good but not great; the meat and potato variant. We dined with Dorie, her husband Bob and their two teenage children, Bill and Mandy. The kids were intrigued with Zee's stories of New York hip hop life. Mom and Dad kept shooting foreboding looks at Zee. By nine-thirty we were back in our room.

I was relaxing on my bed reading *A Lesson Before Dying* by Ernest Gaines. Zee, stripped to her shorts and tee-shirt, decidedly an unmodest Muslim sister, legs folded beneath her, had her tools of the trade laid out on the bed: NATO-issued 9mm pistol, black leather shoulder holster, army bayonet, handcuffs, walkie-talkie, autofocus binoculars; her BDU (battle dress uniform) was hanging up in the bathroom. The whole thing was incongruous. Here was this respectful, deferential young woman cleaning her weapons. This girl, this sister, this woman was a killer.

"Zee, ah, how'd you get into all this?" I lowered my book onto my stomach and looked over at her.

"Oh, I don't know," she shrugged, as she sharpened her knife. "I was always kinda tomboyish, not the proper kind of girl in a Muslim household. Plus, I always admired my Dad. He seemed to know what he was doing."

"Meaning what?"

"Dad always understood his agenda. One god. One race. One destiny," she said repeating an old Marcus Garvey motto. "We have to control and implement our own program for the development of our people. I wanted to know what my Dad knew, so I decided to do what Eric B and Rakim once said."

"I'm older than old school, sister. Drop the knowledge."

"Follow the leader," she smiled and went back to sharpening her knife...a far cry from knitting.

We were expected at the Shandlin mansion by 11 a.m. Actually, I was expected. Zee was going to search the estate for Malika.

The following morning after breakfast I told Dorie that we would probably be leaving town directly from the Shandlin estate. We didn't want to leave our belongings in the room—not that we didn't trust Dorie, but the rules of engagement dictated that we keep our sensitive equipment with us.

The plan was to drop Zee off along the wooded area closest to the camp. Then I would drive back around to the entrance. Zee would do her work, then cut across the estate back towards the entrance were I would pick her up, half a mile down the road.

It was a sight to see Zee work off one set of clothes. She wiggled up woodland camouflage BDU trousers and laced them. Zee put on her shirt and buttoned that up, buckled on a utility belt, strapped on her holster, slid her bayonet into her boot, pinned her shoulder length braids atop her head, placed a crocheted hair net over her pinned locks, and then smudged her face with mud brown, leaf green and flat black camouflage cream.

"The things a woman has to do to get a date," she sighed.

Once her BDU cap was on, it was time to rock and roll. Zee told me to slow down without stopping. I made a U turn and the woman rolled out the car with her street clothes in a nylon black bag.

I'm going to take lessons from her, I thought. Definitely, follow the leader.

A fairly steep incline led up to the Shandlin mansion. The effect was powerful. As my car came closer to the building, it was clear that the mansion was going to seed, in a genteel kind of way. I parked the car near the formal front entrance and heard a flag snapping in the wind. Looking up, I saw a black flag with a green circle in its center and the red MM initials within the circle. I rang the doorbell thinking this was going to be very interesting. In no time the door opened and a young white woman with closely-cropped red hair greeted me.

"Good morning, I'm Nina Halligan. Professor Shandlin is expecting me."

"Yes, please come in," she politely smiled.

"Welcome, sister, to the Republic of Malik." She kissed me, continental style, on both cheeks. "I'm Dominique," she introduced herself. "Sister Eve is expecting you. Please follow me."

We walked down a hallway of portraits that spoke of the Shandlin genealogy. A gaunt, grim and stern looking array of Yankees dressed in the fashions of the 18th and 19th centuries. As we approached one room, a very large black and white photograph hung on a wall near its entrance. It was shot from an overhead angle, perhaps to evoke hopefulness, their eyes watching God. Everybody who was anybody was in the picture: the last great black man himself, Sister Ronnie dressed in African traditionals, Eve Shandlin standing behind Dr. Martin, Roy Hakim and a young Reggie Baxter (flashing a toothsome smile), Roger Conway...everyone except for...Paul Tower. No, wait...there was a body whose face had been erased.

"Ms. Halligan," I heard a husky voice call me.

I turned and saw Eve Shandlin. She was supposed to be in her sixties but looked forty. Money will do that, and genes. But she also looked as if she chopped wood; worked out. She had nice shoulders and a tapered waist. Her hair was faded blond, and combed back flat over her head. She wasn't gaunt and grim like her kinsmen; her face was full, her lips generous. The smack of the black? Eve Shandlin was dressed in a black tee shirt and denim pleated trousers of the same color. She stood near the door of the room where the photograph hung. I walked over to her but pointed my thumb behind me and at the photograph.

"Paul Tower? Is he the erased one?"

She smiled slightly. "It seems you know your history, sister."

I walked into her study which was a mass of books, papers and magazines, a dustorium. She guided me over to her desk which sat before a large window that showcased a panoramic view of her estate. The sun shone through the window, making the atmosphere cheery and inviting.

"Once again, I would like to offer my condolences, Dr. Shandlin." By now NYPD should have contacted her.

She breathed very deeply and slowly. "My greatest loss was Malik and now...." She reached over to her desk, pulled out a tissue from a box and wiped her eyes. While she went through her grieving I gazed around the room, noticing a huge photo of the Minister that was above the fireplace. Across from the fireplace was a couch with a coffee table; this room was her. It was simpler than the hallway and perhaps the rest of the mansion which was a reminder of her family's wealth and inheritance. She was an intellectual, supposedly the intellectual architect of social capitalism. And now working on the theoretical concept of Euro-Africaneity.

"What can I do for you, sister?" Her voice reminded me of a throatier Lauren Bacall.

"Jackie had hired me...."

"For what purpose, may I ask?"

"She hired me to find Malika Martin."

"Oh?" Eve Shandlin slowly straightened up and looked at me.

I decided to throw in the kicker. "Veronica Martin is also looking for her."

"That...that woman," she hissed. Grieving was over and the grudge began. She shook her head in disbelief.

Good. I like a reaction. I like scenes even better.

"Is she out on the loose?" she said in that upper class way that's between a sneer and a laugh. "She ruined a good man...."

"*She*?" I echoed. "I believe I got the story the other way around, Prof—"

"Call me Eve, sister. Of course you did. Everyone got it wrong! She was another one of those show biz hussies who ruined black leadership."

Uh-oh. "What do you mean?" I said, afraid of the answer.

"The government has always tried to confuse strong, progressive black men with petty bourgeois trollops."

I looked at her in a polite but skeptical fashion.

"Oh, don't believe me? Who married Adam Clayton Powell?"

I shrugged my shoulders. Powell had been married at least three times.

"Hazel Scott, a jazz singer! Who did King marry?"

"Coretta Scott."

"Right. She was a pretentious opera singer or wannabe. Stokely Carmichael?" she continued.

I scratched my head. "Miriam Makeba?"

"Rank entertainment! Every black man who's been at the forefront during the sixties was deceived by one of those Hollywood hussies! Look what happened to Malik, the greatest black man that ever lived! He married that high yellow floozy and he wanted to go Hollywood! It destroyed the movement! The woman was a fifth columnist, a sophisticated agent provocateur planted to trick and deceive the noblest of...."

She looked past me and at her missing warrior.

"I tried to warn him. The woman had no depth...Sister Ronnie...Mother of the Nation! She couldn't cut it; she couldn't deal with being the mother of the black nation."

"She saw her man die."

"So did Sister Betty Shabazz! She didn't crawl up into some hole and cry like some Hollywood starlet! No! She raised her girls to be strong black women! The mother of the nation left her child, the fruit of Malik, to be raised by another man...."

"Roy Hakim, right?"

"Yes."

I was going to get back around to that. "Have you seen Malika Martin? Her mother mentioned that she came down here—with Jackie."

Eve sat back in her chair. "Of course she's been here. This is the Republic of Malik, the last refuge for any black person. She's been here trying to get some knowledge about her past...about her father...the last great black man."

"So she isn't here?"

"No."

"When did you last see her?"

"Last fall. September or October."

"And Roy Hakim? Do you know where I can locate him?"

"Roy is incommunicado." she answered. "He's working on a reply to the disgusting theory of Christian marketplace theology."

Her emphasis on the word "reply" was tinged with a deeper meaning, implying that bullets from a M-16 might be appropriate.

"Well," I said as I rose, "I'm sorry to have troubled you, Sister Eve."

"Are you leaving so soon? I didn't offer you anything."

"Oh, don't trouble yourself, sister."

"At least some tea. You know it is a custom in our African home-land to welcome a traveler with some refreshments...Please," she said, rising. "The gods would be angry."

I smiled. "Tea's fine." But if she starts blabbering about being African.... There is a limit to this postmodern hybridity.

"Excuse me." She rose and went out of the room. Her desk was facing a large bay window that overlooked the rest of the acreage. In the distance was the wooded area that hid the camp. I removed a "bug" from my coat pocket and was about to apply it to a spot on the underside of her desk, but Eve's return foreclosed my attempt.

She served spearmint tea and for dessert showed me around the mansion. While walking the halls I kept my eye out for closed doors that might hold a captive.

I said my good-byes and offered my services if she needed them in getting Jackie's body sent home.

When I picked up Zee at the rendezvous point she had already returned to her previous outfit and had stuffed her gear back into the black nylon bag that was slung over her shoulder.

"Well?" I asked her as she entered the car.

Her thumb went up. "They got her."

"Alright," I said. "Now let's git back to the Astonia Inn and plan for this all-girl bust-out."

We arrived back at the hotel and I told Dorie that we had adjourned for the day so that Ms. Shandlin could take care of her personal business. I was about to re-sign the registry but Dorie said that wasn't necessary. We were preferred guests. She smiled and handed me the key and Zee and I took the elevator back up to the fourth floor.

I opened the door to our room and saw Donna leaning against the desk. She nervously smiled and I knew that meant something was wrong. A gun quickly edged out from behind the door and was thrust at my head. I was yanked to the floor and Zee was shoved forward by two men who rushed out of the room behind her from across the hall.

"Don't hurt them!" cried Donna.

It was quick. Our hands were bound with plastic cuffs, the kind that the NYPD use. Then the lights went out as hoods were placed over our heads.

As we were taken down a set of backstairs I head Dorie's voice.

"You got 'em?" she addressed our captors. "Good. I knew there was something funny about them when they didn't appreciate the African room."

33 CHAPTER

After I was shoved to what felt like a wooden floor, kept off balance by the hood over my face and my hands tied behind my back, Zee landed on top of me. We had been both transported by car to a new spot, its exact location unknown.

A door thudded shut.

"Zee?"

"Yeah?" she grunted.

"Here let me help you," said another woman's voice.

My hood was lifted. My eyes adjusted to the subdued light that was filtering in from a high-up window. I looked at the young woman who restored my eyesight.

"Malika? Malika Martin?" I blinked.

"How do you know me?" she asked. She had very sad eyes, sad puppy eyes and a tress of wonderfully nappy, brown dreadlocks that reached down to her back. She was model slim and wore an African print wrap around her and no shoes.

"Your mother sent us to get you," I informed her.

"Oh." She didn't seem either happy or excited about that bit of news.

"Be a pal," I said, "and give my partner the gift of sight."

"Yeah," said Zee. "I would appreciate that."

"Sure," said Malika as she shrugged her shoulder. She pulled the hood off Zee. "Gee, you're cute."

"I'm a female, sister," said the androgynous-looking Zee.

"Just my luck," pouted the first and now only daughter of the last great black man.

"How long have you been here?" I asked her.

"In here or at Camp Afrikana?"

"Both."

"Let me see... I've been here with these pseudo Africans since the fall."

"And in here?" asked Zee.

" 'Bout two months. I'se been a baaad sister," she pouted.

"What did you do?" I asked.

"Do? Do?!" Malika let out a blood wrenching scream. Both Zee and I winced. "Tried to get away from bogus black people like that wacko Eve Shandlin. That's what I've been doing. These corrupt colorzoids: Rudy Downs, Hakim, Eve. They're all pimping the name of the last great black man...my father!" Malika retreated to a corner, sat down and began laughing and crying simultaneously.

We were in a small room, twenty feet by thirty. The cement walls were covered with drawings, scribbles, etchings, all in one semi-continous flow, images and themes seguing, crashing, colliding and bumping into one another. Before me was an incredible re-working of Da Vinci's "The Last Supper" with Malika's father as Christ. You didn't need to be a Biblical scholar to figure out who was depicted at the left hand and right hand of the "black Christ"—or who was Judas. To my right, the wall held a scene depicting the last thirty years of black politics and struggle. This piece reflected a distinct Jean-Michel Basquiat feel. Neo-primitive drawings of King, Michael Jackson, Oprah Winfrey, Reggie Baxter and a host of other black celebs as the "new leaders," with prostrate black forms as the underclass. It was hard to look at, but effective. She had developed a style that was a combination of Basquiat with elements of Van Gogh, Romare Bearden and William H. Johnson thrown in. It was a wild, new style, but it was effective.

Near her, in the corner, was a basket of drawing supplies, and at her feet was a pallet with a cover. This didn't appear to be the proper way to treat the princess of the nation. I figured she was doing time for being an uncooperative mouseketeer in what I viewed as an

African Disneyland complete with obstacle courses and a shooting range, as Zee reported to me on the drive back to Astonia.

"What's going to happen to us, Malika?" I asked.

"Happen?" She shrugged her shoulders. "You'll go before the Committee of the Nation."

"The Committee of the Nation," echoed my second-in-command, Zee.

"That's when the Elder, Mbooma, and that white bitch pretend they are Yoruba deities with the power to pass judgment on your poor black souls." Malika played with her hair as she explained the situation to us.

I looked at her. She was going batty from being cooped up. "Look," I began, inching my way over to her on my knees, "We're here to get you out."

"No one ever escapes Camp Afrikana," she said, smiling like a simpleton.

"Look, we're busting out of here. Now you have a choice. You can stay and rot or you can come with us."

Malika looked at me with her sad eyes. "No one ever leaves Camp Afrikana."

"First rule...No negative thinking." said Zee.

"You sound just like those other motherfuckers upstairs! Always telling other people to have a positive attitude and then they lock your butt up when you complain that neither the circumstances you're in nor what they are doing is positive!" Malika spat back at Zee.

"You mean Roy Hakim's deal with Rudy Downs?" I asked.

"Right on, sister! Right on! You're definitely in here if you know that! That's what got my black ass in here! Uncle Roy was robbing the black nation and when I started talking truth to power I became the first daughter of the nation in a black woman's dungeon! Talking about sending our treasures back to the Motherland but puttin' the gold in his and Downs' pockets!"

My body was sore. I stood up and indicated to Zee to join me in a corner.

"What do you think?"

"About her?" asked Zee.

"I ain't talking my hairdo," I said.

"Slightly whacked." Zee looked back over her shoulder at Malika who was picking toe-jam from between her toes. "Maybe more whacked than I thought before...."

"You think she's motivated enough to get out of here?"

"Yeah, I think so."

"Okay, you deal with her."

"Why me?"

"One, she's your generation. Two, she thinks you're cute."

The door swung open and in stepped two guards.

"You're wanted before the Committee," one of them informed us. He waved his hand for us to come with them and we left the cell. Malika was still playing with her toes when I glanced back.

* * *

We were led upstairs to a large room. At one end of the room was a small raised platform with three hand-carved wooden chairs. Above the chairs was a photograph of Malik Martin.

A few feet from both sides of the platform were other people, mostly black folks but a few whites. Euro-Africans, I concluded. Three bare chested drummers entered playing a rhythm that sounded like an announcement. Mbooma approached the stage dressed in white pantaloons and African slippers, carrying his ebony carved walking stick, with a cheetah-skinned sash across his chest. The First Soldier of the Nation stood before the stage and bowed his head before the photo. He stepped up to the stage, then gazed down at Zee and me.

Eve Shandlin entered from another side of the room. She wore a brightly colored pattern of blue kente cloth wrapped around her. Her arms were exposed, displaying a set of well-toned biceps. She wore no shoes but had cowrie shell anklets. Eve also bowed before she ascended the platform. The drummers intensified their rhythmic playing as the Elder of the Nation appeared.

Roy Hakim wore a Muslim galabiya, a loose-fitting hooded garment. The Elder bowed before the icon of his brother, friend, and mentor, then ascended the platform and took his seat. The drumming ceased and the other two sat.

"Bring them forward," commanded the Elder.

Our guards complied, removed our bindings and forced us to our knees.

We knelt and bowed our heads.

"Rise and state your name and your business."

"I'm Nina Halligan and she's Zee Kincaid," I said. "We're here to take Malika Martin back to her mother, Veronica Martin. She's been released and wants her daughter back."

Hakim focused his eyes on me. "You've been trying to infiltrate our republic."

"I'm only interested in Malika Martin. The rest of your affairs are of no concern to me..."

"What do you know of our business?"

"I know about your insane, stupid plan to attack Paul Tower."

A chorus of hate and rage erupted from the People of the Nation. Voices ushered forth condemnations of Tower: he was a killer, a baby-butcher, a criminal, a faker, a thief, a masturbator, a traitor, and the murderer of Malik Martin. The Elder waved his hand like a magic wand and the chorus subsided.

"Are you aware of what this man has done?"

"Yes, but that doesn't justify your plan. What do you hope to accomplish?"

"It is called retribution, plain and simple. Those who cheat, steal, lie, and murder should not rest or even think that they can escape the people's justice! This is vengeance! A life for a life!"

The people began condemning the traitor of the nation, a so-called black man.

"Look, I think that Tower ought to be punished, but...my God...You'll probably have to kill a great many others to get to him."

"Sometimes," he intoned, "the price of justice is a heavy and exacting one."

I groaned inwardly. Hakim, like Tower, was another calculator; one who added and subtracted other people's lives at no cost to himself.

"For a people to avenge their leader, for an individual to avenge one's loved one, one's honor is," Hakim continued, "an age old custom. And the times demand that Tower pay for his crimes and treachery! The very foundation of his corrupt enterprise rests on the purloined ideas of Malik Martin's social capitalism!"

The Elder of the Nation was seething. Back in Brooklyn he allowed his anger to be part of the audience's, to cajole them, to stir their resentment, but his hatred of Tower was genuinely his, a festering sore he had learned to love.

"Surely, a woman such as yourself, murderously deprived of her family, understands the need to satisfy one's vengeance." He cast an arch look towards me.

"I'm not here to discuss the trials and tribulations of Nina Halligan, Hakim. I want Malika Martin—now!"

"She'll remain with us."

"So she can go out in a suicidal blaze like the rest of you?!" I said.

"She has a duty to perform," added Eve. "She's the first daughter of the nation."

"You people seem to have no compunction about wasting the lives of other people to advance your stupid and bloody schemes! Jackie Shandlin is now dead because...!"

"Silence!" the Elder roared at me while rising. He turned to his guards. "Clear the room. These are matters of state, not community, that are about to be discussed."

The guards cleared the room, leaving Zee and me alone with the troika: Mbooma, Eve, and Hakim. They began talking in hushed but heated voices. When their deliberations ended, Hakim turned an imperious eye back to us.

"What else do you know?"

"More than I care to," I sighed. "The second daughter of the nation—-Jackie Shandlin—-killed Conway and tried to kill Tower. Why? Because the first daughter, Malika, ain't interested in politics. Plus, Malika was about to expose your deal with Downs."

"Go on," he said.

"Also, you were waiting for me to get iced while I spoke to you over the phone, and Tower is probably aware that you are gunning for him. It was your buddy, Downs, who probably set up Jackie."

"What makes you think that?"

"She mentioned over the phone that he had threatened to get Tower's people on her. What was she still doing in town after she had sent her stuff down here?"

"Jackie stayed on to do some coordinating," responded her mother. "She was a warrior."

"And you folks didn't have back-up for her?" I thought about Jackie screaming for my help and the way she died, alone, in a hotel room. So heroic.

"We pulled all our people out of the city," said Hakim.

"And you sent Donna in to get her out, as the sacrificial lamb?"

"We all have duties to perform."

"Since you threatened to put Downs' African art bazaar out of business, he had to get a new backer: Tower. And Tower was probably closing in on Jackie in order to find out what you were doing and when you where going to do it!"

"That faggot!" spouted Mbooma, his fist crashing into his palm. "I never trusted that mothahfucka!"

"Well, whatever he knows about this place I'm quite sure he's filling in the blanks for Tower."

Mbooma turned to the Elder. "I say it's time to strike! Let me get the warriors together!"

The troika huddled again. Their body language seemed to indicate they were going for the countdown to extermination. I leaned my head over to Zee's.

"What do you think?"

Ever the tactician and strategist, Zee was looking around the room, at the doors, windows, and the armed guards. "The desire for vengeance is usually a greater motive than the one for justice."

Was she merely being rhetorical or signifying? Even Hakim had made a less than veiled reference to my personal history. In my part-time quest for Nate Ford, how different was I from them? I reasoned that I wasn't going to shoot up a neighborhood in order to kill one man, but I was hoping and searching for a bloody one-on-one with Mr. Ford. They were planning for a massacre.

The Committee, the troika, was still deliberating when I decided to address them.

"Excuse me, Elder Hakim..."

He held up his hand for silence.

"Look," I began despite his forbearance, "I think an outside voice needs to be added to this."

"This doesn't concern you, Halligan!" snapped Mbooma.

I advanced rapidly and saw the guards drawing their pistols. "The hell if it doesn't!" I thundered. "Anything you do in the name of African people affects me! You people are living in a goddamn fantasy! How in God's name can you call yourselves disciples of Malik Martin, a man who was about the social—social!—recon-struction of the black communities! You three are plotting a war! Murder! As if the loss of jobs, AIDS and the drug trade in our communities haven't done enough damage!"

"The slate has to be wiped clean before a new nation can be reborn. An agenda will be offered to our brothers and sisters," explained Eve.

"There will be no agenda if you go in and do an Afrorama wild west shoot-out!" I argued. "Aren't you people aware of the crime bill that President Benton and Congress passed? White folks are looking for any reason to lock up and shoot to kill!"

"We will not let Tower proceed with his scheme, this attempt to rob the black masses of their churches!" fumed the old man. "This man has conspired against black people for over twenty-five years! Twenty-five years, my sister! His time has come to an end. What we do does not concern you!" The Elder looked at his captain of the guards and nodded. The show was over. The guards began moving towards Zee and me.

"Wait a minute!" I shouted. "I know of a document that'll do more damage to Tower than your bullets!"

"What are you talking about?" asked Hakim

"Do I have permission to speak?" I asked, deciding to get with the flow.

The Elder nodded.

"Dexter Pierson, a *Newstime* reporter, is hot on the trail of an audit report written twenty-five years ago. The report proves that Tower stole the Nation's fund," I said.

Hakim's demeanor slowly began to change, as if he had been vindicated. "Yes! Yes! What happened to it? Some of us suspected Tower of monkeying around with the funds! What happened?"

"FBI," I said. "The audit report was intercepted by the Bureau, then Tower was turned into a Bureau asset. That document will destroy him, especially if we can hook him up to an even greater act of treachery...Black Heat."

Hakim's mouth circled around the words before a sound came forth. "If you bring me this document I will let God handle Tower!"

"What?!!" Mbooma blasted, "We're ready to go and avenge the Teacher! This bitch—"

Eve jumped up from her chair at that word, the B-word.

"How dare you address this sister that way! You know the rules, Brother Mbooma!"

"I don't believe this! She appears and says she has some document to prove Tower's wickedness and you fall for this?! She's a lawyer! A liar for hire! A trickster!"

"No! No! No!" Hakim answered as he shook his head. "She speaks the truth. She knows what she's talking about. For years, I wondered what happened, what allowed that man to make off with our future...."

Mbooma fumed.

"You bring me this document," said the Elder, "And you can take Malika..."

"Will you call off the attack?" I pressed.

"Yes, but only for twenty-four hours. I can't ask them to stand down for much longer. I will put them on alert and also the community. Go!"

Zee and I bowed and withdrew. Our belongings were returned to us. My Dodge had been driven to the estate and awaited us. We avoided Astonia, passed the town and then parked the car. We sat in silence for a moment.

"You think I did the wrong thing?" I asked Zee.

"Only if you can't deliver that document," she replied.

"Yeah." I reached over to the back seat, pulled over my attaché case and got out the cellular to call the Womb.

"Anna?...Nina." I said when girlfriend answered.

"Nina! Where the fuck have you been?! Thank God!" she said, out of breath. "We've been trying to reach you!"

"We had a change of plans" I informed her. "A radical change of plans."

"So have we!" she said. "Veronica has been abducted by Tower! Father Dave said that some men entered the rectory and snatched her! Later she called your office and left a telephone number for you to call. She's called several times, Nina. You have to get back here!"

I told her about my new situation. How I had to go to Washington and help Dexter look for the old audit report.

"You have got to get back here! It's imperative, Nina!" she almost pleaded and demanded at the same time.

"Okay. We'll be home." I switched off. "Tower grabbed Veronica," I told Zee, staring off into the distance, looking at the other vehicles passing by us on the road.

Zee silently nodded her head. "Twenty-four hours," she said softly.

CHAPTER 34

3:27 p.m.

Zee drove while I tried to figure out how I was going to pull this off. We were losing four hours on the road. I'd called Father Dave to see if he was alright; he only wished that he had been thirty years younger to take on the "hooligans" who nabbed Veronica. I called Dexter's hotel in Washington and left a message. I then phoned the Womb. They were trying to figure out where Veronica was, but so far, no luck.

"A man like Tower has many properties. She could be anywhere in the city, Nina," said Anna over the phone. "Where do we look?"

"He wouldn't keep her at BCN," I said. "He's too smooth for that. So that's out."

"I've been racking my brain....We'll wait until you get back" she sighed.

"We don't have that luxury, Anna!" I emphasized. "You and Mustapha have to locate her by the time we get back! Don't be sitting on this shit! I'm depending on you!"

"Nina, this is out of my league! I'm not the surveillance expert in the family! That's your shit!" she shouted.

"I'm not there, girlfriend!" I returned. "Do your job!"

"This isn't my job!"

"Look," I said, wanting to put my foot through the car's window, "you got us into this and you better start working on getting our asses out of it! It's too late to stop now!" I switched off the phone and wanted to ram my head into the dashboard. I hated my life...hated it!!

I suddenly felt a hand on my left shoulder. "Don't worry, skipper." Zee's dark lips smiled at me.

"You know something that I don't know, Zee?"

"Not really. But I've seen how you operate and Dad told me that no matter what the odds are you always..."

"Please, Zee..." I said, softly pounding my head against the dashboard, "don't give me that strong black woman shit. Not now." She kept her hand on my shoulder. I reached over to her hand and gripped it. I knew she was trying to buck me up. "Thanks."

The phone beeped. "Nina," I answered.

"Dexter. What's up?" said the new man in my pathetic life.

"Dexter, how's the search?"

"Voluminous," he replied. "I'm dusty and sweating. I tracked down the firm, McKinney and Clarke. It's one of the very few black accounting firms. The accountant, Walter Palmer, died years ago. The firm now keeps their old records in a huge storage house that's collected twenty years' worth of dust. Sounds like I'm enjoying myself, doesn't it? What's going on with you?"

I explained to him my turn of events—and what I needed from him.

"What? In twenty-four motherfuckin' hours?"

"Twenty-two, baby...and counting. I got to get back to New York and deal with this abduction."

"Call the cops! Call the Feds!" said Dexter. "This shit is out of control, Nina!"

"Look, I know I don't have any deep claims on you as far as our relationship is concerned, but would you do this for me? Do an all-nighter? I really need you, Dexter. I'll be down there as soon as we find Veronica."

"Okay...I'm not promising anything...I'll try. Bye."

"Bye, baby." I switched off the phone and reclined the car seat, listening to the hum of the road as we glided over the turnpike.

* * * *

5:15 p.m.

Zee and I arrived at the Womb. Anna, Mustapha, Yusef, and others were busy at computers, going over lists, and talking on the phones.

"I don't want to hear anything but maybes and possibilities," I announced as I sat down at the round table. I ratched up the tension and anxiety. "Mustapha, what about contingency plans?"

The colonel looked at me as if I were a madwoman. "I can't put a plan together until I know where she's at, Nina." He was at a terminal punching in data with his fat fingers.

"I only have twenty hours, Mustapha! I have to be in Washington! I got a man who's possibly contracting emphysema because of this! Lungs as well as lives are at stake!"

"We're doing all we can, Sister Nina. *Inshallah*," he said. He rose, then crossed the room to embrace Zee. They talked in subdued tones and Zee glanced over at me.

Anna, casually dressed in a tee shirt and slacks, was going over a computer printout of De Lawd's property holdings. I looked over her shoulder. "What have we got, kid?" I winked at her and she smiled tiredly. We were cool.

"It's more like what doesn't this fatherfucker own." The printout showed hundreds of addresses.

"You know..." began Anna. She was interrupted by the ringing of the blue phone, to which all my office calls had been forwarded.

I reached over her shoulder and picked up the phone. "Halligan and Associates."

"Mrs.—Ms. Halligan?" It was De Lawd.

I snapped my fingers and pointed to the speaker. Anna switched it on and everyone in the room stopped to listen.

"You've been ignoring me..."

"I was out of town, reverend."

"Well, now you're back..."

"Let's get down to cases. It's been reported that you have something of concern to me."

"Yes. And I've been trying to get you to supply me with a

certain item."

"How do I know you have it?"

He laughed. "Don't worry. You know I have it or else you wouldn't be talking to me. What do you know about Hakim?" He dropped the vagueness and got right down to what he wanted.

"What makes you think I know anything about him?" I said, clumsily stalling.

"You're a very luscious, clever, and resourceful woman," he breathed.

"If you're trying to make me dampen my panties, reverend, you're not doing a very good job," I informed him. "Besides, my people won't be able to get back to me until tomorrow morning."

"Your people? Why not?"

"Because they don't walk on water," I said icily. "So don't tie up my line. I'll get back to you when I do know something—and you better take care of—"

"Don't worry. I have something as fragile as that kept in the right place. Tomorrow at ten." He hung up.

The proverbial sigh of relief went through the room. I got us some hours, enough time to find Ronnie.

"I think he has a thing for you, Nina." said Anna. "When you have that much power fucking a woman isn't enough."

I rubbed my temples. Finally, it was getting to me. "Do we have that down on tape?" I asked of no one in particular.

Mustapha nodded. The tape was played over and over. I began focusing on the last substantive thing he said: Don't worry. I have something as fragile as that kept in the right place.

"Something as fragile as that..." I mumbled while pacing around in my stockinged feet, massaging my temples.

"...Kept in the right place." Anna finished. We looked at each other. Then we looked at the printout, running our fingers down it. Where would Tower keep someone as "fragile" as Veronica Martin?

Tower Christian Hospital was on the list.

Anna looked up at me. "There?" she pointed. "You think he has her there?"

"Maybe. She was in a hospital recently and her abduction might cause her to have an emotional relapse. That would be a perfect cover. Held in an isolated room, they could easily keep her sedated and physically bandaged to keep her identity hidden. Purrr-fect." I looked over at Mustapha. "Got anybody over there?"

"Yes," he said and began typing into a computer. He waited a few seconds until what he wanted appeared on the screen. "We have several nurses, orderlies, and a few doctors."

"We need to know if and when any new patients have been entered, particularly anyone who fits her description," I said. "We need to know exactly because we're going in to get her."

"I have the right men for the job. Marksmen all!" informed Mustapha.

"No guns!" I emphasized. "Not in a hospital...not in a school or a church. No guns."

"Nina, the man probably has armed Sword of Christ disciples outside her door. What are we supposed to do?"

"I don't care, Mustapha. Mamou has spoken! No guns!" I sat down at the table. "We'll figure a way in and out."

"The men I have in mind won't like this," Mustapha said, slowly shaking his head.

"Then don't recruit them," I replied. "I don't want any cowboys or Afrotopian warriors."

Mustapha stroked his beard, then turned to his ace assistant, Yusef. "Get in touch with our contacts at Tower Christian Hospital. Find out if any patients entered since this morning. See if any unusual security arrangements have been made. We also need a floor plan of the building." Mustapha turned to me. "Does Mrs. Martin have any distinguishing features or birthmarks?"

"Yes. She has a birthmark, a brown discoloration on her left arm near the top of her shoulder. Looks like an inverted triangle."

Anna's eyelids became narrow. "How do you know that?"

"I used to belong to a Veronica Thorn fan club. She was once the most popular Negro actress of her generation," I said. "There were a couple of books, *Two Hundred Things You Need to Know About VT* and *The Complete Veronica Thorn.*

"I think I know how to get her out, Nina," said Zee as she approached the table. "It'll be tricky and it will depend on some timing—and aviation. I'll need two on the outside coming in and one inside the hospital, outside the room to incapacitate the guards. Someone has to go in as a nurse."

"You look good in white, Anna," I said. "With your fine yellow self."

"Forget it, girl. Not my speed. I'm not tactical," she said.

"What do you need?" Zee's father asked her.

"Mainly, a Huey and rappelling equipment." Zee looked at me and asked, "Have you ever rappelled?"

I nodded my head. It was a skill I had picked up recently.

"Good." She then turned to Anna. "That means you're wearing white, Anna," said the captain.

This was a done deal and Anna resigned herself to the task at hand. She sighed, "Okay...what time are we going in?"

"Like Chaka Khan sang, at midnight."

12:05 a.m.

Tower Christian Hospital, located in Queens, was a twelve-storied red brick building, with three hundred beds and four wings. VM was being held in the psychiatric ward, sedated—zoned out—and listed as Myrtle Williams. She was identified by one of Mustapha's people, a Muslim nurse from Pakistan. Two BCN Sword of Christ securitrons were posted outside the room. Dressed in solemn business suits, they did not appear to be armed, but Tower's securitrons were known to be heavy smokers.

Dressed in black SWAT BDUs, our faces covered by black balaclava facial masks, carrying pounds of rope and rappelling equipment, Zee and I tiptoed over the gravel that covered the hospital's roof beneath a moonless sky. We reached the roof's ledge and knelt down to silently confer. I pointed to a door that was a few feet away. Zee went over and made sure it was locked. She then applied a super glue to keep it sealed.

We each wrapped a line of rope around one of the rotating out-lets on the roof and slid the lines through the harnesses that went around our waists and crossed our thighs. We sat on the ledge giv-ing ourselves last minute checks before we went over and down.

Our major problem would be the metal bars over the room's window. After all, it was the psychiatric ward. Since it was after midnight, we assumed that the patients would be asleep, the night staff preoccupied. We set up a pulley on the ledge. Its job would be to hoist up the metal bars after we had loosened it from the window.

I straddled the ledge and waited for Zee's signal. She held up a gloved black thumb and we went over and down. We bounced off the wall, letting the nylon burn our gloves until we came to the intended window. I switched on my nightshades and peered into the darkened room. There was a figure lying still on the bed. I nod-ded at Zee. We fastened the pulley lines to the bars and went to work with our crowbars at the hinges. We started work at twelve-ten, giving ourselves ten minutes to do the job, to twelve-twenty. By twelve-thirty Nurse Anna, dressed in white and sporting bogus eye-glasses, would approach the two guards, pass them, turn and then fire at them with a stun gun. Anna could handle a gun, but she was the wild card. Would she be cool enough to do what was expected of her? Anna was a complex person. Would she be tough? Or would she crumple up and cry like a teen-age reject? At twelve-forty a Huey helicopter was supposed to be hovering over us and ready to take Veronica Martin.

By twelve-twenty-six we had hoisted up the bars and were working on the window. Zee prepared a low-intensity mixture that would burn out the window's metal frame from around the cement. We would then apply suction cups and hoist the window up. We packed the mixture around the edge and put in a detonator and swung to the side to escape the smoke. Zee popped it.

Instead of burning out the metal from the wall, a blast took out the entire window and pelted us with glass. The plan had been rad-ically altered; the elements of surprise and stealth were over. My biggest misgiving would come to pass: guns would have to be drawn. Both Mustapha and Zee had convinced me that it would be suicidal to enter the situation and not be sufficiently armed.

I swung into the room first just as a wide swath of light came into the room from the corridor followed by the two SOC securitrons. They were about to draw their weapons. Behind them was Anna who shot one in the back of his neck with the stun gun. His partner quickly turned around to her. I fired and hit him twice, sending him into Anna who was knocked off her feet and back into the corridor.

I hit the release on my harness and went out into the corridor and pulled him off Anna; her white uniform, in parts, was covered with his blood.

"Come on! We gotta git," I said, yanking her to her feet.

Zee had taken up a position near the door, gun drawn, watching the hallway for any possible unfriendly movement. She also began speaking into her two-way radio.

"Wayward to Assistance. We've been exposed. Expedite your arrival. Over."

My watch read 12:38. The chopper was in the distance and was fast approaching. Anna and I ripped the covers from Veronica and secured binding around her. The chopper's blades began whipping the air around in the room, a sure sign that it was hovering outside the window. Anna reached outside and pulled in the line from the helicopter. We secured it to Veronica's comatose body, lifted her, and gently guided her out the window. Dressed in a hospital gown, her hair blowing in the air, she looked a slumbering Madonna as she was hoisted upward to the helicopter above. Mustapha, aboard the craft, guided her up.

"You're next, Annie." I pulled out a shoulder and torso harness from my backpack and got her into it.

"What about you?"

"Girl marines are the first to arrive and the last to leave." I helped her over the window's ledge and she went up like an acrobatic kung fu star. Zee turned her head and backed into the room.

She closed the door and sealed it with the super glue. We then pushed the bed against the door for good measure. We hooked ourselves up to the lines dangling from the chopper, straddled the gutted window and were soon gone.

CHAPTER

2:30 a.m.

I caught a red-eye flight to Washington. The plane landed at Washington International at 4 a.m. From there I boarded a subway and proceeded to the city's downtown area. After that, a taxi took me to some street off of New York Avenue where Dexter was milling through documents at a storage house.

4:30 a.m.

While being driven to the storage house I stopped at an all-night diner and picked up some coffee and sandwiches. I arrived at the door and rang and rang and rang the buzzer. Finally a bleary-eyed man in his late forties or early fifties opened the door.

"Morning, I'm working with Dexter Pierson."

"Oh, another one of you," said the guard, a brother.

The place was cavernous with rows of metal stacks with cardboard banker boxes. Rats were scurrying about and holding jamborees. At the end of the line was a ray of light splitting the darkness, illuminating a body slumped over a small table with papers and boxes. I stopped a few feet from the table.

"Dexter...?" I said. He didn't move. I went over and touched his back; he was clutching a paper.

"Wha...?!" he croaked and slowly sat up.

Dexter sleepily rubbed his eyes and began focusing them on me. "Nina, God, girl...."

"Here, baby." I handed him a cup of coffee.

"Thanks." He took the cup and drank. "Wow...you're here. What happened?"

I beamed proudly until I thought about the dead Sword of Christ guard. "We got her," I simply said, not wanting to go into details. "What do you have for me?"

"Two hundred boxes," he replied sourly.

"Where are the suckers?"

Dexter pointed to his left, to a dimly lighted area where a stack of boxes stood. I walked over to them, pulled one down and hauled it over to the table. It was a heavy box and I let the weight of it thud onto the table.

"Boy, you're butch," he smiled.

"I'm a killer, too."

"I bet," he said, but he really didn't know.

"Okay, what am I looking for exactly?" I asked as I pulled off the carton's top and pulled out an accountant's index to the box.

Dexter yawned and stretched. "Your marching orders?" he said while yawning. "An independent audit report from the firm of McKinney and Clarke, written and signed by Walter Palmer. Also, possibly attached or enclosed, would be a letter from the last great black man, Malik Martin, asking for the inquiry. Palmer's report would be dated March 1971. It should state something about irregularities and possible criminal conduct. You're an attorney, you know the lingo."

5:07 a.m.

Combing through reams and reams of documents was one of the joys of lawyering I no longer missed. Yet I had to keep my mind on what I needed: the smoking gun, or at least a silver bullet. My mind kept traveling back to the hours before...me pulling the SOC guard off of Anna, her uniform stained in blood. Blood was blood. His blood became mixed up with Lee's, Andy's and Ayesha's...all of it smeared and dripping, oozing...me in a pool of it, crying up to my God, my Lord, and hearing Nate Ford's faux Oxford laughter echoing in my ears....

"Nina?"

"Huh? Did you find it?"

"No...but you've got water coming from your eyes. Something wrong?"

I shook my head. I didn't want him reacting to me the way he had a night or so ago. "Nothing."

"Look, Nina..." he began.

I stopped him by placing my finger to my lips. "Somebody is moving around us. Does the security guard make rounds?"

"That bum—"

Two pops went off and the boxes behind Dexter's head were hit. We both scrambled to the concrete floor, away from the light overhead. I pulled out my gun, aimed at the light and fired. Dexter then crawled over to me and began talking like a real man.

"I'm not going to have an emotional reaction over your tool of the trade tonight. I just want you to know that."

"Glad to hear that, babe." I pulled out my special shades and put them on.

"This isn't the time to go gangsterlene, Nina," he said tightly.

"Night vision, buster."

I scanned the room before us, in the direction of the shots. A dark figure, back-lit in infrared, was yards away, moving back and forth between the stacks. I grabbed Dexter by the hand and we moved in the opposite direction. The man fired again in our direction, the shot pinging off the metal stacks overhead.

"I think this guy may be using what I'm wearing." I fired back and we ran alongside a wall, ducking continuous gunfire. We reached a passageway and darted through it into another row of stacks. We could hear him heavily breathing, huffing and puffing as he trailed after us.

"Sounds like a somebody who isn't used to the active life," whispered Dexter.

I told Dexter that we were splitting up. I gave him my gun and an extra magazine clip.

"What are you going to do?"

"I got the sight and these." I pulled out a handful of kung fu stars. "I'll go up and try to get him from above."

"That's a good way of staying out of my line of fire."

We quickly kissed and he made a step by locking his fingers together and boosted me up. I climbed up to the top and knelt down, trying to get myself situated. Throwing a star from above and not hitting my target could easily expose me to gunfire, especially if I didn't move quick enough. I heard gunfire and flinched; it wasn't aimed at me but below. I saw the stalker darting from the stacks. He fired at Dexter again and Dexter returned fire. I leaped from the top of one stack to another, took aim, and threw. I nicked him on his shoulder. He cried out, spun around, and fired in my direction. The shot was wild but I flattened myself on the top and unexpectedly rolled over and crashed into a pile of discarded boxes. The boxes luckily broke my fall but exposed my position. I scurried off of them and the man fired off two more rounds as I moved to hide behind a stack. I shot a sharp glance around the stack and he fired. I tossed a star over the stack, it landed behind him and he quickly turned to check his rear. I stepped out, quickly threw two stars directly at his gun-hand and dislodged his weapon.

I charged at him, ramming my head into his stomach. He smacked me away as if I was yesterday's newspaper. I was no competition. He was short and built like a tank. The only thing I managed to do was to kick his gun away from him when I attacked. As he ran for his gun, I quickly got to my feet and unleashed my last three stars. All of them ripped into his gun arm, the right one.

"You fuckin' bitch!!" he yelled, switching to his left hand, firing wildly.

Dexter appeared to his right and popped him twice in the chest. The man fell back into the stack, the gun still in his hand. Then he fell face first onto the concrete floor.

I slowly walked over to the body and retrieved the gun. I then knelt down and, with great effort, turned the body over. I shook my head. Dexter walked over and squinted in the darkness. "Who is he?"

I handed him my night shades and Dexter looked down at the man with no neck.

CHAPTER 36

7:40 a.m.

We found the document. It was in the binder that I held in my hand when Kirby began firing. At a D.C. police station I made a statement and told them that I was expected in Astonia, Pennsylvania. I was let go and told to return (which I did later). I took off for Astonia and Dexter remained behind to handle the rest of the police inquiry regarding the two bodies. Kirby killed the storage house's night guard; slit his throat. Kirby's death confirmed my suspicion that he had been a part of the BOSS operation, Black Heat, against MM. It also made me suspect that he was doing a clean-up operation for Tower.

9:36 a.m.

"You are early, sister," said the Elder.

"I don't like to keep my clients waiting," I said.

We—Hakim, Eve, Mbooma, and I—were meeting at the villa,

the "capitol" of the Republic of Malik. I slid a copy of the report across the table over to them.

"What else do you have?" asked Hakim.

I knew that they were hungry for more, but I didn't have the time and Dexter was dealing with the police.

"A dead body," I said crisply.

"Whose?" asked Mbooma.

"Someone whose death you will enjoy, brother," I said, a little sickly. "Harold Kirby."

They liked that. Kirby was on their list. I told them how it happened.

"I want the girl, Elder," I said to Hakim. They wanted to give me a state dinner worthy of a "heroic and conquering sister." My own choice of a virile young warrior was offered (at least they had broken that lopsided sexist custom). I wanted out. I was a busy woman and had loose ends to tie up: getting a young woman home to her mother, reuniting what was left of a family.

Two guards brought Malika from her cell. She had her basket of art supplies and some drawings. At first she didn't want to leave her walls, but I told her that there were even whiter walls to draw upon back in New York. We left the stateroom and made our way out of the house to my rented car. I'd just gotten her in when I heard someone call me.

"Nina!"

I turned to see Donna walking towards me. "Yes?"

"Please don't hate me," she said.

"I don't hate you, Donna. I'm disappointed. I hope you find happiness here in Afrotopia, and I hope I'm wrong about you and Mbooma."

"He's good to me, Nina. He doesn't beat me."

"He better not," I said still feeling responsible and somewhat protective.

"Please come to the wedding."

I looked at her. "You got to be kidding, girl. After the shit you put me through..."

"Nina, I don't have any family."

"You weren't thinking about family when you handed me the key and walked away."

Donna bowed her head. "I was really confused, Nina. I didn't want to lose him...I was afraid of losin' him." She looked up at me. "Don't I have a right to experience some happiness? You had some before your tragedy."

I told her that I would think about it. We shook hands, and I got in behind the wheel of the car. I told Malika to buckle up. She had started to draw on the dashboard. It was going to be an interesting drive.

Mustapha had set up a safe house in Montclair, New Jersey. Mother and daughter were reunited under the watchful but unintrusive eyes of the colonel's people. I returned to the city and dropped the car off, and headed to my apartment, then directly to the shower. I was just stepping out of it when the telephone rang.

"Nina!! Turn on the TV," Anna screamed into my ear.

"Why?"

"Turn on the set!!" she shouted again and I obeyed.

I picked up the remote, aimed it at the Cyclops and saw a fire raging on the station.

"Any particular station, dear?" I was ready to push to another.

"I doesn't matter," she said weakly, "it's on all the stations...."

I zapped the remote and the same image was on another station, the same fire. The angle was different on this station. One could see the entire place and police cars and fire engines. I then recognized the square Tuscan tower, the circular turrets and the flag, the flames eating away at the letters MM....

"I just came from there! What in God's name happened?" I said, while holding the phone to my mouth and staring at the television set. I began pacing the floor, speaking to Anna, switching from one channel to another, getting the same news.

"The government went after the guns..." said Anna. "Hakim declared a state of siege."

Donna...Donna...Donna, was all I could say to myself. "Get over here, Anna. I need you." I put the phone down and watched the flames devouring the Republic of Malik. Thoughts of an unfortunate recent immigrant to that enclave of delusion filled my head.

A few mornings later, a small gathering of us met at the Hudson River. Myself, Dexter, Anna, Shinyun, Mustapha, and Zee were going to say good-bye to Donna. Nothing special, but she deserved better than being remembered as one of two hundred or so charred, unidentified remains.

While packing up Donna's room I discovered a small, wooden box filled with her hair. She had shaved off her hair and saved some of the plaits, tied with red ribbons. Tucked beneath the hair, was a photograph of Donna, Anna, and me. It was taken at a restaurant celebrating Donna's 19th birthday. During her entire life, up to that nineteenth year, Donna's birthdays had never been celebrated. While looking at that photograph I slowly realized that Donna was special, and her death made me face the fact that I had failed her. I expected her to live up to my class expectations, but she had realized that she had a class, a street allegiance. People like Donna, the misfits and disenfranchised, really don't believe in the system or the middle class way of life. As futile as the revolutionary suicide of Hakim and Mbooma was, the middle class reality of daily compromises and smugness is just as corrupting, less deadly but still a slow death of weakness and deceit. Perhaps Donna's last few years with me were preparing her for her destiny, best symbolized by us gently lowering the box into the water and watching it drift down river....

 The media had a field day with the story. Hakim, prior to the fire fight, released a statement denouncing the government's conspiracy to undermine the Republic of Malik. He talked about the audit report from McKinney and Clarke that I had given him. The document was immediately ignored since the issue was, in the eyes of the government, the illegal possession of automatic weapons. No one survived the charred remains of the Shandlin estate, the Republic of Malik, and that was a Godsend to those nationalists who needed dead martyrs.

The fact that Eve and Dominique had "womaned" the barricades as white women gave rise to a series of lurid and sensationalistic stories and features about white women as concubines, the sex slaves of big appendage black men. Twisted articles appeared about blood and sex orgies in which Euro-African bitch goddesses killed some of their white male babies to prove their loyalties to their black masters! Or they that ate the flesh of dead, white males to prove their fidelity to their "heavily hung" black men!!!

Reverand Paul Tower, ever eager to show his *white* credentials, lost no time in appearing on various talk shows (as well as from his tele-cross atop BCN) denouncing the New Nation and applauding the government's swift action in putting down the "insane insurrection that was based on rap and Afrocentrism." Tower repeatedly made a link between ghetto violence, hip hop and Afrocentrism, which was never challenged by the media. Those who had knowledge of what was going on, those independent voices of the black community, were muscled aside by the stature of the most "prominent" and "authoritative voice in black America today," Paul Tower. Even General Calvin Farmer, the former Chairman of the Joint Chiefs of Staff (who was the unannounced but plausible black presidential candidate until Tower) took a back seat.

"I'm not surprised at the turn of events," Tower sagely reflected on PBS's *The Newshour*. "Roy Hakim was always part of the black counterculture, the ultra-radical fringe of Malik Martin's movement. After black power collapsed during the mid-seventies, he retreated to teaching and propagandizing amongst the urban lumpenproletariat—the same social morass that produced the Black Panthers and other pseudo revolutionaries. Hakim produced and financed rap shows. One of the best kept secrets of hip hop is that it was the product of a group of dissidents in the Nation movement, Hakim and Shandlin, and how they conspired with the large recording companies. It was a slow burning time bomb and it has been documented in my book, *Hip Hop and the Euro-Africans: Their Secret History*."

It was a brilliant performance and the media sopped it up. Who could know more about about the macabre goings on in the urban Bantustans of America than De Lawd, a man who was dedicated to bringing marketplace Christianity. To Tower, the root of all that was bad in black America, as Hakim observed, was rap and Afrocentrism. Hakim was off the mark about many things and that had cost him his life, but he was right about Tower's ludicrous obsession.

Lost in all of the media coverage was the curious story of Harold Kirby. He was eulogized as a dedicated veteran, police officer and family man. Yet no one could explain why he murdered a security guard and tried to kill two other people.

I became persona non grata at NYPD. Prior to Kirby's death, the blue wall had more or less embraced me as a victim and fellow crime fighter. But after the Kirby incident, they rejected me as an "accessory to the murder" of one of New York's finest. They did not see it as justifiable homicide or self-defense, as the D.C. grand jury deemed it.

A whispering campaign had begun, instigated by anonymous police sources. It was rumored that Dexter and I were part of a drug network. Yet they could not explain what a New York Police Department captain was doing out of his jurisdiction.

Dexter got sick of it, the innuendoes, the racial slurs, and death threats. He began to fight back, letting it be known that he was working on the investigation of a former police operation called Black Heat. Suddenly, the innuendoes and vicious gossiping stopped...as if it never happened.

That was a mistake. It made us realize that the heat was still burning. It was hot enough to cause others to withdraw their hands from the fire. Dexter wanted to write an article on the rise of Paul Tower, but I told him that the article would be spiked, killed on his editor's desk.

Dexter left again for Washington. He planned to spend more time at the Domestic Security Archives doing research. He also mentioned that some people might be willing to talk off the record about Black Heat. I went uptown to see Murchison, recently promoted to captain, and experienced the coldest walk from the front desk of the station to Murch's office. My pal Petroff threw my visitor's badge on the floor. Blue uniforms coldly eyed me as I walked to the captain's office. One of them was gracious enough to anoint my head.

"You got a handkerchief, Murch?" I said when I entered his office and closed the door behind me. He stood at his file cabinet, fished around in his coat pocket for the requested item and handed it to me. I wiped the saliva from one of my braids.

"A little something from the boys out there...in remembrance of Harold."

"Who did that?!" Murch slammed the cabinet drawer shut and walked over to me.

"I don't know. My back was turned, Murch."

"No-motherfucking-body in my command is going to disrespect a visitor of mine!" He was shaking with rage.

I patted him on his shoulder. "Calm down, brother. They did the same to the kids who integrated Little Rock High School. The kids got over it."

"Nina, I'm not going to have this kind of disrespect in my station!" he continued to fume.

"Look," I said calmly, "why don't you be nice to me and buy me a cup of coffee. Okay?"

We adjourned to a mid-town coffee house. Murch was under suspicion by the men and women in his new command because he was a friend of mine. The circumstances of Kirby's death—the criminality of it—were brushed aside. Murch's association was the focus of the rank and file's rage. He resented that, but he also wanted to know what really happened, and I told him.

"Murch, do you think I enticed him down there? Little ol' femme fatale me?" I said. "You yourself said that he thought I had something on him."

The new police captain sat back, weighing the odds, calculating what was and wasn't in his interest, and what he thought he was obligated to tell me as a friend.

"Nina," he slowly started, shifting his eyes around a nearly vacant cafe, "this is hearsay and if you ever attribute it to me, I'll deny it and call you all sorts of MFs."

This had to be serious.

"Kirby was probably on a clean-up operation. You must've have figured that out. He was a former intelligence officer in the army..."

"And a BOSS man," I kicked in.

Murch solemnly nodded his head. "He was virulently anti-communist, a Goldwater-Birchite-Reaganaut, and a level-one nigger hater. The story is—and it is only a rumor—that he was recruited by an unofficial, clandestine committee of government officials, businessmen and others who were becoming annoyed at the uppity Negroes who were demanding their rights as humans and disrespecting property rights during the sixties and seventies."

I looked at him skeptically. "You sound like Ollie Stone."

"Fuck Ollie Stone—and J.F.K.! As far as I'm concerned Kennedy got whacked 'cause was he *schtupping* other people's wives," said Murch. "Look, sister, I'm talking about home-grown, American style death squads."

"Death squads?" I echoed.

"Look, Nina, they do everything by the book. The formal dictates of our pro forma democracy require that a legal framework needs to be established so that an activity can be performed under the cover of law. You teach law, tell me that I'm wrong."

Was I listening to the same Murch? Mr. Apolitical Careerist?

"So...?" I replied, but quickly began thinking about those COIN-TELPRO documents I had read.

"So," he continued, "during the sixties and seventies people in high places gathered other people to do some dirty work. An American dirty war. Looked at what happened to the Panthers...King...Malcolm...."

"Kirby was one of their boys?"

He said nothing but nodded.

"How do you know this?"

"A nigger on the make has to know these things—or know of them," he answered cryptically.

"So what's the connection between Tower and Kirby?"

"The story, unsubstantiated but loosened by liquor during old blue boy talk, is that Kirby was Tower's contact and handler. The ad hoc committee didn't want anyone formally connected with Washington. The story—unsubstantiated, Nina—is that Tower organized the hit on Malik Martin. He, Tower, knew what was coming down and decided to get rid of Martin."

"What was coming down?"

"The shit, girl!" Murch said. "Look what happened after any slave revolt or the mere rumor of one. White folks go crazy. They start wildly killing anybody or everyone — especially if they look like us. Look at Nat Turner, Denmark Vesey. Look at Wounded Knee, the internment of Japanese Americans...My Lai. Shit, niggers were doing things and they decided to come down hard, but Tower said he could handle it."

Murch looked at me and let the info settle onto my shoulder. "This is all hearsay," he reiterated.

"Yeah, but said by guys who may know," I countered.

"Men are the worst when it comes to gossiping. Look, these folks don't keep shit like this on record."

"Oh, I don't know about that...The Nazis filmed what they were doing," I reminded him. "And sometimes I depend on white folks' arrogance and their methodological compulsiveness to record everything."

Murch disagreed. "Sister, these folks are professionals. They don't leave records behind. You aren't dealing with New Nation headmoes who play revolution. These fuckers own it."

CHAPTER 38

 De Lawd used the media frenzy created by the violent collapse of the New Nation to launch his master stroke: The African American Prophetic Institutes, a Christian marketplace franchise. Usually black ministers are a highly contentious and suspicious set, each jealously guarding their lot and privileges. But Tower seemed to have been able to strike a chord of unity among a majority of them. They willingly complied with his scheme, allowing themselves to come under his wing as "affiliates." "Non-affiliates" didn't seem to present any opposition either. As a matter of fact, Tower made sure they got a piece of the action, creating an under-the-collection-plate tithe. Recognized as the Dean of Deliverers, the most respected (black) man since Martin Luther King, Tower was organizing his base for an assault on the Republican Party nomination.

He appeared on television talk shows where he admitted that he was the source of information that led to the government's attack in

Astonia. He was quoted in news magazines, visited editorial boards, and sent out editorials to black local and community newspapers. His high visibility was making Anna and me wary. We knew this guy was a killer and an operator; we believed that he was weaving an aura of plausible deniability.

We decided that we needed to push back. Tower was becoming more and more powerful. Many blacks were looking at him as the new Black Messiah. Let's face it, I thought: De Lawd had the smell of a winner and the people's noses were wide open.

Anna and I decided to hold a press conference. The pretext was to introduce Sister Ronnie and Malika as "Da Sistuhs," who would carry on the name and agenda of the last great black man. The problem was Veronica. She had to be convinced that this plan was just a show, a preemptive strike to protect her and Malika.

We were seated on the patio at the Montclair safe house. Mother and daughter had some initial trouble re-establishing their relationship, but their relative isolation in Montclair allowed them to close the gap. Malika's "emotional problem" disappeared. She had become clear headed and directed.

"Ronnie," I said, "the point is that you won't be setting up a real agenda, but we have to make you visible so that nothing can happen to you."

"But you can't guarantee that," she said, looking me dead in the eye.

"Yes, you're right. But why make it easy for him?"

"Nina is right, Veronica," added Anna. "Tower would feel less inclined to, uh, tie up loose ends. By you becoming visible and proclaiming your stake—"

"You'll be preempting a possible strike," I finished.

Veronica turned to Malika, held her hand and asked, "What do you think, daughter?"

"I think Nina and Anna are right. Tower is usurping Daddy's ideas and really perverting them," answered Malika. "Not everything Uncle Roy said was wrong." She leaned forward and continued: "I know he became obsessed with getting Tower and really compromised himself with Downs. But he was right about Tower, he shouldn't be allowed to get away with what he did!"

"Must we go through that again?" Veronica sighed audibly, wearily shaking her head.

"Mom, he killed Daddy. He didn't pull the trigger but he gave the order..."

"We don't have proof of that..."

"You know he did it! Uncle Roy knew it! Even Nina has people working to get proof!"

"Honey...we just got back together."

"Veronica, what's the real problem?" I said, sensing something else.

"Nina, I couldn't carry the weight then. Some of the things Eve Shandlin said about me were true...."

Malika shook her head. "No...no...no. That was her class trip, Mom. She couldn't have Daddy in any real way because he was in love with you."

"I couldn't compete with her."

"No one could, Veronica," I said. "The woman had lots of money. She could afford to be a Euro-African! Malika's right. Eve was pulling an I-know-my-black-man-routine."

"Besides," added Malika, "everyone is now going to think that Daddy's message was about violence...guns."

"But what about our people?" asked Veronica. "Remember what they said about me? 'She can't hack it. Coretta could! Betty did!' They're right. I'm just a bougie Hollywood babe."

That annoyed me. "I disagree with the notion that there are no second acts in America. We can't make you do this, but you can give yourself and our people a chance," I said.

Anna and I picked up the dishes from the meal we had and went into the kitchen. Mother and daughter remained outside talking. Veronica was shaking her head and Malika was kissing her mother's hand. The sun was setting; its rays made their skins glow. Maybe I was thinking that Veronica had to be tough—like me—and get on with the business of getting back, not letting those men think that she's permanently damaged. But I was damaged. I was the one who woke up in the night screaming my children's names, thinking that my perspiration was their blood. Veronica had been locked up for years. She knew what the public's scorn felt like. She couldn't live up to the black mythology of being a strong, progressive black woman.

I decided not to push it. Tower was behind the assault on Astonia, but if I wanted him I was going to have to get him on my own.

Malika came into the kitchen. "Give her some time," she said to both of us. "I think she'll do it. I'm trying to fire her up. I've got years of Uncle Roy in me," she winked. Veronica was left on the patio with the sun's rays.

"Nina?" said Malika.

"Hmmm?"

"Is that cute guy still around?"

"What guy?" I thought she meant Dexter, but I knew she hadn't met him.

"You know, the guy who came with you to rescue me."

"That guy has the same type of plumbing as the three of us, Malika," I said. "Zee is her name. She's a very upright Muslim sister who's looking for a progressive man. She's also a captain in the U.S. Army Reserves. So forget about it."

"Oh, no," she said innocently. "I was only curious about her. I wouldn't mind having her sit for me...you know, drawings." Malika ran her fingers along the counter and across the refrigerator until she left the kitchen.

Anna looked at me. "She's in love!!"

"Don't start, Anna!" The telephone rang and I picked it up. My conversation was brief, my face solemn.

"What" said Anna dreading the worst. "Who's dead now?"

"Not who's dead but who's alive," I said.

"Huh?"

"The First Soldier of the Nation is back!"

CHAPTER 39

As we drove back to New York I explained to Anna what I'd been told on the phone. Apparently, Mbooma had arrived at my office. Zee, still acting as my assistant, recognized him despite his shabby clothes and haggardness. She said he seemed disoriented and was mumbling that Donna had sent him to find me.

Zee took him to my apartment. Anna and I found him there, looking like a defeated puppy. All his bluster and bombast had been knocked out of him. Seated on the couch, he was agitated, straining to get his words out. Zee sat on the other end of the couch; Anna sat in the armchair. I stood with my back against the bookcase listening.

"The shit was comin' down hard. Hard!" Mbooma continued. "The mothahfuckas had everything and everybody. Tanks. Personnel carriers. SWAT. Feds. Helicopters! We never had a chance...."

"What did you expect?" I said, somewhat coldly. "How'd you escape?"

"The Elder ordered me to go."

My look must have read cowardice.

"He did! Honest!" he almost pleaded. Mbooma glanced around furtively. "The Elder ordered me to retreat," he said, his voice deepened. "He wanted me and Donna to reconstitute the Nation. He wanted us to be the Adam and Eve of the second regeneration of the Nation...."

"What happened to Donna, Mbooma!"

Mbooma's eyes shifted, his voice softened and he hung his

head. "We were going down the stairs of the mansion. The Elder...you know...and Sister Eve too...they were dead. The place was burning...smoke everywhere...Donna and I were heading down the stairs when some SWAT mothahfuckas came in. I started shooting, but Donna was hit. I threw her over my shoulder and we went down to the basement, to the escape hatch. She was losing a lot of blood...my shirt was soaked. We had built a tunnel that goes out miles from the Republic. We had a car on a track and we rode out. At the end I pulled the switch and blew the sucker up with the explosive we set up. I took it out...I tried to help Donna with the medical kit but...." Mbooma shrugged his shoulders and clasped his hands. "It was just too late for my queen. I buried her with my own hands. I wrapped her up in cloth and plastic, like a body bag. The fuckin' dirt wasn't good enough for her."

Anna wiped her eyes. Zee was staring very intensely at Mbooma; I couldn't read her.

"She told me to get to you while we were riding down the tunnel. She kept saying 'Mamou...Mamou...' I knew that was you, so...."

Mbooma pulled a yellow bandanna wrapped around something out of one of his pockets and handed it to me. It was a bandanna that Donna often wore around her head. It still had her scent.

"I'm sorry about Donna," he said quietly. Mbooma stood near me as I unwrapped the bandanna. Inside the cloth were her last personal effects: wallet, rings, earrings, a gold chain with a small pendant shaped like Africa. I folded the cloth and placed it on a shelf; I didn't want to think about what had happened to Donna. I had already done my mourning.

My silence made Mbooma uncomfortable. He looked around waiting for something, a tear, a thank you.

"She shall be revenged, sister," he informed me. "I'm going to fulfill my last mission...Tower," Mbooma said with finality.

I sucked in my breath and closed my eyes. "Don't you think there's been enough violence? Enough killing?" I finally looked at him. "You just buried Donna, your queen...."

"And now I'm going to bury him." That must have been his cue, for he strode towards the door. I grabbed his coat sleeve and jerked him around to me.

"I'm tired of you knuckleheads posing as nationalists!" I snapped.

Mbooma contemptuously spat. "I don't have time to listen to any bullshit!"

"That's because you're too busy feeling your dick getting hard when you have that cold black steel in your hand! You're just another death freak, Mbooma! No different from the ice people you rant about! What have you ever done that didn't involve death or bad-mouthing?! Huh! What?!" I fumed. "Nothing!"

"The New Nation has got to hit back!" he announced. "The First Soldier of the Nation is back to collect!"

"Don't you understand?!" I said. "There is no New Nation! It's dead! You and Hakim killed it!! You took on the national security and a billion dollar apparatus like BCN on their terms and lost!"

But Mbooma wasn't interested in Reality 101. He broke for the door but found it blocked by Zee.

"She's right, brother," she said to him. "Talking mau-mau merely gives the powers that be a legal provocation to destroy you."

"So Tower gets away, huh? He killed the minister and the Elder and now he gets to be the head nigga in charge?! Is that what you're telling me?!"

"No, brother," I said, softening my approach. "I'm saying that Tower's Achilles heel is power and you have to attack that base, the source of it."

"How?" he asked skeptically, not convinced that it could be done.

Zee and I both tapped our heads with our index fingers. "By using the ultimate weapon, brother."

Mbooma didn't seem to be totally convinced yet he wasn't in as much of a hurry as before to get out into the street. Zee approached him, placing a hand on his shoulder. "You know, brother, it is the lioness that brings home the meat."

* * * *

The press conference was held at the Women's Center for Constitutional Concerns (WCCC). Press releases were sent out. The media—in the wake of the shoot-out at "Afro Astonia"—were in full attendance. Two days prior to the conference, I met with Mimi Goddard , a reporter from the *Greenwich Post* and a producer at radio station WBAD. I slipped her the Hakim-Downs tape recording: this was deep background. We had an off-the-record discussion about Professor Rudy Downs. The day before the Martin press conference her newspaper ran a story on the front page: "Profscam: The Secret Life of Rudy Downs."

Downs cried libel and the newspaper produced the tape. When it was authenticated, the postmodern professor, a leading black intellectual, dropped out of sight. The police also wanted him for questioning.

I dropped the newspaper in Mbooma's lap and tapped my temple.

"One down."

As I said earlier, the subtext was to give Veronica and Malika a parameter of protection by high profiling them, mother and daughter reclaiming the mantle of their fallen man. Seated at the table with a bank of microphones that eerily looked like rifle barrels pointed at their faces, Veronica, aka Sister Ronnie, and Malika sat between Anna Gong and Sonia Baraka, the director, cited as "the most dangerous woman in America" by conservative radio talk show hosts.

The sisters announced the formation of the Malik Martin Social Initiative Center, an organization dedicated to implementing the ideas of the late minister, particularly his emphasis on social capitalism. The media, of course, was more interested Veronica's response to the shoot-out. She let them have it with both barrels.

"Roy Hakim was caught in a time warp," she began. "He thought, like many others, that armed struggle is the only way to achieve black liberation. Let me say that it is my understanding that his motive was to punish a person whom he felt betrayed my husband and the Nation—"

"Who was that?" asked a reporter.

"Let me finish, please.... Roy Hakim knew he couldn't rely on the judicial system, due to the fact that the government had acted to undermine my husband's program while he had neither committed a crime nor broken any laws."

The media wolf pack wasn't interested in a historical perspective. They smelled the blood of a name, an easy peg to tie a story around. "Who did Hakim suspect?"

"Paul Tower."

The heat and the voices in the room went up. Shouts of: "Proof?" "Evidence?" "What did he base that on?" rained down.

Veronica raised a document, the McKinney audit report, and said, "I have here in my hand an audit written in March 1971 that cites the illegal transfer of funds by Paul Tower when he was the treasurer of the Nation. This report was written but never released. It was stopped by the FBI. They wanted to blackmail Paul Tower into spying for their illegal operation called Black Heat! I do not have the evidence at this time of the government's complicity in my husband's death, but I do believe that the death of police Captain Harold Kirby was in some way tied to that operation and that Paul Tower was engaged in the betrayal of my husband, the movement and black people in general! This man is unfit to be the head of the Black Christian Network. My daughter and I will lead organized protest marches against him and his McChurch scheme!! Thank you."

Sister Ronnie and Malika left the media hanging. They wanted more and called out question after question. How did she get the documents? Exactly what was Black Heat? What about Harold Kirby? Was Black Heat part of COINTELPRO? What is the Paul Tower connection?

* * * *

In the wake of Veronica's explosive press conference, De Lawd's public relations team issued the following statement: "Reverend Paul Tower will not comment on the lunatic ravings of a woman who has been incarcerated for almost twenty-five years. It is a typical ploy of those of the left, feminazis, to use confused black women to try and bring down traditional African-American leadership."

Then Mel Farmington, the jerri-curled minister, chimed in: "We have got to stop the vicious smearing of our black leaders. Paul Tower is known to have increased voter participation in our communities, and this attack on him is by certain known forces! Veronica Martin and her group have an agenda: to destroy traditional African-American leadership."

Farmington didn't want to call a gonad a gonad and say male. It was rumored that he was preparing a campaign, his sixth, during the same year that Tower was to seek the Republican nomination, and he was getting funds from De Lawd. What made Farmington's defense of Tower so slimy was that he was a Democrat and Tower a Republican. But they both belonged to the most unchallenged mafia in America, the ministry.

Ronnie and Malika marched in front of BCN headquarters. Days before, the numbers were quite small, a group of ten. The protesters held signs that read "Thou Shall Not Steal," "No Fried Religion," "Tower - You have Profited but Lost Your Soul." The police presence was at a minimum until the end of the week; it rose when the numbers began to be fifty or sixty marchers circling before the building. Tower's image on the cross's monitor denounced them in prophetic marketplace terms, but he came down to talk when television cameras arrived on site.

De Lawd sought to embrace his "long lost sister," but was intercepted by a well-wisher who wanted the great man's signature. Tower was on the move but couldn't resist a prospective voter. He stopped, signed, and the man left him with a subpoena for him to appear in court to answer the charges of conspiracy to fraudulently take over the Nation.

Flustered at being outmaneuvered, De Lawd fumed and tore up the subpoena on national television, an act of contempt, decried the court later.

"Who do you think you're messing with?" he exclaimed at the mother and daughter who continued marching. "You won't get near my network! It's my network! I own it! I built it!" he shouted. His entourage tried to get him to cool it before the cameras, but he continued to fuss "about those people" and mumbled audibly about "doing something about those bitches!"

My eyes were glued to the TV, as the saying goes, when the phone rang. "Nina," I said into the mouthpiece.

"Ms. Halligan?" It was De Lawd himself.

"Reverend," I said cheerily. "I was watching your stellar community outreach performance. Temper, temper. What can I *not* do for you?"

"I want to speak to you."

"Shoot," I said, switching off the television.

"Not over the phone. At my office—now!" he demanded.

"I don't cross picket lines, Reverend Tower and I don't care to be in your presence. There's nothing that you can say to me that I care to hear," I calmly told him.

"My God, what are you trying to do to me?!"

"*Moi?* Me? I'm not doing anything," I said. "You don't understand, do you? You have a mother and her daughter upset that you iced—"

"I did no such thing!" he countered.

"That's what you tell yourself every night before you go to sleep so it won't be a troubled one! Even God doesn't believe it—or what you call God!"

"If you don't..." he threateningly began.

"Look, sucker," I said, "don't talk to me as if I'm one of your stooges, Farmington or your boy Stonewall. I don't work for you!" I slammed the phone down and got up to make myself another drink. The phone rang again. This guy was annoying.... I picked up and went on the offensive.

"Am I speaking Swahili or something?" I snarled.

"Sounds like heated English to me," replied Dexter.

"Baby, where are you?"

"Back at the ranch, Nina. I want you to come over."

"What's up?" My antenna rose and was picking up a vibe.

"Just get over here," he said in a sexy but demanding way. Now here's a man who knows how to talk to a woman.

"Okay." I hung up the phone and began licking my lips in anticipation of tasting him. My brain began to click, spin and whir, wondering if he found anything that would implicate that fraudulent you-know-who. I wanted him to take a big fall. With Nate Ford momentarily off my radar, De Lawd would be a preliminary execution.

CHAPTER

I arrived at Dexter's with a bottle of red wine and a pair of red lips. I walked into the living room and saw a 16mm film projector and a screen.

"Aren't you being a little retrograde, baby?" I asked. "X-rated 16mm went out years ago. Is this a collector item? Some Vanessa Del Rio?"

"Nina, cool your jets," he replied. He smiled and embraced me, really hugged me. His arms wrapped around me like a man who's truly glad to see his woman. "I'm sorry...I got things on my mind," said Dexter. He kissed my forehead and left for the kitchen. I went over to the projector and looked at the film canister:

TOP SECRET RESTRICTED TO AUTHORIZED PERSONNEL ONLY.

I turned to Dexter as he returned with the uncorked bottle of Merlot and two glasses. "Exactly what is tonight's selected feature, *mon frere*?"

"The Death of a Nation," he said, and flipped the switch on the projector.

There it was in grainy black and white: a young Paul Tower facing a young Harold Kirby in what looked like a cheap hotel room. Tower was seated on a bed with Kirby standing over him. De Lawd wore an Afro, dark suit and a white turtleneck with a black fist hanging from around his neck. Kirby? The only thing different were his slots and ball bearings. They were wider then, the slots, and his eyes registered the faintest glint of humanity.

"Are you ready?" asked Kirby.

"Yes. They know when to come down. He'll be backstage and they'll come down from the ceiling," said Tower. "They've been instructed to shout 'Die, nigger die!'"

"Well, I hope for your people's sake that things will cool off. We expect some hot heads to start trouble in a few cities but we've got them covered. Others are interested in rounding up the whole lot of you under the Internal Security Act," said Kirby.

"Why should we all pay for the activities of a few?" said Tower. "With Martin gone, blacks won't be willing to do anything. Most Negroes are exhausted. The nationalists are just into rhetoric. They don't have a program or a plan."

"Except the Panthers..." added Kirby.

"You're taking care of them. Martin is my department..."

"It better not fail..."

"It won't. You told your people to stand down, right?"

Kirby nodded.

"It won't fail, then. Martin's security people are incompetent—except for Conway."

Kirby smiled, or made an attempt at it, and said, "That's because he's one of us."

The film abruptly ended. Dexter rose, turned off the projector and turned on the lights. I just sat there. That film was the smokin' motherfuckin' gun! That sucker was going down. I felt elated for a moment and then my feelings unexpectedly crashed. I looked at Dexter and he was wearing the same stone face as when I'd entered.

"Good work, Dexter, " I commended.

"Luck," he replied, "and an agenda."

"An agenda? Whose?"

He pulled off the film reel from the projector and placed it back into the can. Dexter came over with the can and sat down next to me. "Ever heard of Monroe Phillips? Know anything about him?"

"No. Should I?"

"Not really, I guess. I told you that someone might be willing to talk about what they knew, people in spookville—the intelligence community."

I sipped my wine. "Uh-huh...Is this Monroe Phillips a spook?"

"No. He works for someone who used to be a degree or two away from the intelligence community."

"Who?" I asked, my eyes squinted inquiringly.

"Calvin Farmer."

"The General?" I said, referring to Farmer by the title that most Americans, white and black, called him.

Farmer, explained Dexter, was a member of the preceding administration's National Security Advisers team. He had resigned from the army to take the position when that president ran into trouble and had to revamp his NSA apparatus and Farmer, a black soldier who had served a tour of duty in Vietnam and on the military-politico circuit, caught the eye of various men in high places. He was smooth, sharp, polished, professional, and a plausible Negro who could be groomed for a high profile, if not powerful, position down the road. After managing several spectacular post-Cold War invasions, the General retired and people speculated about his presidential stock.

Tower was on the road engineering his nomination in the Republican Party—a party that wasn't big enough for two black contenders. They were already making the most racist and fascistic elements of the GOP's right grumble. After all, the right-wingers had already bolted from the Democratic Party because that party, in their view, had become a captive of welfare niggers, testicle-eating feminazis, and McGovernite limo liberals.

"Monroe Phillips and I had a meeting in Washington, he dropped this on me," said Dexter. "He said this was the kind of reality-based advertising that others might use against Tower. This is a preemptive strike..."

"Someone else's agenda."

"Right. My first instinct as a reporter was 'Great!,' but then I thought about it. I don't want to be doing Farmer's dirty work."

"And you think it's from him?"

"Yes. He would have access to this. He has clearance for this type of stuff. If my newspaper publishes this, guess who goes up and who comes down?"

"Tower killed Martin," I reminded him.

"And how much better is Farmer? He masterminded the invasion of—"

"That's different, Dex! He did that under constitutional auspices. He was a soldier."

"Couldn't Tower argue that he did so in order to keep the government from rounding up blacks en masse?" argued Dexter.

"Not when we know that he stole money. Two different cases, Dexter," I countered. "Totally different situations."

"They probably filmed this just so they could keep Tower in check. In case he got uppity," he speculated.

"Well, he is, in the eyes of Farmer!" I said.

Dexter looked at me, then took the can from the table and handed it to me. "Do what you like. Don't mention Phillips, Farmer, or my name."

"Dexter, what's wrong?"

"It's the same thing, Nina...the same thing...the same old shit."

"What is, baby?"

"Tower whacked Martin," he sighed. "Hakim planned to get back at Tower, but is annihilated by the government...and now Farmer is planning to neutralize Tower..." he trailed off. "Where does it end? When?" He finished his glass and looked at me again.

"This shit has been going on since Booker T. Washington and W.E.B. Du Bois, and Marcus Garvey...black leaders sniping and trying to pick each other off. Look at the stuff that went on between Davis and the NAACP. Baxter running around talking about "It's our time" and not one real idea or organization. Farmington wants to run for the Senate and that guy even snooped for the FBI! The same agency that spied on King and Malcolm! I'm just sick of the whole thing, Nina. Everyone is pimping and promising black folks things they can't deliver...Hakim! Mbooma! It's such a farce! I'll never win a Pulitzer this way," he sighed to himself.

I left my seat and went over to him. "What do you mean?"

"I don't have what it takes to play the great game—what the Brits once called their skullduggery. To be a reporter on the high profile track entails a certain level of duplicity and back scratching, all under the cover of the people's right to know and the First Amendment. In short, a dog for someone else's policy."

"Dex..Dex..." I cooed, putting my arms around him and nestling my face in the crook of his neck. "You got scruples."

"Yeah," he said bitterly. "I'm taking a leave of absence from the paper...I'm getting out of Dodge." He looked at me and made sure I got the message.

"You mean you're also taking a leave of absence from me," I said. He couldn't look me in the eye.

"Yeah...something like that."

Two scarred people...One who was trying to cleanse himself and the other willing to stick her hand into the bloody muck of life a little deeper.

41

CHAPTER

Things were becoming hotter and hotter. Sister Ronnie and Malika appeared on local TV talk shows, and spoke on talk radio. When on television they waved the McKinney-Clarke report; on radio they read from incriminating COINTELPRO documents that named Paul Tower as an "asset."

They marched before the McChurchs of the nation and challenged the franchised clergy members. They were backed up by angry black women who had often seen their children and men cast aside. They wanted to know what were these "churches" really doing in their neighborhoods, and why were the ministers fronting for a thief like Paul Tower. Local leaders of the MMSICs deplored that kind of activity and stressed peaceful demonstrations and sit-ins inside the McChurchs. The police hauled Sister Ronnie and Malika from the churches and the television cameras captured it all, reminding viewers of the golden days of the civil rights era.

Tower declared a state of religious emergency: "I say that the soul of black America is under siege by the forces of hip hop and Afrocentrism, the twin pillars of black fascism!" he exhorted his fellow ministers at the National Black Clergymen Association. "We have weathered many crises and struggles during our captivity and advancement, but this plot, this goal, this agenda of rap, afro-fascism, and feminism is the most diabolical since the spread of communism almost fifty years ago! The Lord, my precious Lord, my invincible savior, has sent me to deliver the teachings of marketplace theology and I...will...not...be...thwarted...in...my mission!" he defiantly and dramatically hammered the lectern. He also sweated bullets...big bullets.

It was that performance that led me to believe that he would eventually crack under the right pressure, exquisitely calibrated, for I had yet to release the film. Sister Ronnie and Malika were effective: they chipped away at Tower's facade of respectability. He could only answer with retorts of "misguided sisters," "confused black women." That sold some brothers, but others were suspicious.

De Lawd's persistent line on the hip hop conspiracy gave me an idea. The plan called for the recording of a smokin' jam that would be released, and the video of Tower and Kirby to be held in reserve. This would be Mbooma's swan song, for the Feds would really be after him once they realized that he was not dead. He would be, to borrow from Ice Cube, "America's most wanted."

"I'm down. Let's do it," was his only response when I broached the idea.

Acting as the executive producer, I contacted the people that Mbooma recommended as he worked on the lyrics to *Death of a Nation (The Eternal Black Situation?)*. I knew what the brother had been through but thought the title was too morose.

Mbooma knew what he had to do. It had to grab the listener by the throat. Before we went into the studio to lay down the tracks, Mbooma sampled some riffs from other rap records, soul, jazz, and r & b.

The team assembled was waiting for us in a studio called The Cellar. Everybody wanted to know who the mystery artist was. Screaming and crying filled the room when Mbooma dropped his hood. It was as if Christ had returned and revealed himself to his disciples.

I snapped people back into reality when I slapped the tape of Tower and Kirby into a VCR and instructed them to watch the deal of the century.

"That's your objective: Paul Tower! Get him!" They got the message and got to work. Half way through the night Mbooma and I got into an argument about the title, *The Death of a Nation*. I thought it was too much of a downer, the type of nationalist morbidity that "noble warriors" are wont to engage in. I insisted on changing it to *The Deal of the Century*.

CDs and tapes consisting of various mixes and remixes of "The Deal" were released. Masking ourselves as PRB, we slapped on "For Promotion Only" labels and the kids began taking them around to parties. Mustapha had associates in different cities mail them out to hundreds of Urban Contemporary and College Alternative radio stations around the country. We also sent them to critics and record reviewers. The initial response was lukewarm. No one believed it was really Mbooma.

I didn't want Mbooma to expose himself, but he wouldn't listen. He started calling radio stations to let people know that the First Soldier was back to denounce the "high agent of Satan, Paul Tower." Within weeks, *The Deal of the Century* had made its way into the mainstream press. People were beginning to ask questions....

Tower fired back and tried to have the courts issue an injunction, but the PRB didn't exist. It was a phantom recording company. *The Deal*, as it was called by now, was the hottest song in the nation. De Lawd was being punched, kicked, hit, slapped, and cold shouldered from all sides. When Reggie Baxter and Mel Farmington, both certified members of the black minister mafia and all-around strategic opportunists, withdrew audible support from Tower, it was only a matter of time. Tower himself angrily appeared on his television show; his smooth and once powerful articulation became disjointed and out of context. He only knew of two things: rap and Afrocentrism. Anything prior to the 1980s he couldn't or wouldn't account for. The *Times* and the *Wall Street Journal* reported his deteriorating political fortune and the financial sections spoke of the even more rapidly declining profits of BCN, his pride and joy. Tower finally got around to denouncing yours truly and the Martins as "those bitches of all bitches," over the airwaves, and shocked the faithful with the crudeness of his slurs.

The overclass must have huddled together and begun to wonder about him. Tower was longer invited to prestigious and swank policy convocations. His op-ed pieces were no longer accepted in mainstream and corporate newspapers and magazines. As a matter of fact, those outlets began to come to a different opinion, for the tone of their editorials changed from denouncing the underclass to "Why doesn't Tower answer the charges?" The establishment media, which   for years had suspended any critical evaluation of Tower's Black Christian Network, suddenly began to look into the history of the Nation, Malik Martin, and Paul Tower. As for the white overclass, Tower was becoming a political liability. He was only allowed into their inner sanctum for one reason and one reason only: he had assured them that as a   black leader—in process as a race-transcending negotiator—he could "control" his own people. Now he could no longer do so, thus his services were no longer needed. In short, De Lawd was in race-transcending trouble with everyone.

CHAPTER

The showdown occurred when Gary, my brother, demanded my presence at his Wall Street office. His investment bank, Warren and Grimke, was considering an infusion of cash into BCN's operation, but this ruckus was making things iffy. I packed up the documents and the film footage and took a cab downtown. The cabbie, a Trinidadian, had the radio on and it announced that the body of Rudy Downs had been found. It was reported that he was last seen leaving a Tribeca neighborhood bar with two men, thought to be Nigerians. These men had been looking for him and had gotten into an argument with Downs over artwork that had never made it back to the motherland. One truly down, I thought and patted my briefcase. The Great Mother works in deadly ways....

I got out of the cab and stepped into the dark shadows cast by the gray canyons of Manhattan. I entered the building owned by Warren and Grimke and took an elevator flight up to the fortieth floor.

Warren and Grimke was laid out in "old money" brown wood and green leather furniture with toe-thick, plush burgundy-colored carpets. It had that air of breeding and good taste, what I call pseudo-British decor. And the decor tried to mask over the fact that the firm was a con job of sorts. Warren and Grimke wasn't a real "old money," blue blood firm but an affirmative action product. It had earned its money the post-civil rights way: minority set-asides and as a front for white investors who wanted a slice of the business that was earmarked for so-called minority-owned firms. What was annoying about Warren and Grimke was that it acted as if it were "old money." It took offense when others accused it of "racial preference." Warren and Grimke, like many graduates of affirmative action academies, had cut its deal with the white overclass and was becoming highly skittish about the anti-affirmative action fever that was going down in its own party, the Party of Lincoln.

I walked into the reception area and was greeted by canned classical music and the smile of the receptionist. She told me to go straight ahead. I was a known and expected entity.

I approached the area outside of my brother's office and spoke to his secretary extraordinaire, Gertie, a woman of about fifty or so. "What's up, Miss G?"

Gertie looked from her computer screen and shook her head. "Girl...I don't know about you..."

"Yeah? What don't you know about?" I feigned.

"Your brother, Mr. Warren, and Reverand Tower are in there..."

"Tower's in with Gary and Mr. Warren?" I echoed. That was a surprise. I thought Gary was going to sit me down and tell me to call it off. It was a good thing I brought along some other documents that would come in handy. I mentally shifted to my former Assistant District Attorney mode.

I inhaled and exhaled, knocked on the door and entered my brother's plush, spacious office. Mr. Charles Warren was seated on a couch below a picture of Frederick Douglass. Paul Tower was seated in front of Gary's desk. He watched me as I walked over to them; his eyes tried to sear me into submission.

Mr. Warren, last of the great black patriarchs, was a short man with slicked back, brilliantined hair gone grey; his skin had a faded yellow pallor. He faintly resembled Carter G. Woodson, the author of *Mis-education of the Negro*, a tome popular with the black masses nowadays. Warren was of the old Negro elite that had lost social power during the sixties. His class was the "high yellow" gentility that ruled over us darker breeds and often got the nod and play from whites. He was of a generation that was able to take advantage of the doors opened by the Great Society programs of Lyndon Johnson and Richard Nixon's black capitalism, "a piece of the action," as the evil prince of American politics called it.

The old man couldn't figure me out. I was a lost cause in his eyes when I left the legal field and didn't take a job at his firm. But he changed his opinion somewhat when I tracked down a hot, sleek "protegé"—an embezzler—who made off with ten million dollars of the firm's money.

"Gary," I said. "Mr. Warren." I studiously ignored De Lawd.

"Sit down, Nina," replied Gary, who had his suit coat on, so I knew this was a formal matter. "The reverend has made some very serious charges about you and your client, Veronica Martin, regarding blackmail."

"Did you tell him that I was a card carrying member of the Union of Strong, Progressive Black Women?"

"This isn't funny, Nina," Gary tersely replied.

"Okay," I demurred. I kept my eyes on my brother, but felt a nearby set of eyes lasering my face.

"I know that you're not a blackmailer, or an extortionist, but you could influence those who are leaking these lies..." said Gary.

"Not lies, Gary," I countered. "Statements of fact. History. Documented. Certified by the National Security Apparatus."

"They are lies!!" roared Tower. I turned and looked at him. His face was slack but his eyes had the rage of fire in them. He was gripping the chair's arms. "You and those Martin bit—"

I leaned over and pointed my finger. "You say that word and I'll smack the black off you," I calmly warned him.

252

"Nina!" snapped Gary. "This is a discussion, a meeting, and we're trying to iron out these disagreements in a professional and courteous manner." Gary was very disturbed by this. He was the person who had initiated the review of the investment to BCN and now the old man was watching him to see how he handled this mess.

"Then tell him not to address or refer to my clients in such a vulgar manner," I pleasantly informed him. "These women have been through an ordeal."

Gary looked at me as if I weren't his sister: I was from the planet Zotz. "The stuff that's being aired by the media...rap songs....Even the kids at home are listening to it," he continued.

"Yeah? Do they like it? Huh?" I was enjoying this.

Tower, however, bolted from his chair and pointed his finger at me. "Your sister may enjoy this as a game, but she and her clients are trying to destroy me! Trying to destroy all that I built—"

"Stole," I corrected.

Tower snatched me from my seat and I was head to head with him.

"Reverend Tower!" exclaimed Gary as he rose from his leather chair.

"Paul!" shouted Mr. Warren who also rose, shocked at the manhandling of a member of the weaker sex. The old man walked to our circle of imminent fire.

De Lawd was trembling with rage.

"Take your hands off of me," I said evenly. I detected an unmistakable mixture of rage and lust, hatred and love in his eyes. I was probably the only woman who had ever thwarted him and that made me an exciting combination; someone to love, fuck, and kill. He breathed into my face and shoved me back into the side of my chair. I fell back in quite an unlady-like way. Good thing I wore slacks and not a skirt or dress. De Lawd fumed as he walked around the office like a wounded animal.

"All my life...all my life I worked for our people..." he began to preach.

"Until you began stealing from them."

"Will you stop instigating!" cried my brother.

The Tower of virtue wheeled around. "Everything she says is a lie! An ungodly lie!"

"A lie, huh?" I rose from my chair and pulled my attaché case over to Gary's desk and opened it. I took out several folders marked "FBI Documents: Operation Black Heat," and handed them to Gary and Mr. Warren.

"What are these?" asked the patriarch.

"Photocopies of documents from the FBI's file. Marked 'Top Secret—Black Heat'," I said, with particular emphasis on the last words. Tower turned to me, his face drained of color, an amazing feat for a son of Africa.

I explained to them the history and the chronology of events regarding Black Heat and Tower's connection in it as he walked around the office screaming "Lies! Lies!" But it was all in print.

Charles Warren, called Chas but not Chuck by his friends, looked up at his old friend. "Paul...?"

"Lies, Charles. I'm running for the presidency.... This woman is part of their dirty tricks! The Martins also! Look, they couldn't take down Clarence, so they are coming to get me!" he said, thumping his chest. "These people are liberal Democrats!! Agents of Jeff Benton!"

I wanted to say Calvin Farmer but I was enjoying De Lawd's second greatest performance since that night in his office. He would never believe that it was the work of the general, a man many thought too decent to be Machiavellian.

Warren and Gary looked at me. I pulled out the video coup de grace. "Gary, activate your monitor."

He switched on the monitor and I strolled over to the forty-inch screen and placed the cassette into the VCR unit that was embedded in a wall.

"Show time," I announced. "Dim the light and get your popcorn, boys."

Gary activated the unit and we watched Tower and Kirby.

Tower looked at his treachery of twenty-five years ago without emotion. "They filmed it?" was his only reply. "They filmed it?" He staggered over to the screen and soon blocked out the view. The film ended and the room was eerily quiet.

Tower turned to face his old friend and fellow Republicans. "They...they," he began, his mouth seemed dry, his lips trembled. "Kirby told me that they were going to round up the whole lot of us, all blacks. I figured that they were getting scared about Martin's talk about social capitalism and redistribution. To whites it all sounded like communism, black communism! I told them that I could arrange for Malik to be taken care of if they left the rest of us alone. It was just one man...once he was gone..."

"Why didn't you say something, Paul?" asked Mr. Warren. "Go to the press or something?"

"They had me...I was caught with my hand in the till, Charles. The McKinney report is true," he said as he mopped his face with a red silk power handkerchief.

"And you decided to sacrifice another?" said Mr. Warren. "To save your misbegotten black ass?"

"Charles, don't you remember what it was like back then?! They don't!" he said. "We had to do something to prove that blacks were a responsible people! That we were a responsible leadership!"

Warren exploded, "My God, what kind of man are you?!" He looked at Tower with awe and contempt. "How could you agree to such a thing, Paul?"

"It was the only way to save the race! I had to do something!!" defended Tower.

Warren scoffed, "You don't expect us to believe that, do you? You can do better than that, Paul. Was it the money?" asked the old man, who oozed class contempt at the dark petty bourgeoisie that Tower represented.

"No...you don't understand...Malik Martin was dangerous. He was planning to continue with Malcolm's plan...."

"That being?" asked Warren.

"He was going forward with Malcolm's idea of bringing charges of human rights violations against the United States for racism," replied Tower. "It would have been treasonous! We were prosecuting a war and he was going ahead with Malcolm's plan to compromise the national security of our country before the United Nations!"

We all looked at him; we were not impressed. De Lawd had picked his master and as a faithful dog sought the bone of the Republican Party, his reward.

He walked, staggered, over to the man who was distancing himself from De Lawd. "But I made up for it with BCN...."

"You mean you made it up to yourself! You stole it," replied the financier who was becoming a moralist. Then I realized that the men and women of his generation had something that mine lacked: integrity. De Lawd was an affront to that.

"You're a disgrace! A goddamn, hypocritical disgrace!" Warren lashed out. "The problem is, what do we do with you?" The old man looked at me.

"The media hasn't seen this—yet," I informed him.

"Do I hear a proposal?" piped up Gary.

"Well..." I said. I thought about the other documents I had with me.

"You see! She's ready! She's trying to blackmail me!" cried the reverend. He knew his fate was now being decided by others than himself and he didn't like it.

"What?" asked Warren, smelling a way to extricate himself, a member of BCN's advisory board, and his firm's good name. "What are you proposing, counsel?"

"The reverend steps down from BCN and turns it over to the Martins."

"Are you mad??!!" screamed Tower. "I refuse!"

"You want to go to jail for murder?" I retorted. "It doesn't belong to you, Tower! Get used to it! You are out!" I reminded him. I was tired of coddling this punk preacher. I reached into my case and handed another document to Gary and the old man.

"What's that?" asked De Lawd.

"Your letter of resignation and an instrument that will relinquish your ownership—lock, stock, and barrel—of BCN and forward it to the Martins!"

"This is blackmail! Extortion!"

"This is justice!" I hissed. I had to fight the urge to back-hand slap this double-breasted crybaby. He disgusted me. Instead, I whipped out Gary's Mont Blanc fountain pen and extended it to Tower.

"You're mad if you think I'll sign that. That's a death warrant. I won't..." De Lawd backed away from as if I were a vampire going for his jugular vein.

"You'll sign it!" broke in Mr. Charles Warren III. "You'll sign it or go straight to jail from this office! A scandal like this would destroy what is left of the civil rights movement!"

The old man was right—but off by fifteen years. The civil rights movement died when Reagan entered office and cold shouldered the movement that had turned into a service industry for the black middle class. And with a so-called New Democrat like Jeff Benton slowly selling out blacks, anything could happen. A scandal like this would convince the black masses that people like Tower and Warren were a class of sell-outs, igniting class warfare amongst blacks.

"If he signs this, then what?" asked my brother.

"This discussion will be kept in this office," I informed him and his boss.

"But I can save it...the movement," said Tower, sounding like a small boy. "I have a plan...the church will deliver us back into the Republican Party, the party of the emancipator!"

Mr. Warren scowled at Tower who had become a pathetic supplicant. "For God's sake, man, you are through! Washed up! You're a crook, murderer! A bloody Judas!!" said the old man. That word, the J-word, hit Tower hard. He looked around at our unsmiling faces. Your own people can call you out in a way that outsiders can never affect you. He was out. Socially dead.

"I'm not going down alone, Charles," said Tower. "I'm not the only one who has sinned!"

"What are you babbling about?" asked Warren. "You have nothing to bargain with. You're finished!"

Tower began to look composed and assured. "I'm not the only one who stands to lose a great deal. What about you, Charles?"

"Well, what about me, Paul? I'm not a thief, a crook, or a co-conspirator."

"No you're not. You have always maintained a correct and upright image, " replied Tower. "A paragon of rectitude."

"I live the way I talk, Paul," said Warren. "Nothing more, nothing less."

"That's quite correct—up to a point," stalled Tower. "You were always somebody who I looked up to and admired...until I found out that you were an abominationist!"

Tower had dropped a bomb by using a code word from the Bible.

"What are you talking about?" asked Gary.

"You don't know, do you, son?" smirked Tower; the heat, his own black heat, was off of him. "About your boss's secret life? His illicit desires? Tell him about it, Charles. Let him know."

The old man sighed and his proud frame contracted somewhat. Tower had something on him.

"Tell him, Charles!" triumphed De Lawd. "Tell him about it. Your...your *alternative* lifestyle."

"What is it, Mr. Warren?" said Gary.

I was getting angry at my brother for being so thick, having to ask Warren to humiliate himself in front of us. "He's gay, Gary! That's what Tower is trying to blackmail him with!"

"Oh, now I'm the blackmailer?" said Tower. He was catching his second wind.

"And less than that!" I retorted. If I'd been armed I might not have been able to restrain myself.

"Yes," said the old man. "I'm a homosexual. Been one all my life...and will die one."

"But you're married...I mean you had a wife and children..." said a confused Gary. Warren was like a second father to him.

Tower crowed, "It was a marriage of convenience."

"Because people like you, Paul, won't let us be!" defended the old man. "Phyllis understood me...and we worked out an arrangement...had children. I loved her and I love my children and grandchildren!"

"Lived a life of sin and abomination!" cried Tower. "Now who's fit to judge whom?"

"I don't see how you can equate an innocent party's sexuality with your thievery and murderous machinations!" I interjected, bringing the issue back to him. "This is about you, mister! Not him!"

"Quite correct, counsel," he said. "I'm just not going down without a fight. And it's not just Charles, either. His lover, Melvin Webster, might also be concerned about this sudden divulgement of information."

Tower was even going to out the publisher of *Black Finance*. I didn't care about which way these titans swung or who they slept with. It was none of my business, but other black folks, the masses, may not be so forgiving. Some tossed out "faggot" as quickly as some others said "nigger." Most of them didn't even know that the March on Washington was organized by the likes of Bayard Rustin, a gay man who was a friend of our father and whom I addressed as "uncle."

"Well, Charles...?" asked Tower solicitously.

"Well, what?"

"A deal? You call off this bloodhound, Ms. Halligan, and you and your friend's private lives will be kept as such. A deal?"

The old man walked over to Tower, who clearly had the advantage of height but not the old man's moral stature. "What do you have, Paul?" asked Mr. Warren. "Nothing but rumors. This girl," referring to me, "has concrete things: documents and film footage. What do you have? Huh?"

"Do you want to gamble that I don't have something?" edged Tower.

"This is Wall Street!" he thundered like a black god, tired of playing with nickel-and-dime mortals. "We play for keeps down here! Big money! You have something or you don't!! I don't think you have anything other than stale rumors about me and Melvin! Nina didn't come down here to play games and I bet she's ready to release this stuff on you!"

"That's correct, Mr. Warren," I confirmed. "I have people standing by to release this via faxes and to the Internet, to television news shows, network and cable."

"Even if you do expose me," continued the old man, "by the time you get back to BCN, every black man woman and child will have assembled at your building, threatening to kill you. As a matter of fact, by the time you get to your car you'll be dead when people learn that you killed Malik Martin. Paul, the only thing worse than an old faggot is a dead nigger!"

The old man had calculated the pluses and the minuses and made his decision: he wouldn't be blackmailed. Tower looked at us and his lips trembled. He began sweating again, a sure sign that he was whipped.

"I'll sign...I'll sign. May God have mercy on your soul, Charles..." he desperately uttered, always ready to clothe his skullduggery by invoking the Almighty.

Warren looked at Tower and I knew he had squelched an impulse to slap him. "You cheap, pathetic Negro...." Tower was the kind of person who even took dignity out of the word Negro when it was applied to him. He was the last of a discredited phenomenon, the corporate preacher.

Warren walked over to me and took the pen from my hand and handed it to Tower with deliberate authority. "Get Gertie in here," he said to Gary. My brother called his assistant over the intercom and she came in and watched Tower sign the document. Gertie then affixed her name as the notary. Mr. Warren signed as a witness. Gertie took the original and went out to make copies. The deal was done. Tower was now the living dead, and that would be his ultimate punishment. No power. No fame. No glory. Nada. Nothing.

Tower collapsed into a chair and began moaning. Gary and Mr. Warren stepped over to the door and began speaking. I watched

Tower and thought of the past months, weeks, and days...time filled with blood. He was quietly sobbing, crying over the loss of his BCN.

"Nina?"

I turned and walked over to Gary and Mr. Warren near the door. I kept an eye on Tower but turned to face them. Gary wanted to know if the Martins would be satisfied with Tower's relinquishing of BCN.

"They don't even know that this was being discussed," I said.

"I beg your pardon?" said the old man.

I heard a sound in the direction of Gary's desk and turned and saw Tower sliding open the glass door that led to a small terrace outside Gary's office. Tower was going to get some air. He needed it.

"I'm sorry about all this Mr. Warren," I offered.

"Nonsense, my dear," he replied. "You did nothing wrong. I just never realized what a desperate scoundrel he was. I'm glad you are on this case...and maybe I can stop living a..." Mr. Warren stopped and squinted, looking past my shoulder.

I turned and saw De Lawd raising his leg up to the small railing that ran along the length of the terrace. There was a 40-story drop outside Gary's office. He had one last card to play, his death. For a hot second I envisioned a series of testimonials, tributes, and movies and speeches given in his honor, elevating him to the pantheon of black heroes and that was more than I could stomach.

The Nina Express flew across the office to the terrace and I grabbed Tower by his coat and yanked his black ass down from the ledge. He fell back onto me and we tumbled onto tiled terrace.

Tower rolled on top of me and began slamming fists into me, calling me bitch this and bitch that. For a nanosecond I wished he had jumped off. Wedging a knee up to his groin, I applied pressure and shoved him back into Gary who had come out to assist me. Gary's wind was knocked out of him when Tower's back flattened him against the wall of the terrace. That gave me enough time to scramble to my feet.

De Lawd swung at me and I blocked his arm and delivered a blow with my fist to his abdomen and jammed my palm into his chin. His head reared back and he went back towards the office but both of his hands caught the terrace's aluminum door frame. He was about to launch himself over the edge and if I didn't get out, take me with him. Quickly, I brought the heel of my cha-cha shoe down on the bridge of his foot and that loosened his grip. He yelped and I squarely slammed him—once, twice, three times—into his jaw, sending him back into the office and onto the floor. De Lawd lay sprawled on the carpet, his arms spread out to his sides, his legs straight, the perfect symbolic ending to his career.

"You're not getting out that easy, mister..." I said as I stood over him. I wobbled back onto the terrace and helped Gary to his feet and brushed off his suit as we walked into office.

"Girl," said Mr. Warren approvingly, "you're something! Good God. You are a dynamo and a half!

"Yeah, I'm an army of me," I said, wiping a small trace of blood from my mouth.

He smiled. "You deserve something more than a medal, young lady. What can I do for you?"

My first thoughts were of a drink and a new boyfriend, but something else was more outstanding in my heart. "You want to know what I'd appreciate, Mr. Warren?"

"I most certainly do, young lady," he enthusiastically replied. "Name it."

"Well, let's go somewhere else and talk, mon general."

Mr. Warren offered me his arm and I began tucking in my clothes as we proceeded to the door.

"Mr. Warren?! Nina?!" said Gary, surprised. "What about him? Reverend Tower? We can't just leave him here?!"

"Gary, my boy," said the old man, "we always let the cleaning people handle the garbage. Good night. And don't stay too late...."

We strolled. Case closed....but not my heart.

About the Author

A native of Washington, D. C. Norman Kelley currently lives in Brooklyn. He has been residing in New York State since 1982 and edits *The Bedford Styvesant Current*. He is also a member of the National Writers Union.